Storm Shelter

To Jeannie
Enjoy!

Also by J. L. Delozier

Type and Cross

Storm Shelter

J. L. Delozier

WiDō Publishing
Salt Lake City

WiDō Publishing
Salt Lake City, Utah
www.widopublishing.com

Cover Design by Steven Novak
Book design by Marny K. Parkin

ISBN: 978-1-937178-90-1
Library of Congress Control Number available on request

Printed in the United States of America

For Mom,

my most patient critique partner

Chapter One

Philadelphia VA Hospital
September 2006

"What are you afraid of, Bradley? What keeps you awake at night?" Dr. Persephone Smith's questions were gentle but direct. She'd been asking him those same questions in a more oblique manner for the last two months of his therapy, and they'd gotten nowhere.

Sgt. David Bradley broke eye contact and fumbled with the folds of his pants, hemmed to hide the scarred stumps of his amputated legs. When the silence dragged on too long for comfort, Seph prodded him again.

"David?"

"It's the storms." He blurted it out like a confession.

"The storms?" The baby-faced Marine sitting in front of her was missing one arm and both legs. Seph expected to hear about bombs and ambushes. An IED blast had sent Bradley's Humvee skittering across the desert sand as if it were a giant tumbleweed, and he was afraid of a little weather?

"Go on." Seph resorted to using one of her stock phrases. She pulled one out when she couldn't think of anything more appropriate or profound to say.

"A sandstorm isn't like a thunderstorm here in the States. When it hits, you can't see anything around you. You're blind, dead in the water. You can't breathe because you're choking on sand, but when you try to take a deep breath, you choke worse.

It's as if the sand is alive, crawling into your eyes and lungs like a parasite until you're so disoriented anything could happen. Something horrible, something deadly could be standing right in front of you, but you'd still be caught off guard, completely helpless."

Bradley's voice rose with his agitation, and he hunched forward in his wheelchair to hide his terror-stricken face. He took a few deep breaths to reassure himself he still could before settling back in his seat.

"Now you know. Stupid, isn't it? To be afraid of going to bed. It must be the darkness; it gives me that same helpless feeling. It's even worse if I hear thunder approaching. My brain screams 'storm!' even though I know it's not the same as when I was in Iraq. How could it be the same?" The young man resumed picking at his pant legs, tearing at loose threads until his hem threatened to come completely undone.

"David, look at me."

Bradley's troubled eyes focused on her chin. "Is that crazy, Doc? I mean, am *I* crazy?"

Seph relaxed her face and shook her head back and forth. "Not at all. You don't even reach a two on the nut-o-meter."

"If that's the case, I'd hate to see what a ten looks like." He laughed, which was the intent. "You mean there's hope for me yet?" Bradley seemed lighter already, as if confessing his fear had stripped an eighty-pound rucksack from his shoulders.

"Absolutely. Especially now that I know what's been bothering you. We can work on it together, starting with your next session." They were out of time. Seph held the door so Bradley could maneuver his wheelchair out of her room, and they journeyed down the hallway together.

"Are you gonna tell me what keeps *you* awake at night? Don't think I haven't noticed those dark circles, Doc."

"Not a chance." Seph smiled to remove the sting from her firm response. "This is a one-way street. Unless you decide to get a degree in psychology. Then . . . maybe."

"You never know, Doc. I could back to college. I haven't used my GI Bill benefits yet. I might hold you to that someday." Bradley waved on his way toward the main exit, skillfully weaving his electric wheelchair through the throngs of veterans in the waiting room. "Enjoy your weekend. You've earned it."

Seph was thrilled to hear him mention his future, even if only in jest. A few weeks ago, the young sergeant hadn't been able to think past surviving another nightmare, much less plan his future education. They'd made a real breakthrough today.

She returned to her office, drained after a long week but happy to have ended on such a positive note, which was never a given. The bad weeks forced her to question her career choice. The good weeks sustained her.

She powered down her computer and removed her white coat, hanging it behind the door. Most doctors of psychology chose not to wear a lab coat, but Seph was different. She needed a protective barrier, a layer of separation, between her and her patients. Her psyche demanded it.

The coat stayed locked in her office along with all the horror stories she'd collected during the week. She never took them home with her. Not intentionally, at least. Occasionally, she suffered a stowaway. She was working on that.

On the way out, she paused at her secretary's desk and prepared to bob-and-weave around any last-minute jabs Luna planned to throw her way. Their end-of-the-work-week ritual was not a pleasant one. Luna seemed incapable of allowing Seph to leave the office happy.

Luna was the scheduling secretary for the entire psychology department and, in true karmic fashion, was herself a miserable orb of insanity whose blackness was brightened only by the neon pink streaks in her raven hair. She rarely smiled, but when she did, it was a wide, toothy, sinister grin which never failed to send a chill racing down Seph's spine.

Thanks to the pink hair and maniacal grin, Luna bore more than a passing resemblance to the Cheshire Cat—a comparison supported by the sign Luna displayed on her desk. "We're all mad here," it proclaimed, winking slyly at the mental health patients as they waited to schedule their next counseling sessions. Luna found the inside joke hilarious, a sentiment not shared by her supervisor, who periodically demanded the sign's removal. It would disappear for a few days, only to resurface after the supervisor had moved on to bigger and more important infractions.

Luna sat checking her email when Seph stopped at the desk. "Anything I need to take care of before I leave for the weekend?" Seph asked. She hoped Luna was too distracted to offer anything more than her usual grunt. No such luck.

Luna interlaced her fingers and smiled. Always a bad sign. "No, but you should keep your cell phone on tonight. The Weather Channel says there's a hurricane brewing in the Gulf. You know what that means. The disaster coordinator already sent out a mass email. All DEMPS personnel have been put on notice. Looks like they're expecting it to be a doozy." She cracked her knuckles like a boxer readying for a brawl.

Seph sighed. "Great. Thanks for the heads up. Hopefully you won't end up having to reschedule all my patients for next week."

"Yeah, that would totally suck. But not as much as being deployed." *Jab. Duck and cover.* The smile widened, and out came the teeth. Luna snapped her bubble gum and lowered her gaze to finish trolling through her email. Seph made a break for the door.

"Oh, by the way . . ." Luna's smirky voice floated over Seph's right shoulder. ". . . Mr. Payton shot himself in the head yesterday. His son showed up a little while ago with the death certificate and wanted his dad's medical records. 'Every last page of it,' he said." *Jab, cross, and hook*. "Have a nice weekend."

Seph felt Luna watching her, her kohl-rimmed eyes burning a hole through Seph's back. Seph resisted the urge to spin around and smack the grin off Luna's face. She willed her voice to sound neutral. "Thanks for letting me know." She hurried out of the office, her mind roiling with a slurry of expletives.

Once she was safely outside, Seph sagged against the corner of the decrepit brick building. Mr. Payton, a sixty-something-year-old Navy veteran and amateur inventor, had a wickedly morbid sense of humor, and she'd grown fond of him over the last year of his treatments. His depression was so well-controlled, she hadn't seen him for months.

Seph fingered the pocket rosary dangling from her purse and murmured a prayer for his troubled soul. *What happened?* She tapped the back of her head against the wall behind her. *Why didn't he reach out and call? Did I miss something during our last session?* Another tap, harder this time. A tiny piece of brick crumbled to the ground. The only one with the answers to her questions was lying in the morgue with a bullet in his brain.

Tony, a street vendor who'd claimed this particular block of real estate as his own, ducked out from behind his cart to shoot her an odd look. "You're gonna give yourself a helluva headache, sweetheart." Seph stopped mid-motion, and a flush colored her cheeks. She was mumbling like one of her patients.

"Wanna pretzel? Philly's finest!" Tony grinned. He knew she hated soft pretzels. She told him so every day. He hit her up anyway, and twice on Fridays. She figured he had a pricey weekend habit to cover.

Seph averted her eyes and trudged down the street toward the subway station. Mr. Payton wasn't her first patient to commit suicide, and he was unlikely to be her last. She remembered all their faces, all the time. She was fresh out of school, and her boss took every opportunity to remind her she needed to toughen up or she wouldn't last long in their "biz"—as though they did something terribly glamorous for a living. That's why she'd volunteered for DEMPS. Her first deployment made her regret her decision. She'd hated every miserable minute of it.

Seph's Blackberry burbled a welcome distraction. A quick check of her messages confirmed Luna's warning. Sure enough, Seph was on "priority one standby" for deployment by the federal government's Disaster Emergency Medical Personnel System—DEMPS for short.

She buried her phone in her purse and scowled. So much for going to the gym and beating the crap out of a heavy bag. Instead, she'd be spending her evening with Jim Cantore of the Weather Channel. And Ben and Jerry, of course. May as well drown her sorrows in a pint of something sweet. She rubbed the sore spot on the back of her head and jogged down the grungy stairs to the platform.

Before starting at the VA, Seph was oblivious to the fact that civilian federal employees were deployable to any disaster the President deemed to be of a large enough scale. Every employee from all the federal agencies could, in theory, be mandated, but medical personnel were especially prone. And if you happened to be young and childless, you might as well volunteer in advance. You were going anyway, and volunteering at least made you look good. In her three years as a civil servant, Seph had already been deployed twice. Both were for hurricanes. Neither was pleasant, yet Seph felt no tougher despite the dreadful experience.

The subway shuddered to a stop at 36th and Market, and Seph hit the freezer section of the closest Wawa before hurrying the remaining few blocks to her studio apartment. She tossed her keys on the table and, spoon in hand, plopped in front of the television. Hurricane Ignatius was all over the news. Already a category one storm, it was aiming for the Gulf and, if it followed its projected course, Galveston Island was toast. The meteorologists predicted it would rise to a category four hurricane before making landfall. FEMA was in the process of opening federal medical shelters around the San Antonio area—a safe distance from the coast. Her deployment, it seemed, was imminent. Seph clicked off the TV and took a final bite of her rocky road. Time to pull out the bin.

"The bin" was a large plastic tub Seph kept stashed in the back of her closet. It lay dormant and buried under a mishmash of rumpled rejects—shirts missing a button, pants needing to be hemmed—until called into action. She stocked it with a duffel bag and all the necessities, from clothing to toothpaste to earplugs, so she could grab and go on short notice.

She'd learned the hard way. On her first disaster deployment, aflutter with anxiety and given only four hours' notice, she'd forgotten to pack underwear. She'd arrived in Mississippi to discover what few stores were open carried nothing smaller than a 2X. She'd spent two weeks washing out the same pair of Hanes.

On her second deployment, Seph had forgotten to pack a belt, which at the time didn't seem like such a big deal—not compared to the underwear debacle. However, after a week of sweating in the hot Louisiana sun, Seph had lost so much weight that even the slightest of movements placed her in serious danger of dropping her drawers. She was forced to tie her pants in place with a snippet of twine, which was neither comfortable nor professional. It did, however, prevent her from mooning her coworkers every time she bent over, which would've been infinitely more embarrassing.

The above situations taught her Rule #1 of disaster work: Always keep an emergency kit packed and ready at all times. Going commando with rope burns around her waist made an already bad situation feel so much worse.

Once she had her gear transferred to a suitcase, Seph pondered her next move. Waiting around for the inevitable phone call was nerve-jangling, so she filled the time by making a flurry of calls of her own. The first person to call, the first person she always called, was her older sister, Grace. She and Grace were less than a year apart in age and were as tight as twins. Their bond had strengthened even more since their mother's recent diagnosis of lung cancer.

"Hey, Gracie. How's life on the beach?" Her sister was a Navy Lieutenant with the Personnel Support Detachment in Norfolk, Virginia.

"The President's declared a state of emergency for the Gulf Coast, and our storm chasers are predicting a lot of chop as far north as Virginia Beach. We're moving the ships out to sea 'til the storm's over. Once I get everybody where they need to be, life will be good again. You headed to Texas? I saw the governor's evacuating Galveston Island."

"Yep."

"Crap. Sorry. I know how much you hate deployments. You remember to pack some undies this time?"

"*Yes*. What are we going to do about Mom?"

"Well, if you ask Mom, she'll say 'nothing.'"

Their mother, fiercely independent and stubborn as an old mule, had refused to leave her modest South Philadelphia home to move in with either Seph or Grace during her chemo.

"Grace, you know I don't think mom should be alone right now. Granted, she's in remission, but she's still kind of frail. The chemo knocked her for a real loop."

"I know. I'll see what I can do. I've told you before what a jackass I have for a commanding officer, but maybe if I ask real nice, he'll grant me emergency leave." Grace's boss was the son of a state senator and was quick to mention how he was destined for bigger and better things than his current position. "How long do you think you'll be gone?"

"Two weeks, give or take. Officially, the government says they limit deployments to fourteen days, but sometimes if they don't have someone to replace you, you're mandated to stay."

"Right. I'll let you know ASAP if I can come home, okay? Are you gonna call Mom, or am I?"

"I'll call her. You've got enough to do."

"Great. Settle in, pour yourself a drink . . ." Grace chuckled. Their mother loved to talk, or, more specifically, argue. A two-minute call often morphed into a debate of presidential proportions.

Seph smiled wryly as she hung up the phone. She took Grace's advice and forced herself to sit on the sofa, adopting a relaxed demeanor. She inhaled deeply and dialed the phone.

"Hi, Mom. I . . ."

"You're being deployed."

"How'd you know? Let me guess—Uncle Chick told you." Dr. Sal "Chick" Rizzo, the chief of staff at the Philadelphia VA, was the reason Seph had gone into psychology and Grace had joined the navy. He and their maternal uncle served as medics together in Vietnam, and after the war, Sal used the GI Bill to put himself through college and medical school. He'd risen through the VA ranks through sheer determination and hard work. He was Seph's hero—and her biggest fan.

"No, Chick did not tell me. I had a nightmare about it last night." Her mother, pragmatic in most other ways, believed she was psychic, especially when it came to her daughters.

"You probably spent too much time watching the weather before you went to bed. Besides, you don't have nightmares, Mom. I'm the one with the nightmares."

"When mothers have nightmares, they're usually about their children. I don't want you to go to this one, Persephone. It's gonna be a disaster."

"That's why they're called 'disaster shelters,' Mom."

"I'm serious. I saw bad things. Blood. Lots and lots of blood. And . . . madness. I saw faces—a witch with grey hair and a black man with sad eyes—their faces were swirling and fusing like someone was finger painting them together. Stay home. You've done your share. It's someone else's turn. Can't you get out of this one?"

Seph paused. Her mother had fussed a bit with her prior deployments, but never like this. "I . . . I can't. Imagine how embarrassed and disappointed Uncle Chick would be if I flat-out refused. The government never has enough warm bodies to staff these things. Besides, everyone goes a little crazy in the shelters, Mom, which is why they send me in the first place. I'll be fine." She changed the subject. "I asked Gracie to come stay with you while I'm gone."

"You worry too much."

"Look who's talking. At least in my case, it's part of my job. I get paid to worry about people."

"No, you don't. You get paid to help other people stop worrying."

Seph refused to further the argument. "Whatever. Semantics. Anyway, it won't kill Grace to come spend a week or two with you while I'm away."

"I don't know about that. She's been having an awful lot of trouble with her commanding officer. He's stressing her out. She doesn't handle that stuff well, you know—not like you do. Remember when Dinah died? She was catatonic for days." Dinah was Grace's pet hamster.

"She was twelve, Mom. Since then, she's survived the Naval Academy and moved six or seven times already. I'm not going to feel guilty about asking her to come home. Besides, strength is a subjective attribute. According to my boss, I'm nothing but a giant green weenie."

"Your boss doesn't know his ass from a hole in the ground. Chick needs to have a talk with that man, set him straight. Anyone who's overcome a condition such as yours . . ."

"No, Chick does *not* need to talk to my boss, and don't you dare ask him to!" Seph waved the phone in the air like a madwoman before terminating the conversation with a little white lie. "You know what, Mom? I've got a lot of packing to do." Squabbling with her mother was exhausting, and Seph needed to conserve her mental energy for the stressful weeks to come.

"Okay, okay. Did you call Steve yet?"

"I'm calling him next. We're breaking up."

"He's a nice boy."

"Nice and boring, Mom."

"Yes, and not too smart either, is he? Bless his heart. Call me as soon as you can." She paused. "Try not to be too sensitive, okay?"

"I'll try." Seph lied again. Her sensitivity—her *condition*—wasn't something she could turn off, and her mother, of all people, should know that. Since childhood, Seph suffered with what a psychiatrist labeled as, for lack of a better term, "enhanced empathy." Seph could read people with astonishing accuracy and feel what they were feeling, as if their emotions were her own. She used this inside information to predict their actions, often before they themselves knew what they were planning to say or do. The disorder became her greatest career asset—unless things went badly and her gift let her down, like with poor Mr. Payton. Then that emotional connection, so difficult for her to break, became a curse.

She'd chosen to study psychology because of her gift, with Uncle Chick playing a large part in Seph's decision. He'd recognized her innate abilities early, while she was still bouncing on his knee, and he'd encouraged her to funnel those talents into a career helping others. When she'd received her acceptance letter to grad school, it was Chick who bought Seph her books.

The phone beeped, dragging her back to the present. Her mother had hung up. Seph circled the tiny apartment, stopping to stare longingly at the empty ice cream carton in the garbage. She'd been rehearsing her final phone call for weeks, but somehow she always managed to talk herself into granting her soon-to-be ex-boyfriend a last-minute reprieve. Now the hurricane gave her both a reason and an excuse to finally get it done.

Steve hadn't done anything wrong. In fact, he'd done everything right. He was, as her mother suggested, super nice—truly, sincerely, puke-in-your-cereal-bowl nice. But Steve's brain functioned like a hybrid engine. When he was parked, it shut down, allowing him to sit, stare, and idle for lengths of time inconceivable to someone such as herself, who existed in a perpetual state of overdrive. Steve was a Prius, and Seph needed a Hemi.

The call went as expected. Steve's mind operated too slowly for him to realize he'd just been dumped, and by the time he figured it out, she'd be in Texas and unreachable. With her to-do-list complete, Seph was back to waiting.

Her landline jingled, snapping Seph's nerves. She glanced at the caller ID, raised the receiver, and slammed it down again. Damned telemarketers. She needed to get out of the apartment. Time to pay Sammy a visit. Seph crammed her cell into her pocketbook and headed downstairs to the bar.

The ground floor of her high-rise apartment building had a restaurant with a quaint, hole-in-the-wall bar which reminded her of *Cheers*. Seph enjoyed hanging out with Sammy, the bartender, when she didn't want to be alone with her thoughts, which was a lot of the time.

The crowd was thin for a happy hours Friday, so Sammy spotted her as she walked through the door. He flipped the towel from his shoulder and polished her a spot at the bar.

"You're here early," he said. "Betcha ain't even had dinner yet. Rough day at the office?"

Sammy was a good guy, as old and as rough as an opened bottle of cheap gin, and he told a great story. Seph smiled as she settled onto a stool. She'd kill some time, have a nice glass of wine, and listen to Sammy spin some tales.

"Not really. But I'm expecting a tough night."

Sammy raised his eyebrows. "Do tell." He reached beneath the counter and pulled out an aged bottle of Patrón, setting it in front of her with a wink. "I keep this tucked away 'specially for you."

"My favorite."

"I know." He poured her half a shot and shoved the amber liquid her way.

"That's it?"

"You don't need to get shit-faced every Friday night, you know. Besides, you said you have plans."

"Thank you, Father Sammy." Seph raised her glass for a toast. "*Salute.*"

The Patrón tickled her lips, and, as if on cue, her cell phone rang. Seph slammed the glass onto the bar.

"Darn it!" She grimaced at Sammy. "I told you so." The drink would have to wait.

Chapter Two

Seph sat on the plane with her head bowed and hands clenched in her lap, praying that her mother's prophetic nightmare hadn't included a plane crash. Her fingers periodically wandered to the dainty gold cross hanging around her neck. The storm system triggered turbulence which buffeted the plane mercilessly, and Seph's prayers got louder and more fervent with each stomach-jolting change in altitude. She was thankful she'd bypassed the shot of tequila before her trip. She doubted it would've stayed down.

To her surprise and relief, the plane landed in San Antonio without a hitch. Seph disembarked, bolting to the restroom like a greyhound let out of the gate. She was staring at herself in the mirror, patting her clammy forehead with a cold paper towel, when she realized she was alone. Really alone. "No one else in the terminal" alone. She paused to listen. The people mover hummed outside, its artificially perky voice looping a reminder to distracted travelers. *The moving walkway is coming to an end. Please watch your step*. Otherwise, the terminal was silent.

Perhaps her concern was unwarranted. After all, the plane had been mostly empty, occupied only by a few relief workers—people like herself who were either overly cavalier or else mandated to fly into the coming hurricane. She peered outside the ladies' room door. No one sat waiting at the gates; no one stood working behind the desks. The other passengers from her plane had proceeded directly to baggage claim, leaving the hallways preternaturally bare. The people mover was preaching to an empty church.

Seph crept out of the bathroom and cringed as her rubber soles screeched on the granite floor. A trickle of sweat rolled down the middle of her back. Empty airports were about as creepy as abandoned malls. She wouldn't want to have to spend the night here. She slung her backpack over her shoulder and followed the signs to baggage claim, sprinting as fast as her carry-on would allow. She was supposed to be picked up by a driver from the local VA hospital, but she'd never gotten his name and, although she had her contact people back home, she didn't have one here in Texas.

That's the way these deployments worked. You went where they told you to go, trusted the logistics to them, and prayed—a lot. Usually she was a little more careful. Seph had learned a thing or two from her prior deployments (Rule #2: Never take more luggage than you can carry by yourself), and she typically had a backup plan should she need to get the hell out of Dodge in a hurry. *He'll be there.* She fought to quell the rising panic as she jogged down an escalator and hustled along another empty hallway. *Have a little faith.*

Baggage claim held a smattering of other travelers, some of whom were wearing the VA's standard-issue blue polo shirt with the yellow DEMPS logo. The carousels lay dormant except for one, and she slowed her pace, allowing herself to catch her breath before joining a trio of men waiting for their luggage. One was a federal police officer, one a chaplain of uncertain denomination, and the third appeared to be a doctor, based on his fine leather carry-on bag. Seph smiled, giddy with relief. *Three men walk into a bar . . .*

She wasn't witty enough to flesh out the joke in time for introductions, so instead she simply extended her hand. "Hi!

I'm Dr. Persephone Smith, a psychologist with the Philadelphia VA. You can call me 'Seph.' I imagine we're all going to the same place?"

"I suspect we are indeed." The chaplain was the first to reply. "I'm Father Barnabas, but I go by Father Barney. Figured I would rather be associated with a purple dinosaur than a bloodsucking creature of the night."

"You mean a vampire?"

"Ah, you must be too young, my dear, to remember the television show *Dark Shadows.* I'm guessing it debuted right about the time you were born. But trust me, those of us with a few more years under our belts remember. Isn't that right, Doctor?"

"Humph." The doctor peered over his bifocals at Seph. "What kind of physician are you?" He didn't bother to offer his hand.

"I'm a doctor of psychology, not a medical doctor."

"Humph," he said again, turning his back to face the baggage carousel in a curt and obvious dismissal.

Seph's smile faded. Miffed but not surprised, she aimed an invisible thwack at the back of his chauvinistic head. She knew his type well. Snooty, middle-aged, affluent, white, male doctor. Stereotypes remain stereotypes for a reason, and this one was alive, well, and standing in front of her. He wouldn't deign to acknowledge Seph's existence unless he had a wigged-out psych patient he wanted to dump in her lap. She crossed her fingers he'd be assigned to a different shift than hers.

"I, for one, am glad you're here. We always need lots of people like you. The last time I deployed to one of these shelters, I felt like I was riding the crazy train, and I'm not talking about the Metro-North." The police officer jumped in, filling the awkward silence and extending a hand the size of an ape's. "I'm Chief Shane Bishop, Bronx VA. You buckled up and ready for the ride?"

Seph laughed. "I've done this once or twice before as well. I think I'm good." She beamed him a smile. Rule #3: Always make friends with the shelter police. "But speaking of rides, anybody know how we're getting from point A to point B?"

"School bus." The chief laughed at Seph's incredulous expression. "Seriously, they're running a transportation loop back and forth between the airport and the shelter via school bus. It runs every hour, so if our bags show up soon . . ." He glanced at his watch. ". . . We shouldn't have long to wait."

As if on cue, the baggage carousel buzzed and shuddered to life. The tiny crowd cheered. Seph and the others claimed their belongings and headed outside.

"Whew, Lordy!" Father Barney tugged at his shirt collar. "It might not be raining yet, but it sure is *hot*!"

"It's not the heat; it's the humidity. Isn't that what they always say?" Chief Bishop grimaced as he wiped beads of sweat from his forehead.

"Yes, well, it's that, too!" The chaplain panted in the thick, oppressive air and cast a worried eye heavenward, where the angry clouds loomed dark and ominous.

"At least there's a breeze." Seph tipped her head back and closed her eyes. A sudden gust lifted the hair off her shoulders and wrapped her neck in its warm, sticky embrace. Her throat clenched under the weight. She felt the storm coming, smelled its proximity. The pressure in her sinuses told her the rain would be starting soon. "Do you think we'll make it to the shelter before all hell breaks loose?"

Father Barney clasped his pudgy hands in front of his chest. "Let us pray."

The yellow school bus drove straight through the check point, unattended since Kelly Air Force Base was decommissioned several years prior. The sun had not yet completely set, but the twilight seemed unusually dark due to the approaching storm, and the scenery around them blended into a haze of dreary browns and greys, adding to the general air of neglect. They'd beaten the rain.

Seph stared out the window as the flat landscape gave way to a cluster of drab, abandoned buildings and asphalt driveways. Base housing. The bus zipped by a playground, now lifeless and forlorn. Only the swings retained any spark of residual energy. Their chains, whipped by the mounting wind, swayed back and forth, twisting and tangling at a frenzied pace as if being pushed by the ghosts of children past.

They left the housing units and playground behind and continued west, toward an overgrown field. A runway peeked from among the weeds. The bus followed along its path until a mammoth steel structure appeared on the horizon. It grew larger and more imposing the closer they got. The air hangar had a football-sized parking lot in which two dozen vehicles were already parked—yellow school buses similar to their own, white cargo vans bearing the VA logo, and a smattering of military vehicles.

Despite her prior experience, Seph was overcome by the sheer size of the current operation. This was by far the largest shelter to which she'd ever been assigned. On her last deployment, FEMA had converted a Louisiana university gymnasium into a shelter capable of housing two hundred evacuees. This place could hold five times that, with room to spare. A thousand frantic people crammed into an airplane hangar for two weeks or more was a mental health emergency waiting to happen. Seph slumped in her seat and rubbed the back of her neck. She was going to be one busy psychologist.

The driver eased the bus into position between two orange pylons and left the engine idling. He disembarked for further instructions. Seph pressed her nose against the glass, trying to get a closer look.

The scene could best be described as an organized mess. Wooden crates and four-foot square plastic bins clogged the intake area. Workers in ball caps and heavy gloves buzzed around, hustling to unload and stage as much of the equipment as possible before the weather set in. They'd created three traffic lanes: one for supplies, one for evacuee buses, and one for employee transports. The evacuee lane was thus far devoid of vehicles, which was a relief. Getting a shelter up and running was tough enough without screaming children and their harried parents milling about.

The driver re-boarded the bus and plonked behind the steering wheel. He bobbed up and down on the raggedy seat like a jack-in-the-box with a broken spring. "Dee-troit is gonna take y'all from here." He nodded over his shoulder at the huge man lumbering up the steps beside him. "I've got one more pick up t'make before dark."

"Dee-troit" stood in the front of the bus, his bulky frame blocking the entire exit. "I need you to come forward one at a time so I can check you off my list and tell you where to report." With a radio in one hand and a pen in the other, he surveyed the passengers before pointing to Seph. "As always, ladies first, and since you appear to be the only lady on the bus, follow me."

Seph gathered her backpack and trundled down the narrow aisle, hurrying to keep up. They halted next to a folding table, which was covered by a jumble of clipboards, each labeled by location. Phoenix, San Juan, Detroit . . .Seph counted a dozen different cities.

"Where ya from?" he asked.

"Philadelphia."

He routed through the piles until he found the appropriate clipboard. "State your name for me."

"Dr. Persephone Smith."

He checked her off his list with a Detroit Lions pen. "Greek goddess or something, right?"

"Sort of. The daughter of a goddess, which technically makes her a demi-god. But close enough. I'm impressed, actually. Most people don't have a clue. You know the story?"

In the Greek myth, Persephone was the daughter of Demeter, the goddess of the harvest. One day, while picking flowers in a Sicilian field, Persephone was kidnapped by Hades, the God of the Underworld and taken underground to be his reluctant wife. Demeter searched for her daughter, and while she wept, the Earth wilted from neglect. When she finally located Persephone deep underground, she appealed to Zeus for her daughter's release. After intense negotiations, Persephone was permitted to return to the surface for nine months out of each year. The other three she spent in hell with her captor. During that time, her mother mourned, and the Earth suffered through three months of wintery desolation.

"Dee-troit" nodded. "I know the basics. I'm a film buff—huge fan of *The Matrix* movies, in particular. Researched all the characters and the origins of their names. Monica Bellucci played her, remember?"

Seph pursed her lips. "Noooo, can't say that I do."

"Look it up. And whatever you do, don't challenge me to movie trivia. You will lose. Badly. You've been warned." He grinned and tossed her a fluorescent orange armband. "Welcome to Hell, Persephone. Make sure you wear it at all times, even to bed. Consider it your new best friend."

Seph caught the strap and wrapped it around her upper arm. The bands were a simple but effective way to identify the federal workers from the hoard of evacuees, which was no easy task. After a couple of weeks in a shelter, everyone began to look and smell the same—like they'd just crawled out of the sewer.

She scanned the surrounding area. "Don't you think you're exaggerating a wee bit? It looks bad, but not 'Welcome to Hell' bad."

"Nope." He pointed toward the roof. "Says so right there. See for yourself."

Seph craned her neck to examine a decrepit metal sign clinging to the roof by one corner. Years of neglect had left it battered beyond redemption, and it dangled and danced in the mounting wind, shrieking its agony with each gust of air. The word "Kelly" had lost its "y," and the "K" had rusted and faded into a smeared facsimile of itself, making the sign indeed appear to read, "Welcome to Hell FA."

"Okay, I'll give you this one, Dee- . . ." Seph stopped mid-sentence. "What's your real name? I'm betting it's not Dee-troit."

"Nope. It's Lewis. Lewis Liddell, at your service." He swept his arm forward in a mock bow. "But you, my Greek demigoddess, can call me 'Lew.' I'm your go-to guy for any personnel issues. My job is to keep track of everyone, where they're from and what they're assigned to do. You, Dr. Smith, will be occupying the right side of the hangar, which has been designated the medical ward. The left side is the housing part of the shelter and will be managed by the Red Cross. Enter through the door in front of you, turn right, and report to the first person you see with a clipboard and a walkie-talkie. That'll be either Dr. Anne Parrish or Dr. Peter Dodgson. One of them will assign you from there."

A sudden gust of wind fluttered the papers on the clipboards, and the first drops of rain began to fall. "Better hurry, Doc, or you'll get soaked. This one's gonna be a nightmare. I can tell." Lew frowned at the sky before turning his attention back to his list. He poked his head through the door of the bus. "Next!"

The light rain changed to a torrential downpour in the short time it took Seph to sprint across the parking lot and reach the entrance. In front of the solid metal door was a concrete patio, which held a gaggle of federal workers, puffing and dragging on what were likely to be their last cigarettes for the next few days. Alcohol and tobacco use were prohibited in the shelter; once the full, hurricane-strength winds hit, no one would be allowed outside, so the addicts nicotine-loaded while they still could, ignoring the soaking rain to get their full hit.

The savvy smokers brought extra nicotine patches, gum, or even liquid nicotine and sold it on the shelter's soon-to-be-active black market for a hefty sum. Such practice violated all federal employee conduct laws, but many of the laws didn't apply during emergency situations, and the ones that did were tacitly ignored. The black-market nicotine fell into the latter category.

Seph stifled a cough as she weaved her way across the crowded patio. Her mother smoked, but neither Seph nor Grace had acquired the habit. Seph did light up from time to time when it suited her, mostly while nursing a tequila. But she didn't *need* to smoke, and she held little regard for those who did. She saved her sympathy for the alcoholics; liquor was confiscated at the door.

She nodded congenially at the herd as she approached the door and took special notice of one particular woman who was staring her up and down. The woman's plaid shirt was two sizes too big and missing some buttons, and her leggings had holes in both knees. Her grey hair, flattened against her skull by the rain, had been chopped into random-appearing layers, and her eyes blazed with the intensity seen only in those with mental illness, substance abuse, or both. Their eyes met, and the woman slowly bared her nicotine-stained teeth in a malevolent imitation of a smile. Seph shivered despite the heat, picturing Luna forty years in the future. This woman and she could be twins.

Another grey-haired woman with kinder eyes crushed her cigarette underfoot and tugged on the heavy door. "After you, honey," she said. The rain collected in the deep lines of her face and funneled downward to drip off her chin. "I'm already soaked."

"Thank you." Seph dashed through the door, only to stop short, her mouth agape. Despite the shelter's imposing outward appearance, she was unprepared for the daunting vastness of the hangar's interior. The workers had attempted to make the space more manageable by breaking it into rectangular units, stacking empty crates and bins in long lines to create separate "rooms." Instead, they'd created a rat maze. The hangar was so large and the light so dim that Seph's eyes refused to focus on anything beyond ten feet.

"Huge, isn't it? They say a long time ago, the space program in Houston was transporting the shuttle *Columbia* on top of a Boeing 747 and had to make a pit stop here overnight. Ran outta gas, or something. The whole kit and caboodle was parked right where we're standing, inside the hangar. I'm inclined to believe them. I'm Selma, by the way." Selma had followed her inside and was attempting, without much success, to brush the water off her face and arms. "I'll be working in the kitchen, if you want to call it that."

"I'm Seph, a psychologist. And I have absolutely no idea where I'll be working."

Selma chuckled. "Just you wait, honey. Once those evacuees start rolling in, this space will feel positively claustrophobic. They're expecting a whole slew of them, I hear. I'll take you to the command area. They'll be able to help. Follow me."

Seph followed Selma to the far-right corner, where a glass-enclosed room stood separate from the main area of the hangar. Tattered maps, yellow with age, plastered the upper half of the room's only solid wall. The lower half housed a built-in array of radar screens, electronic gadgets, and control buttons, all coated with a fine layer of dust. A folding conference table anchored the middle of the room and held two laptops as well as a mishmash of phones and other communication equipment.

Through the glass, Seph saw a forty-something woman clad in a red polo shirt and the requisite orange armband. She cradled a phone in one hand and a clipboard in the other and was doing laps around the table as she talked.

Selma dragged her finger across the cloudy glass. "This used to be the radio control room. I was stationed here with the Air Force, back in the day, which is how I heard the story about the *Columbia*. Now the whole base has been left to rot. It's sad." Selma wiped her dirty finger on her jeans. "Anyway, behold Dr. Parrish. Handle with care. I don't like to gossip, mind you, but I already saw her ream out one of the maintenance guys. Chewed him up and spit him out in pieces. I thought the poor man was gonna bawl. It's a shame Dr. Dodgson isn't here for you to talk to instead."

"I'll be fine, Selma. Thanks." Seph smiled and raised her fist to tap on the door. "Oh, hey, Selma—before you go—who was the woman outside? The one in the plaid shirt. She wasn't wearing an armband, but I didn't think any evacuees had been bussed in yet."

"Carol came with one of the social workers. I overheard Lew talking to Dr. Parrish about her. He said Carol was sitting at the Galveston VA outpatient clinic with the homeless veterans' coordinator when the governor ordered the evacuation. She refused to leave the clinic because she 'didn't have anywhere else to go and no way to get there if she did.' The homeless coordinator got his deployment orders and decided to bring Carol with him. Figured she'd end up here in the shelter at some point anyway. She got a backstage pass, you might say."

Selma lowered her voice. "She seems kind of strange, if you ask me. Bless her heart. I guess we're all strange in our own special ways."

Dr. Parrish noticed them hovering outside the glass and shot Seph an inquisitive look. Selma twirled to face the other direction. "Time for me to leave. See you at dinner time, I guess. I'll try to cook you up something nice. Good luck!" She left with a wink and a wave.

"Thanks, Selma. I'll look forward to it." Seph rapped on the door and was waved in by Dr. Parrish, who was still on the phone. She motioned for Seph to take a seat while she finished her conversation.

"I think we need to be prepared for an outbreak of a stomach flu, what with having no running water. Yes, I know we have plenty of hand sanitizer, but the alcohol-based sanitizers don't deactivate gastrointestinal viruses. Listen, all I'm saying is we would appreciate having more Imodium and IV fluid bags sent before Ignatius shuts down our supply route. Right. Thanks."

Dr. Parrish tossed the phone harder than necessary onto the plastic table and rolled her eyes. She smiled through gritted teeth. "You'd think I was asking for all the gold in Montezuma's treasure. Instead, I'm just trying to prevent Montezuma's revenge!" She laughed at her own joke and waved her clipboard toward Seph. "And who might you be?"

"Dr. Seph Smith, psychologist, Philadelphia VA." While Dr. Parrish flipped through the list searching for her name, Seph analyzed her new boss.

Dr. Anne Parrish's short hair and rectangular, black glasses made her look like Elvis Costello and Winona Ryder's love child. She seemed amicable enough, but thanks to Selma's warning, Seph knew better. The doctor's jocularity was a practiced façade.

Seph observed the tension in the doctor's grip and the permanently etched frown lines at the corners of her mouth. A volatile temper simmered beneath her polished surface, ready to erupt on demand. Selma was right: Dr. Parrish would require careful handling if she was to be managing Seph's deployment. Rule #4: Never antagonize the one in charge of your way out.

"Ah, here you are." Dr. Parrish slashed Seph off her list with a red pen. "Dr. Persephone Smith from the City of Brotherly Love. Welcome! You've been assigned to work the twelve-hour night shift with me. I'll be doing double duty as the physician in charge as well as the shelter commander for the night shift. Dr. Dodgson . . ." She scanned the area outside the glass walls until she located a man dressed in identical garb to her own. "... Is the day shift commander. As such, you won't interact with him much. I'm your man, so to speak!" She chortled again.

Seph's stomach dropped in disappointment. She managed a polite smile. "Will we have a psychiatrist as well?" she asked.

"No. We have a couple of behavioral health social workers and one other psychologist, and they'll be working days. You and I will handle any psychiatric emergencies at night. According to my information, you've done this twice before, so you know how shelter protocol works. I'll be giving a general briefing once the last employee bus arrives. We should have an hour or two until the evacuees start to roll in. We'll gather in the dining area in a few minutes."

Dr. Parrish pointed to the vacuous central area of the hangar which looked nothing like a dining area, save a few lonely plastic picnic tables floating like deserted islands in the middle of a concrete ocean.

"In the meantime, head to the back and pick out a cot. That'll be where you sleep during the day. You can stash your stuff there, too. And call me 'Annie,' by the way. All my friends do."

Someone knocked on the glass behind them. Dr. Parrish flashed a perfunctory smile and lowered her gaze back to her list. "Get the door on your way out, will you?"

Seph bit back a tart response and turned to march out of the control room. Chief Bishop hovered on the other side of the partition. He opened the door for her with a gentlemanly flourish, cocked his head toward Dr. Parrish, and questioned Seph with his eyes. She pursed her lips in response, and he grinned at their silent but effective interchange. *No way in hell would they be calling her "Annie."*

Seph stomped to the employee rest area at the back of the shelter and claimed a cot at the end of one of the long rows. She didn't like being sandwiched between two other people. The cots were situated within arm's reach of each other, with barely enough room to sidle in between. She'd rather be next to a concrete wall than have someone punch her in the mouth while stretching in bed.

A piece of paper dangled from the foot of the cot, secured to the metal frame by duct tape. Seph wrote her name next to the big "N." The employees shared two-to-a-cot between day and night shifts in order to save space and supplies. As an afterthought, Seph scribbled a smiley face next to her signature. Might as well be neighborly. After all, she and "D" would be sharing the same pillow.

Seph squatted, stashed her backpack under the low bed, and tallied the rows. She estimated about eighty federal workers were expected to report. Only a third of them would end up working the night shift with her.

Day shift fed, monitored, and entertained the evacuees—a considerable task. Stress and boredom led to trouble, and trouble led to chaos. The most experienced employees brought distractions with them—coloring books for the kids, decks of cards for the adults. These small items became as important to the evacuees as the shoes on their feet. The social workers were busiest during the day as well, interviewing each family for their "exit strategy" out of the shelter. *Do you have a place to go if your home's been destroyed or isn't livable? Any family in the area?*

The answer was always "no." People with means evacuated themselves by private vehicle to a hotel or a relative's house—anywhere but a shelter. In Seph's experience, shelters like this one held the social fringes—those too ill, too poor, or too stupid to get out of harm's way on their own. Exceptions existed, of course, but it was the norm that kept the social workers hopping. A shelter could not close until everyone had somewhere to go.

But night shift was oh-so different. After the evening meal and medicines, the commander issued her nightly reminder to please be courteous to those around you, especially mothers fighting their children to sleep. The lights dimmed at eight and turned off at nine. The constant hum of the shelter, a beehive of activity during the day, ceased with the click of a switch.

The social workers ruled during the light of day, but people like Seph ruled the night. In the darkness, the shelter transformed into an entirely different animal, and the neuroses crept out to play. Sundowners—dementia patients who got confused in the dark—began to shriek with agitation. *Help*! *Help*! Their pathetic cries mixed with the sounds of children wailing, men snoring, and mothers struggling to break down as quietly as possible.

Predators prowled, nightmares flourished, and Seph was at her busiest. This shelter promised to be particularly challenging. The university gymnasium from her last assignment had been bright and cheery. By comparison, the hangar was a grungy, vast space with dark corners and jagged shadows everywhere. The feral noise of the wind howling over the roof added an extra layer of angst and hinted at the destruction occurring outside the heavy, metal doors.

Seph had worked night shift once before, and she'd hated it. The only good thing about the experience was the valuable expertise she'd gained in dealing with mental health crises. During that deployment, she'd worked alongside a fabulous psychiatrist. This time, she'd be working with Dr. Parrish.

"Shit move in the dark, you know."

Seph jumped at the sound of a voice close to her ear. "Lew! Holy moly, you scared me! Don't you know you're not supposed to sneak up on people like that?"

Lew stood behind her with both hands in the air. "Sorry, Doc. Not my intent." He lowered his hands. "I'm pleased to report I finished processing the last employee bus, so I came to stake my claim on a cot before all the good ones were taken. Looks like you already garnered yourself a prime piece of territory." He grinned. "'Holy moly'? Seriously, we need to teach you some proper cuss words."

"I know plenty, thanks. I'm from Philadelphia, remember? I try not to get into the habit." His initial words finally registered. "'Shit move in the dark?' What's that supposed to mean?"

"You like that one, huh? I wish I could say I came up with it on my own, but I didn't. I was rappin' with one of the maintenance guys from New Orleans—I won't even try to copy his accent—and he let it fly. We were talking about night shift. You know—how during the day everything seems so nice and shiny and perfectly in place, and then—*bam*—out go the lights, and suddenly nothing is where it was or as it seems. It's *ugly.*"

"Weird. I was just thinking the same thing. Minus the shit-moving part, of course."

Lew laughed. "Of course. This guy from the bayou—he said back in Louisiana the phrase refers to alligators skulking around at night, but since we don't have gators in Detroit, I'm gonna have to search for other reasons to say it. I like the sounds of it. Like right now—I was referring to your cot. You need to remember where it's situated so you can find it again once the lights go out. Because . . ." He waited expectantly.

"Shit move in the dark. I get it."

"Bingo." Lew located an open spot in the back row, inspected the flimsy mattress, and threw his duffle bag on the floor beside it. "Perfect. Home sweet Hell."

"I take it you're on the late shift, too?"

"Yep. Assigned myself to it. I like working night shift, butt-ugliness and all. There's a smaller, tighter group of people with a pack mentality. They watch out for each other, you know what I mean?" Lew unzipped the front flap of his duffel and removed a half-empty pack of cigarettes. "Don't you worry, Doc. We have a good team. I made sure of it." He kicked the bag under his cot.

"Even Dr. Parrish? You've worked with her before?"

"No. Word on the street is she's good at what she does . . .but don't piss her off."

"I figured that much out on my own."

"What, you got ESPN or something?" Lew grinned at the confusion on Seph's face. "It's called a joke, Doc. It's from a movie. You know, ESP . . .never mind." Lew dangled an unlit cigarette from his lips and sauntered toward the front of the building. "I got time for one more smoke before our mandatory group hug. See ya soon."

"Hey, Lew!" Seph yelled after him, and he stopped in his tracks. "I just got it! That ESPN joke was a real knee-slapper, you know."

He flashed a broad grin and waved one hand in her direction as he continued his jaunt toward the exit. She chuckled at his retreating backside. Dr. Parrish may be a bit tight-cheeked, but Seph and Lew were going to get along just fine.

Seph navigated her way back to the center of the building. The dining area now held dozens of folding chairs in addition to the picnic tables. Most of the federal workers were already assembled, and they milled about, making good use of the one and only time they would be gathered together in one place with nothing to do.

Carol was there, too, standing alone, as forlorn and bedraggled as a feral cat. She reeked of tobacco and fiddled obsessively with an object in her pants pocket. Every few seconds, she'd stop, pull it out partway, and take a furtive peep. Satisfied, she'd thrust it deep inside her pocket again, eyes darting back and forth, worried someone might have caught a glimpse of whatever it was she held so dear.

Seph sidled alongside, determined to get a better look. She needn't have bothered. When Dr. Parrish stepped to the front of the crowd to begin her announcements, Carol whipped the object out of her pants with a flourish and held it high in the air for everyone to see.

"It's time!" She crowed like a rooster, face to the sky, right hand holding a gold pocket watch. The crowd fell silent.

"Thank you, Carol." Dr. Parrish's voice was surprisingly devoid of any patronization, which seemed to please Carol immensely. She preened with satisfaction as she returned the watch to her pocket. She stood at full attention and waited for Dr. Parrish to speak.

"Welcome. If anyone has not checked in with either Dr. Dodgson or myself, please step forward."

No one did.

"Excellent. We're off to a great start. Many of you have done this before and know the drill. You'll be working twelve-hour, seven-to-seven shifts except for tonight, when I'm allowing the night shifters to rest until ten p.m. so they can acclimate to their new schedules. The buses will start arriving soon, and we need everyone processed to either the area managed by the Red Cross . . ." Dr. Parrish pointed to the left-hand side of the shelter. ". . . Or to the medical ward on the right. The maintenance workers are doing their best to get the HVAC system up and running and the water flowing. Until then, it's bedside commodes in the medical unit, and all of you, no matter what your job titles may be outside this building, are on potty duty. We don't want any outbreaks here. Any questions thus far?"

A young man in a tropical print shirt raised his hand. "How many patients are we expecting?"

"Good question. We anticipate roughly two hundred medical evacuees from nursing homes and hospital units, but we have to be prepared to handle any medical issues from the Red Cross side, too. I'm requiring the federal workers to stay on the medical unit at all times unless responding to an emergency. This place is huge, and I don't want to have to hunt you down if I need you. Doing so would make me extraordinarily cranky, and I'm sure none of you wants to see that."

Dr. Parrish peered over the top of her glasses at the man in the tropical shirt, who quickly shifted his eyes to the floor. "Any other questions?"

No one else spoke.

"Great. Chief Shane Bishop is in charge of security. Chief, do you want to say a few words?"

"Yes, I do." The chief strode forward. "The plastic barriers positioned down the middle of the shelter mark the border between the two halves, but we didn't have enough to run them clear to the back. The deepest part of the hangar is therefore open and accessible to both sides. It has a lot of small storage rooms and closets capable of hiding criminals searching for an easy target. I don't want anyone going back there alone. It's dark, it's confusing, and I don't have enough officers to patrol the entire space.

"If you absolutely have to go somewhere isolated, use the buddy system. I have a couple of two-way radios I can lend out if needed, but we expect to lose all other forms of communication shortly, once the storm takes out the cell towers. When we're back up and running, we'll let everyone know."

"Thank you, Chief Bishop. Although we hope to have little use for you and your fellow officers, your presence is reassuring and much appreciated."

The chief nodded and rejoined his group of sergeants.

Selma raised her hand. "How do we reach security if we need them?"

"Another great question. You scream. Loudly." Dr. Parrish said it lightly, but the twitching muscle in her jaw gave her away. Her words were no joke. The crowd tittered. The chief took a brisk step forward, but Dr. Parrish held up her hand and changed the subject with the breezy finesse of a career politician.

"I'd also like to introduce our chaplain, Father Barney. He's here to attend to the spiritual needs of both the evacuees and the staff, and he'll lead religious services for as long as the shelter is open. He has a blessing to offer to those who are interested. Those who are not can head to their stations. Thank you."

The mob dispersed, most moving to congregate around Father Barney. Carol, however, remained locked in place. Her right hand resumed its compulsive fingering of the watch in her pocket. Seph cleared her throat and glued a smile to her face. *Time to break the ice.*

"Hi, Carol. My name is Dr. Persephone Smith. I'm a psychologist from Philadelphia. I'm pleased to meet you."

"What kind of stupid-assed name is 'Persephone?' You a foreigner or something?"

Seph blinked. "No, as I said, I'm from Philadelphia. I guess some people might consider Philly a foreign country, huh?"

Silence.

Seph tried again. "Would you like to join me over by Father Barney?"

"Why would I want to do that?" Carol's voice was harsh and deep with suspicion. Her lips curled, and out came the teeth.

"To get a blessing, of course. It can't hurt, right?" Seph strove to sound as friendly and non-threatening as possible, despite an alarming sense of dread rising within. Carol had managed to set off Seph's empathic sensors, and they were just getting started.

"God doesn't bless people like me, Miss Persephone." Carol's tone was mocking, challenging Seph to refute her words. Seph rose to the bait.

"I believe he does. Why would you think otherwise?"

"Because every night I sleep with two men, Smith and Wesson, and God don't like that much. You run along and get your blessing now, ya hear?" Carol stalked away, muttering obscenities under her breath.

Well, that went well. Seph shook her head as she joined her fellow employees gathered around Father Barney. She had other patients like Carol—wounded, distrustful animals who snarled to cover their fear. Maybe, with God's guidance, she could help Carol heal while they were stuck together in the shelter.

Seph's hand clasped the gold cross dangling around her neck. She closed her eyes, using her gift to sense the moods of the individuals around her. She noticed some jitters, for sure; but the prevailing temperament was one of quiet determination, which both pleased and calmed her. She bowed her head and listened to the chaplain work the crowd.

"Nature's fury is God's way of prepping the earth and our souls for bigger and better things to come. At times, we must be stripped to our foundations, laid bare in order to build solid, new walls, to grow and strengthen as human beings. Fear not this process, for the Lord's hand guides us in our transformations, keeping us safe in the face of fury until we are home once more. Here in this shelter, you are not only public servants, federal servants, but servants of the Lord. May His grace shine upon you, illuminating that which has been darkened by the storm. Amen."

Seph sighed with contentment, soothed by the chaplain's blessing. She touched her forehead, then her chest, tracing the Sign of the Cross. *Amen. So be it, truly.*

Chapter Three

The First Night

The giant overhead fluorescent lights flashed on and off at ten p.m., jolting Seph from a dead sleep. After the invocation, she'd chatted with the guy in the tropical shirt—Joaquin, a wound care nurse from the San Juan VA—before returning to her cot for a short cat nap. She'd planned to call home before the phones went out. Unfortunately, she'd underestimated her travel fatigue.

There was no point in calling home now. Her mother always went to bed by nine, unless Nick at Nite happened to be showing a particularly juicy *Columbo* rerun. Seph stretched her stiff muscles, sore from being cramped in the tiny cot, and wrapped the orange armband around her bicep.

A man with a bullhorn and a U.S. Navy Veteran ball cap shoved aside the flimsy rolling partitions cordoning off the employee rest area and shouted the arrival of a bus full of evacuees in the docking bay. "All hands on deck!" He marched through the aisles of cots and shook the feet of those slow to heed his call. "Time to get to work."

The next several hours passed in a blur of activity. By the time the last bus rolled in and the hordes of patients and other evacuees were settled into their assigned pieces of real estate, it was four a.m. The shelter still hummed with an undercurrent of suppressed energy as its new occupants—wide-eyed, soaked, and too terrified to rest—lay awake in their cots. The hurricane loomed large now, its imminent threat visible in the flickering lights and shuddering doors.

Once the patients were triaged according to severity of illness, Dr. Parrish assembled the twenty-six night shifters assigned to the medical ward for a quick but intense huddle. She wasted no time. "How many of you are fluent in Spanish?"

A dozen hands went up.

"Excellent. Register with Lew. Check-in reported many of our patients speak little-to-no English. Also, do any of you have special training or skills I might find useful? For example, any OB/GYN nurses here?"

Her hopeful expression collapsed when no one stepped forward. "Crap. We have a pregnant lady in the shelter who's full term and ready to blow. Let's hope she delivers on day shift. I haven't delivered a baby in eons."

Joaquin raised his hand. "I can't assist with the deliveries, but if it helps, I'm a wound care registered nurse and something of a diabetic specialist, by virtue of personal experience." He lifted the edge of his scrub top to reveal a small box clipped to his pants. A tiny tube and even tinier needle ran from the box to the skin of Joaquin's abdomen, where it was meticulously taped in place. "An insulin pump, for those of you who are unfamiliar."

"Your wound care expertise will come in handy." Dr. Parrish lowered her already-hushed voice. "Did you notice the two gangbangers who arrived on the last bus?" The gang members would've been hard for anyone to miss.

"You mean Tweedle Dee and Tweedle Dum?" Joaquin replied, with a cheeky grin.

"Man, I dare ya to say that to their faces." Lew hijacked the conversation, matching Joaquin's grin with a broad smile of his own. "I double-dog dare ya!"

"I wouldn't recommend it." Chief Bishop did not share their amusement. "They may appear . . .unusual, but make no mistake: The big one's tats identify him as a member of the Aryan Circle, a prison gang known for its brutality. He's not likely to be fond of either one of you." He nodded toward Lew and Joaquin. "Let's just say they take their white supremacy very seriously."

"Nice." Joaquin wrinkled his nose. "So what do my wound healing super powers have to do with them?" he asked Dr. Parrish.

"The little one has an ulcer on his ass. A 'sacral decubitus,' if you prefer the correct medical term. He'll need twice daily dressing changes and packing of the wound, and you just volunteered." Dr. Parrish poked him in the chest with her pen. "Make sure you have someone within shouting distance in case he gets feisty."

Seph raised an eyebrow at Dr. Parrish's understated description. Twisted and deformed, "the little one" resembled some kind of grotesque tarantula/human hybrid, a creature more likely to be found on Dr. Moreau's island than in a storm shelter in Texas. Unable to walk due to the ravages of muscular dystrophy, he possessed just enough strength to push himself up on all fours, arms and legs thrusting his abdomen skyward, so he could creep across the floor, like an inside out spider.

His quivering limbs couldn't support him for long, though, and gradually his torso would begin to sag, causing his rear end to drag along the ground as he slowly sank back to a supine position. His wasted muscles made his head appear too large for his body, and the overall effect was that of a lab experiment gone terribly wrong.

"Thad and Delmas," Seph said. "Thad's 'the little one.' I overheard them talking as they were checking in." Delmas—tall, tattooed, and broad enough to be intimidating—had carried Thad into the shelter on his shoulders. They'd claimed adjacent cots closest to the front exit, where Delmas had gently placed Thad onto a mattress, tucking the sheets around his "brother's" deformed legs. The first thing Seph had noticed was not Thad's bizarre appearance, but the amount of deference he commanded from Delmas.

Delmas doted on Thad, exhibiting a respect which seemed both genuine and profound. Behind their relationship was a story begging to be told, and Seph was a willing audience. She planned on getting to know them better. Maybe the four of them—Delmas, Thad, Carol, and she—could have coffee together. She shook her head and smothered a giggle as she pictured the surreal image. *Good times, good times . . .*

Seph dragged her attention back to Dr. Parrish, who was running through a list of patients she considered to be at high risk during their stay in the shelter.

". . . And, lastly, we have Mr. and Mrs. Condo, who have active tuberculosis. They need to keep their masks on 24/7 except while eating, and they're supposed to report to pharmacy twice daily for their mandatory meds. I've made the pharm tech responsible for ensuring they do so." Dr. Parrish lowered her list.

"You have your assigned roles, but remember—in an emergency shelter, everyone does everything. We're all scut monkeys here. You do what needs to be done, whether it be emptying a urinal or ordering the Condo's to keep their masks on. Work hard, don't whine, and we'll be singing 'Kumbaya' by morning." Dr. Parrish flicked her pen toward the chief. "Who do we need to monitor from a personal safety standpoint?"

Chief Bishop consulted his clipboard. "We tried to run everyone through the law enforcement databases as they checked in. We got several hits for minor offenses—shoplifting, DUIs, the usual stuff—but a few people stood out. Turns out our beloved gangbanger number one, Delmas Duchenne, was recently released from prison after a decade served for murder. While incarcerated, he earned a degree and is now a licensed practical nurse. And a model citizen, I might add."

Joaquin snorted, and Lew slapped his back. The chief ignored them.

"You'll also notice a guy strutting around in cowboy boots, a ten-gallon hat, and a whole lotta gold chains."

Lew interrupted. "I've already had the pleasure. Dude bummed a Marlboro off me while I was checking him in. Way too much bling for a middle-aged white guy. Let me guess—he thinks he's a pimp, or something?"

"Wrong. He gave us a hit on the national sex offender registry. Pedophile. We'll be keeping an eye on him as well."

"Better wear your shades," Joaquin said. "The reflection off those chains is blinding."

"Enough." Dr. Parrish glared at Lew and Joaquin, who giggled like a couple of teens bonding over a beer. "Settle down, you two. Anyone else, Chief?"

"We also have a prostitute running around propositioning old men. While she distracts them with her God-given assets, her boyfriend rifles through their valuables. They both have records, but nothing violent. I think that sums it up. Everyone needs to remember what I said earlier. Use the buddy system, exercise common sense, and stay safe."

"Great advice. Thank you, Chief." Dr. Parrish looked over the rim of her glasses at Seph and the rest of the night shift team. "Okay, you know what to do. We've got three hours until day shift takes over. Anything you accomplish tonight will make the rest of your weeks here easier, so get to work.

Alice, you're the charge nurse for night shift, which means you're with me on rounds."

Alice, with her grey hair and serene demeanor, was the perfect foil to Dr. Parrish's intensity. Clipboard in hand, she glided into place next to Dr. Parrish, effortlessly matching her stride as if the two of them had worked together for years. Together, they headed to the first row of cots to review each patient in more detail.

The rest of the team dispersed as well until only Seph and Lew remained. She waited until Dr. Parrish was out of earshot. "Way to get on the boss's good side. 'Don't piss her off,' you said."

Lew shrugged. "Take a look around, Doc. Soon the boss lady'll have bigger fish to fry than little, ol' Lew. Sharks, with sharp teeth and gold fillings." Lew smiled, flashing his own pearly whites. "Besides, gotta have a little fun when you can. Otherwise, it'll be a long two weeks. She don't bother me. Joaquin don't care, either. He's from San Juan. She's straight outta Boston. As long as she's not planning to transfer to Detroit any time soon, I'm good."

"Not bloody likely."

"Exactly. Where you headed?"

"I think I'll wander around and see if anyone's still awake and wants to talk. Might give me a better idea of who's going to require some support over the next few weeks. You?"

"Time cards. I gotta start time card records for every single employee on night shift. It's not sexy, but hey—someone needs to make sure all you fine people get paid. Trust me—you'll thank me for it once you get home. You'll be like, 'you know, that Lewis guy was all right!'"

Seph smiled and patted Lew on the shoulder. "I think you're all right now, Lew. I wouldn't dream of keeping you from your time cards. Catch up with you later."

"I'll look forward to it."

Seph worked her way to the farthest row of the medical unit's cots and hospital beds so as not to interfere with Dr. Parrish's rounds. She tiptoed by the patients, attempting to memorize their faces and names from the papers that hung from the ends of their beds. A few were wide awake, so she introduced herself, making quiet conversation with those who appeared interested in her services.

At the end of the last row, Seph spied Thad propped next to Delmas, who was shuffling a deck of cards. She wandered over to watch, hoping they'd give her some kind of opening to work with. Instead, Delmas ignored her and dealt the hand.

Thad picked up his cards one by one. He took his time and studied them with great care, communicating a clear lack of interest in his audience. Seph took the hint. She'd already made a small move toward the next cot when Delmas, without lifting his gaze from his handful of aces, decided to acknowledge her presence.

"What are you?"

"I'm Dr. Seph Smith. I . . ."

"You can't follow directions, or else you don't pay much attention, do you? I asked *what* you are, not who you are."

Delmas dripped of sin, with a voice so silky and deep, it conjured up images of supple black leather and aged bourbon. He splayed his cards on the blanket and tipped his chair back on two legs so he could examine her without craning his neck. His blue eyes skimmed over Seph's face and roamed her toned figure, stripping her bare.

Seph's throat clenched, and she ached for the protection of her white lab coat. Despite a valiant attempt to remain calm, her voice assumed a strange and unfamiliar edge, and her eyes wandered to the concrete floor.

"I'm a psychologist. A counselor, if you like."

Delmas and Thad exchanged amused looks at her prim response, and Seph's irritation surged. Intuitively, she knew what she needed to do.

"What are *you*?" she asked.

The bold counterattack surprised Delmas, and his eyes narrowed in suspicion. "What do you mean?"

"Exactly what I said. You asked me what I am, and I told you. Now it's your turn. What are you?"

Delmas cocked his head and perused Seph's face, as if trying to discern her motive. The corners of his mouth curled into a salacious smile. Seph quivered, but she held her ground and managed to steady her wayward gaze.

"I'm a nurse." Delmas broke the uncomfortable silence with his carefully crafted response. He nodded toward Thad. "And he's my only patient."

Thad snickered, and Seph leapt at the chance to divert her attention away from Delmas and his hypnotic gaze. "You must feel pretty lucky to have someone like him helping you out, huh? I saw how well he treated you during check-in."

Thad's face grew wary as he debated her sincerity. "Uh, yeah, I guess so. Delmas does a good job."

An earsplitting shriek from several rows over preempted Seph's response. Delmas cursed and lurched forward in his chair, smacking its metallic front legs against the concrete floor with a clang. Seph spun around in time to see Carol bolt to an upright position in her cot. She began rocking back and forth while staring at the pocket watch in her right hand.

"It's late. Too late. It's too late." Her muttering gained both speed and intensity as she rocked faster and faster in place. The cot's aluminum frame, not designed to handle such aggressive activity, squealed in protest. The darkened room swelled with the irritated murmurings of those awakened by the din.

Delmas scowled at Seph and swung his head in Carol's general direction. "That one's fucked up. She's the one you should be talking to, not us."

Seph frowned. "Carol is mentally ill, not 'fucked up.' She needs our help." Carol released another high-pitched wail, and Seph took off running. She weaved her way through the maze of beds toward Carol's row, knocking into clipboards and tripping over luggage in her haste to reach Carol's side. "Carol, hey, remember me? It's Dr. Smith. What's the matter? Can I help?"

Carol halted mid-rock. She glowered at Seph and thrust the pocket watch into the psychologist's face. "Don't you see what time it is? It's too late, and I can't sleep. It's the storm. It's the storm's fault. I need some sleep, and the storm won't let me." The wind howled a vociferous response to her accusations. Carol dropped the watch and covered both ears, cowering in terror.

Seph glanced at the gold watch. In the dim light, she was unable to distinguish the numbers on the dial, but she could tell one thing for certain: The timepiece was not ticking, and the second hand was not moving. The pocket watch did not work.

"I know it's late, Carol, but I promise it'll be okay. You're safe in here . . ."

Carol wasn't listening. She half-rolled, half-fell out of her cot and onto the concrete floor, landing hard on all fours. She rooted underneath the bed's frame, throwing clothing right and left before settling on her prize—a small metal box, similar to a money box, which she tugged from under the bed with a whoop and a sigh. She hugged it to her chest as she stumbled back to her feet, cradling it as if it were her most precious possession.

"What's in the box, Carol?" *I sleep with two men—Smith and Wesson.* Seph recalled Carol's defiant proclamation from a short time ago, and it made her nervous. The police searched everyone during check-in, but it wasn't hard to imagine them missing a small item here or there amidst the chaos. And if that small item happened to be a gun . . .

Seph peered over her shoulder and saw Dr. Parrish and Alice assessing the situation from a few rows away. Seph caught Alice's eye and gave her a subtle head shake—all the communication the wise, old nurse needed to realize something was amiss. Alice and Dr. Parrish exchanged a few words before Alice bustled off, presumably to find the police. Dr. Parrish headed toward Seph.

Carol perched on the edge of her cot and squeezed the box even tighter. "Go away." Her bloodshot eyes stared at an invisible spot on the floor.

"Okay, Carol." Seph kept her voice calm but firm. "I'll go away and let you get some sleep—as soon as you tell me what's in the box."

Dr. Parrish rounded the corner, with Chief Bishop and Alice not far behind. Carol's head jerked up at the sound of their approaching footsteps.

"What did you do?" Carol screamed at Seph, skewering her with a glare of such intense hatred that Seph took an involuntary step backward, tripping as her ankles caught the edge of the cot behind her. Carol used the extra time and space to fling the box open, reach inside, and stuff a fistful of something into her mouth.

"Carol!" Dr. Parrish knelt beside her and tore the box from her hands. "Whatever it is, spit it out! *Spit it out!*"

Carol shook her head violently, sending her stringy hair flying around her puffed-out cheeks. She patted the blanket up and down, searching for her lost watch. Her fingers touched upon the chain, and she shoved the watch deep inside her pocket before belly flopping onto her cot. She buried her face in the pillow and balled her fists at her side.

Chief Bishop arrived to stand next to Dr. Parrish, and he shined his flashlight into the bottom of Carol's box. Inside were hundreds of loose pills—one of every shape, size, and color, it seemed, with no bottles or instructions in sight.

"She skittled," Seph said. She touched Carol's back and received an angry swat in return.

"She did what?" Dr. Parrish sounded more annoyed than concerned.

"Skittled. Like the candy. It's the 'in' thing among teens these days. They mix a whole bunch of medications like Xanax and painkillers in a big bowl, set it on the coffee table during a party, and pop pills at random. Stupid and dangerous, of course. Maybe even crazy."

"Great. That's just great." Dr. Parrish reached into the box and plucked out a shiny, green capsule with small letters stamped across its surface. Squinting, she held it up to the light. "I recognize this one. It's Seroquel, a commonly prescribed antipsychotic."

She waved her hand over the open container. "I'm guessing these represent the prescription meds Carol's supposed to be taking. Instead, she's been hoarding them for God knows how long. It'll take pharmacy several days to sort through and identify them all, if that's even possible. In the meantime, we have no idea what she took, how much she took, and how it's going to affect her."

"Plan for the worst; hope for the best," Alice said. "What else can we do?" She watched Carol's back move up and down with each breath and counted her respiratory rate. "Her respirs are slowing down already. Whatever we decide, we need to do it soon."

"Do we have any of that syrup here?" the chief asked. "You know, the stuff they give you in the ER after an overdose to make you throw up?"

"Ipecac. No. It's fallen out of favor. Too many bad experiences with it. You don't want someone who just drank Drano, for instance, vomiting it back up. Burns on the way down; burns on the way up. Nasty." Dr. Parrish wrinkled her nose in distaste.

"We might have activated charcoal," Alice said, tucking a wayward strand of curly grey hair into the braided bun atop her head.

The chief sputtered in surprise. "You're going to give her charcoal? As in, the stuff I grill with? You've got to be kidding me!"

Dr. Parrish nodded her approval. "Good idea, Alice. Charcoal, when given early in an overdose, can bind to the medications and prevent them from being absorbed into the bloodstream."

Carol lifted her head from the pillow long enough to burp and curse. Dr. Parrish rolled her eyes. "Convincing an agitated patient like Carol to drink a slurry of chunky, black particles is often nigh to impossible. Which leaves us with the option of cramming a tube down her nose and into her stomach and force-feeding the charcoal to her. No shits and giggles there, either. What do you think, Alice?"

Alice's glum expression indicated the prospect was less than appealing.

Carol made it easy for them. She turned her face toward Alice and exhaled with a soft sigh. Her hands, which had been clenching the side rails of the cot's frame, relaxed, and Carol went to sleep. Her back movements slowed to a stop.

Dr. Parrish and Alice sprang into action, rolling the unconscious Carol into the fetal position and assessing her pulse. Carol gasped and resumed breathing but failed to awaken from her stupor.

"Help me move her closer to the nurses' station," Dr. Parrish said. Chief Bishop lifted one end of the cot, and Seph helped Dr. Parrish with the other. Together they shuffled Carol, cot and all, toward an array of folding tables which constituted the shelter's nurses' station.

"A little help here!" Dr. Parrish shouted commands as they set Carol's cot down as gently as possible on the concrete floor. "Alice, get an IV kit, and see if the pharmacy has the charcoal in stock. Even better, see if they happen to have any Narcan or Romazicon. And don't forget the NG tube!" Alice scurried away, while Joaquin, who was manning the station, swooped in to help.

Within minutes, Carol had an IV in her arm and the opening of a plastic tube taped to the side of her nose. Dr. Parrish managed to suction a rainbow of partially dissolved pills out of Carol's stomach and replace them with the liquid charcoal. Alice and Joaquin hovered over their new patient, monitoring her vital signs every ten minutes and documenting every twitch and gasp on a makeshift chart. Dr. Parrish and Seph positioned themselves within earshot at the nurses' station.

"Do you think she'll survive?" Seph asked. Carol's slack face appeared ashen in the dim light.

"We only have to keep her alive for two more hours." Dr. Parrish's mouth curled into a grim smile. "Then she's day shift's problem."

Their conversation lapsed as Seph, taken aback by the callous nature of Dr. Parrish's response, simply nodded. She felt the adrenaline surge ebb away, and as fatigue set in, she was reminded of the late hour and her own lack of accommodation to working twelve-hour shifts. She hadn't pulled an all-nighter since her last deployment.

Seph sagged back in her chair and let her eyelids drift shut. She would've been happy to spend the remaining two hours silently watching Carol sleep off her overdose, but Dr. Parrish wouldn't allow it.

"So, Persephone, right? Great name. I'm sure there's a story behind it."

Seph forced her eyelids open and launched into a dutiful recitation of the Greek myth, but Dr. Parrish cut her off.

"I know the origin. I meant the story behind why your parents chose the name."

"Oh."

Tired, cranky, and put off by her boss's pithy inquiry into her personal life, Seph dismissed Dr. Parrish's curiosity with an apathetic wave of her hand. "Annie" seemed hell-bent on bonding whether Seph wanted to or not. "There's no story, really. Nothing interesting, anyhow. My mother was a big fan of Greek and Roman mythology, and she liked the name. The end."

"Mm. You're right. That's not much of a story. I've got a better one. You wanna hear it?"

Seph did not want to hear it. She stifled a yawn and feigned profound interest in a sudden switch in the nurses' previously synchronized activities. Alice had Carol's vital signs under control, so Joaquin rushed to collect an armful of tape, gauze, and other wound care supplies. The situation with Carol had put him behind schedule. He juggled his equipment and hustled to change the soiled bandage on Thad's seeping ulcer before day shift arrived.

"I'd love to hear your story," Seph said, hoping Dr. Parrish was too egocentric to notice the insincerity of Seph's words.

". . . But first I want to sneak a peek at Carol's watch while she's gorked out. I noticed earlier it wasn't ticking, and I'm curious as to why she finds a broken watch so special."

"Seriously? Who cares? Carol is mentally ill—a paranoid schizophrenic, if I had to venture an educated guess. The watch is her toy, something for her warped mind to attach itself to." Dr. Parrish shook her head in disbelief and skewered Seph with her sharp gaze. Seph squirmed like a worm in a petri dish.

"You're a bit strange yourself, aren't you, *Doctor* Smith?" Her boss placed a subtle emphasis on the word "doctor," as if implying the title was a sham.

Seph forced a smile. "Maybe I am. But collecting stories is what I do best. Right now, I'm most interested in Carol's. I'll be back for yours next." She strode toward Carol's cot, leaving a bemused Dr. Parrish sitting alone at the nurses' station.

Alice was bent over, checking Carol's blood pressure when Seph approached. "Any change?" Seph asked.

"No. She's stable at the moment." The hissing cuff deflated. Alice left it positioned on Carol's upper arm for the next set of vital signs. "But things can change in an instant depending on which drug hits her system next. Thank God the pharmacy had Narcan in stock. It reversed the effect of the narcotics, but it won't help with the benzos."

The petite nurse straightened to full height and stood guard, Carol's personal guardian angel, waiting for Seph to state her purpose. "She won't be awake for quite a while yet. Not enough for you to talk to, anyhow."

"I know. I want to take a look at Carol's pocket watch, if you don't mind. I promise to stay out of your way."

If Alice found the request odd, she didn't show it. She stepped aside and allowed Seph to access Carol's pocket. Seph removed the watch for closer examination. It felt heavy in her hand and was obviously of fine quality and high gold content. She would've expected a homeless veteran like Carol to have hocked it long ago.

The face read, "*Jaeger-LeCoultre*." She flipped the watch over, squinting in the dim light. The back of the gold case bore a worn inscription, engraved in fancy, cursive letters. Aware of Alice discreetly straining to peek over her shoulder, Seph read the words aloud. "To Harry, the best of the 8th. Bombs away, old chum! Charles Lutwidge, Flt. Lt. London, 1944."

Seph stuffed the watch back into Carol's pocket. "Well, that doesn't help much, does it?"

"Oh, but it does, Doctor." Alice surprised Seph with her perky reply. "My father was originally from Bermuda and served in the Royal Air Force during World War II. The navigators and bombardiers always used pocket watches not just for convenience, but because their split-second timing allowed for perfect bomb groupings. The United States, specifically the 8th Air Force, participated in joint operations with the RAF in 1944. The British flew by day, and the Americans flew by night. I loved to hear about my father's secret missions when I was a child."

"So, you think Harry, a World War II bombardier, was Carol's father?"

"Yes. He probably passed his watch on to her when she joined the military. It's a family heirloom. That would be my guess, anyway. A nice story, don't you think?" Alice brushed a lock of damp, stringy hair off her sleeping patient's forehead.

"If it's true. It would explain why she didn't sell it, I suppose."

"Far too precious for that."

Seph nodded in agreement and, lost in thought, traipsed back to the nurses' station where Dr. Parrish lie in wait. She pounced the minute Seph arrived.

"Did you find Jimmy Hoffa?"

"What?" Seph, bewildered by Dr. Parrish's taunting question, glanced at the closest nurse for assistance. He shrugged and went back to his charts.

"Never mind. I think we left off with how I got my name."

"Sure." Seph was still too preoccupied by what she'd learned about Carol to conjure any semblance of enthusiasm. Undaunted, Dr. Parrish launched into the history of her name.

"Anne Parrish was a renowned American novelist, writer of children's books, and a cousin of Maxfield Parrish, the famous artist. She lived most of her adult life in my hometown of Claymont, Connecticut. My mother adored Anne's books and read *Knee-High to a Grasshopper* to me every night before bed—I swear to God—until I was, like, twelve. She was convinced we were distant relatives, even though there's zero proof our genes ever crossed paths with Anne's!"

Dr. Parrish erupted into her hearty, yet somehow insincere, laugh. Her eyes cruised around the nurses' station, inviting everyone to join the merriment. Seph managed a polite smile.

"Naming me 'Anne' was a no-brainer until my mother discovered Anne Parrish had died of a brain hemorrhage. Mother thought it was a bad omen and wanted to change my name, but my father wouldn't hear of it. So they started calling me 'Annie.'"

Seph sidled away from the desk. "Makes sense to me. Thanks for . . ."

"I'm not finished!" Dr. Parrish actually stomped her foot, and Seph froze in place, unsure if she should be amused or frightened.

"As I was saying . . . The weirdness started five years ago, when I developed these wretched migraine headaches. All I could think about was this story from my childhood. I convinced myself I had an aneurysm; I was surely going to die of a cerebral hemorrhage, just like my namesake. I turned into a genuine neurotic—the real deal. The more obsessed I became over Anne Parrish's death, the more excruciating my headaches became. Thankfully, a normal MRI cured me of my affliction. To this day, I insist people call me 'Annie,' though—never 'Anne.'" Dr. Parrish chortled again, but this time her amusement was short-lived. Delmas was strolling their way.

He had the slow, stealthy gait of a predator—low center of gravity, cautious, always on guard. He passed by Carol's cot and sneered at her charcoal-streaked face and the tube jutting from her nose. "I told you baby girl was whacked, didn't I?" He aimed his silky drawl squarely at Seph.

Dr. Parrish spoke before Seph could stutter an answer. "Can I help you with something?" Her voice was cool with a hint of disdain. Seph hoped it was too subtle for Delmas to notice. No such luck. He visibly bristled at Dr. Parrish's tone.

"No, Your Highness, I don't think so. I'm actually here to help *you.*"

"Really? Do tell." Dr. Parrish's condescending attitude was now on full display, and Seph cringed. Disrespecting an ex-con white supremacist without back up is generally considered poor form. Here, in the close confines of a shelter, it was an especially dumb move. They were trapped together in the same building for the next two weeks, and Delmas had the ability to wreak havoc if he chose to do so. But Dr. Parrish didn't seem to care. She crossed her arms and waited for Delmas to finish what he'd started.

"Your boy, the can-kicker you sent to work on Thad's ulcers, he wigged out. Started acting all weird and shit—shaking, sweating, chanting in his *loco* Puerto Rican Spanish like some kind of nut job. Then he ran off. Didn't even finish the dressing change. Left Thad's ass hanging out to dry. I don't know what he's coming down from, but it must be some serious shit. I thought you might wanna know."

"Which way did he go?" Dr. Parrish, suddenly too worried to act pompous, dropped her attitude and readied one hand on her walkie.

Delmas gestured past the employee rest area, toward the dark void at the rear of the shelter where the chief had forbidden them to go alone. "Somewhere back there. Listen for the jabbering. You'll find him."

Dr. Parrish pointed to Seph. "Go get Alice. Tell her to bring a glucometer and as many tubes of instant glucose as she can find. I'll notify the chief. I suspect Joaquin is having a severe hypoglycemic episode, and he could die if we don't find him quickly." Dr. Parrish lifted her walkie to her mouth and strode away, leaving Seph the sole recipient of Delmas's attention.

Seph stiffened and braced herself to handle another visual undressing. "Thank you," she said, since Dr. Parrish did not. After all, the white supremacist may have just saved Joaquin's life. A simple expression of gratitude was the least Dr. Parrish could've offered.

Delmas winked as he watched Dr. Parrish's back disappear between the rows of cots. "Don't let the Red Queen boss you around. She's a real bitch, you know." He looped one thumb in his waistband and sauntered back to Thad.

Seph exhaled and searched the medical ward for Alice, whom she found sternly lecturing the husband-and-wife tuberculosis patients about wearing their masks. She rushed to update the head nurse on Joaquin's disappearance. Alice, calm as ever, gathered the requested supplies, and together they joined Dr. Parrish in the central dining area. The chief had cobbled together a ragtag search party and was barking out orders.

"I have enough radios for five teams of two people each. I want one medical and one non-medical person per team. Dr. Parrish believes Joaquin may be suffering from sugar shock, and he could be confused or even combative. The first team to find him should announce their location over the walkie immediately. I'll take the back storage areas of the shelter. Doc . . ." Chief Bishop waved his radio at Seph. ". . . You're with me. I want each team to check in every ten minutes. Move out."

Seph fell into place next to Chief Bishop. They walked together in silence past the employee cots and rolling barriers until they arrived in the deepest part of the shelter, where they halted in front of an array of doors. The portable generators couldn't handle a facility of this magnitude, so the unoccupied storage areas remained unlit. The blackness was absolute and limited Seph's vision to whatever happened to lie in the path of the beam of Chief Bishop's Maglite.

Seph inched closer to his side and struggled to hide her jitters. "Please tell me you put fresh batteries in that thing."

"Sure did." She imagined him grinning at her discomfort. "Are you afraid of the dark, Dr. Smith?"

The shelter shrieked in response to the latest blast from the strengthening wind, and Seph jumped. Raindrops pounded the metal roof, slowly at first. *Drip, drop*. The staccato rhythm picked up speed until the shelter sounded as if it were being hammered by a thousand drummers from a thousand different symphonies, all playing different songs. The storm had fully arrived.

"Normally, no. But this situation is far from normal."

"Agreed. Let's move on. We'll circle back and check out each of these rooms once we've secured the perimeter."

They shuffled forward, searching for any sign of Joaquin's presence. The chief clenched his flashlight like a club, and the muscles and tendons of his forearm bulged under the strain. The darkness blanketed them on all sides, wrapping them in its suffocating embrace until Seph could bear it no longer. She touched the chief's bicep.

"I've been meaning to ask you since the airport—how does someone so young get promoted to chief?" Seph guessed him to be no older than Dr. Parrish. His sandy hair had only the slightest tinge of grey at his temples, and he didn't seem the type to worry about dyeing it.

"Says the girl who looks like she should be living in a dorm." He flicked his light to Seph's face, and she blinked. "Doesn't matter how old you are. The brass thought I was the right man for the job. When you're good, you're good."

"Humble, too. And I'm not a 'girl.'"

"You don't say? My keen observational skills must be failing me, then—right when I need them the most." The chief's steps faltered as they reached a blank wall. "This hallway's a dead end. We need to make sure the rooms we passed are empty before we pack it in and rendezvous with the others. I'm guessing they're supply closets of some kind. Shouldn't take long."

They traced their steps backward until they returned to the series of doors, none of which bore any signs to indicate what might lie within. "Care to guess what's behind door number one?"

"No, I do not." Seph frowned at him, though she knew it was too dark for him to see. "I'm hoping it's Joaquin so we can get the hell out of here."

"Hmm." The chief reached for the door's handle, then froze in place.

"What . . ."

"Shh!"

Seph held her breath, trying to discern what had caught the chief's attention. The howling wind and the rain made it almost impossible to hear anything else, but if she closed her eyes and concentrated . . . Seph picked out a low-pitched hum or a muttering, perhaps, emanating from somewhere nearby.

"I hear it," she whispered.

"Where?"

"I don't know."

Disoriented by the darkness and the metallic echoes, Seph and Chief Bishop struggled to pinpoint the sound's exact location. Every few seconds, the muttering swelled in volume and then disappeared, leaving Seph to strain against the silence until the cycle started over again. Seph, fingers splayed like antennae, rotated slowly in the darkness, waiting for the next surge to echo around her.

"There!" Seph pointed to her left, and the chief swung his light down the empty corridor. "I think it's coming from the third door down."

"Are you sure? Because I thought I heard it best this way." He waved to the right.

"No, I'm not sure," Seph snapped. "How can I be? The only thing I can say for certain is that it's not coming from the door in front of us."

The noise swelled again, and Seph thrust her palm toward the third door on the left. "Did you hear that? I really do believe it's coming from this direction."

"Okay, Doc. Whatever you say. Let's check it out." They crept forward and positioned themselves outside the door, where they waited for the next cycle to begin.

"*La muerte. La muerte viene por mí.*" The mumbled words were barely audible.

"Joaquin?" The door was locked. The chief rattled the handle back and forth and pushed with his broad shoulder until the hinges groaned, yet the door refused to yield. "Joaquin, it's Chief Bishop. Let us in."

"*La muerte*!" Joaquin shrieked in fear.

"Screw this." The chief lifted one leg and slammed the sole of his steel-toed boot against the cheap lock. The door flew open with a bang, bathing them in a rush of hot, stagnant air tinged with the scent of bleach. The chief shined his light into what appeared to be a tiny utility closet. Joaquin sat huddled in the corner with his back to the wall and eyes clenched shut. Sweat poured down his forehead and nose, mixing with the tears on his cheeks. His whole body shivered even though the room was easily one hundred degrees.

Seph crouched beside him while the chief radioed the others. "Joaquin, hey. It's Seph. You're gonna be okay. You hear me?" She placed her hand on his shoulder in an attempt to strengthen their connection. "Look at me so I know you can hear me." Her touch invited him to share his terror and confusion, and she reeled from the psychological onslaught.

Joaquin's eyes flew open, and he grabbed at the front of Seph's shirt, scratching her neck with his nails. He scrunched the fabric into a tight ball and tugged. Caught off guard, she wobbled on her heels until a second tug toppled her forward in an ungainly heap. Seph landed with her palms on the floor and her cheek next to his—close enough for her to smell his foul breath. He whispered in her ear. "*Ángel de Dios, ayúdame.*" His hoarse voice trembled with the desperation of a dying man.

"Whoa there, partner! Easy now." The chief leaned over and covered Joaquin's fist with his own, forcing Joaquin's fingers to relax enough for Seph to wriggle away.

She scrambled to her knees and fingered the red welts forming on her neck. "We need to do something!" She shoved her trembling hands into her pockets and rummaged through her stash of emergency munchies. Her fingers touched upon a crinkly wrapper, and she extracted a packet of Sweet-tarts.

A triumphant Seph held them high in the air for the chief to see.

"Ta da! I don't know about you, but I can't imagine these are much different than prescription glucose tablets. They have to be ninety-nine percent sugar."

Seph ripped the wrapper apart with thick, fumbling fingers and cursed when half the contents scattered through the air like confetti. She carefully removed one of the remaining candies, waving the bright pink disc in front of Joaquin's line of vision.

"Here, Joaquin. Take this. It'll make you feel better."

He didn't move. She persisted, adopting a firmer tone.

"Joaquin, open your mouth!"

He stared at her but did not comply. Seph rolled her eyes at the chief who, realizing what she wanted him to do, sighed. "You know the others will be here in less than five minutes. Six, tops."

Seph raised her eyebrows, and he threw up his hands in defeat. "Fine."

The chief reached forward and used one burly arm to pin Joaquin against the wall, and the other free hand to force Joaquin's jaw open. "If I lose a finger, it'll be your fault." But Joaquin, fading fast, offered little resistance.

"If anyone loses a finger, it'll be me." Seph popped the piece of candy on Joaquin's tongue, pushing it as far back as she could, and the chief let go. Joaquin grimaced at the sour taste but swallowed the candy.

"There. Success. Just like pilling a cat." Seph pulled a second colorful disc out of the wrapper and held it under Joaquin's nose. "You want another one?"

This time, Seph positioned the candy in the middle of Joaquin's palm. He inspected it, puzzled at first, but finally raised it to his mouth and ate it, followed by another. By the time Seph heard the footsteps of the rest of the search party echoing through the darkness, Joaquin had started to come around.

"How is he?" Dr. Parrish arrived first, with Alice close on her heels.

Seph backed out of the way to allow Alice and her equipment to pass. "Better. He was confused when we first found him, but I gave him some candy, and he seems to be improving. You were right about the low sugar, I think."

Alice squirted a tube of glucose gel into Joaquin's mouth, and he gagged at the treacly taste. While he was distracted, she pricked his finger, drawing a single, perfect droplet of blood which she used to check his sugar. The machine read thirty-two.

"What's normal?" Chief Bishop asked.

"Seventy, eighty . . .one hundred would be nice." Alice's hands flew in and out of her duffel bag as she reloaded her testing equipment with a clean strip. "It's amazing he's still conscious when you consider those results occurred *after* you'd already given him some candy. Imagine what his sugar was before." She opened a second box of instant glucose and awaited orders. "Should I administer another tube?" she asked Dr. Parrish.

"No." Dr. Parrish watched as Joaquin's eyes began to regain their focus, and his trembling stopped. "The critical phase appears to have passed. Let's get him back to the nurses' station for closer observation, and recheck his sugar in another fifteen minutes. The level may continue to rise as the glucose gel is absorbed into his bloodstream. We don't want to overshoot our mark and end up with a sugar of six hundred."

Chief Bishop and one of the med techs helped Joaquin to his feet, and together they half carried, half dragged him back to the medical ward. They placed him on a cot next to Carol, who was somehow managing to snore despite the tube blocking her nose. Alice glided between the two of them, assessing vital signs and periodically pricking Joaquin's finger for more blood.

Dr. Parrish loomed over the foot of Joaquin's bed and supervised his care. "He was lucky you two found him when you did. Another ten minutes, and he would've been ready for the freezer." She seethed, furious at Joaquin for daring to almost die on her watch. "Not that we have a freezer."

"Why do you think this happened?" the chief asked. "Joaquin said he was an expert at managing his diabetes."

Dr. Parrish pointed at the insulin pump clipped to Joaquin's pants. "He probably is—at home. Here he's eating, sleeping, and working on a different schedule, and he has a different level of activity. But the pump doesn't know he's been deployed or that his sugar's out of whack. It keeps supplying insulin at a steady rate no matter what—unless Joaquin adjusts it, which he obviously didn't do."

Her scowl deepened, and she glared at the prostrate nurse. "I should've predicted something like this would happen the minute he mentioned he wore a pump. But with juggling everything else, it simply didn't occur to me to ask him if he'd adjusted his settings. It was his responsibility, and he should've known better. I'm here to run the shelter, not babysit the staff."

Joaquin stirred. He pushed himself up in bed, groaned, and lowered his head to his palms. Alice pulled one hand aside and rechecked his sugar.

"Eighty-four, Dr. Parrish." Alice announced Joaquin's latest reading, which Dr. Parrish acknowledged with a terse response.

"Sweet. Pun intended."

Joaquin and Alice traded a few quiet words, and he removed his insulin pump to tinker with the settings.

Dr. Parrish lowered her voice. "I'd bet he has a killer headache. Worse than a hangover, I'm told. Serves him right. He should turn that damn thing off while he's here and switch to insulin shots, but I know he won't agree. Nurses make the worst patients—almost as bad as doctors. We'll have to keep a close eye on him from now on, because, like I said earlier, the next time he may not be so fortunate. And I'd bet good money there'll be a next time."

Joaquin clipped his pump back to his pants and tried to stand, only to sag backwards into the cot.

Dr. Parrish hissed with irritation. "Chief, assign members of the search party to check on Joaquin every fifteen minutes. I want to know where he is at all times. No more disappearing. I will *not* have him slipping into a coma on my shift. And try to be subtle about it, okay?"

Chief Bishop bowed. "Got it. Lucky for you, 'subtle' is my middle name." He cupped his hands around his mouth and hollered at the dispersing search team. "Hey, guys! Hold up." He thundered off to brief them on their new orders.

Seph and Dr. Parrish exchanged wry smiles. For one fleeting instant, Seph contemplated calling her "Annie," but the shared moment quickly evaporated. Chatter from the back of the room prompted them both to check the time. Six forty-five a.m. The day shift was rising. Seph had survived her first night, and so had everyone else. Only thirteen more to go—give or take. Hopefully, they'd be less eventful.

Seph smothered a yawn, and Dr. Parrish nodded wearily in agreement. "Yeah, I know. We still have to sign out to our respective day shift buddies before we can hit the sack. I'll ask Lew to start circulating the check-out sheet." Dr. Parrish plodded off to find him.

As soon as Seph was alone, Father Barney, who'd been hovering nearby, sidled up beside her. "Quite the night, wasn't it?"

"Yes, it was. Glad it's almost over."

Father Barney pointed at Carol. "I noticed you talking to that poor woman earlier, before she overdosed on her medications. I was thinking I could sit by her cot and pray, maybe anoint her feet. Do you think that would be okay?"

"Honestly, Father, if Carol woke up and found you touching her feet, I suspect she'd bonk you over the head with her pocket watch. I didn't get the impression she was terribly impressed with God or his clergy."

"I see." Father Barney considered Carol's pale face. His own was solemn. "Those are the souls who need God the most. Perhaps I'll take the chance."

Seph smiled. "Suit yourself, Father, but remember—you've been warned. You might want to consider a helmet."

The overhead lights, which were dimmed overnight, began to click on, one row after the other, until the vast space was filled with their fluorescent glow. A crowd of employees, both night and day shifters, gathered around Seph and Father Barney. They jockeyed for position, eager to give and receive their reports and get on with their morning activities.

Lew stood in the middle of the fray, ticking people off his list as they reported for duty. Seph managed to catch his eye, gave him a little wave, and gestured with her thumb toward the back. He signaled an A-OK, and Seph escaped the hubbub to the relative tranquility of the employee rest area, where her cot awaited. Storm or no storm, she would sleep well tonight.

Chapter Four

The Second Night

Seph did sleep, and soundly at that, which was always a pleasant surprise. Plagued since childhood with nightmares, she could count on one hand the number of nights she'd managed to sleep a solid eight hours. Her mother, tired of Seph awakening night after night screaming in terror, had finally taken her to a psychiatrist. When he threw up his hands at her "unusual mix of personality traits: excessive empathy balanced by a dearth of sympathy, with a tendency to judge," her mother dragged her to counseling.

During the day, Seph absorbed the world's evils—every horrific thing she saw, heard, or read—and at night, she reflected those horrors out through her dreams. Counseling and trigger avoidance helped some, as did partaking in the occasional shot of tequila, but the nightmares never completely resolved.

Like the relationship between a comic book superhero and her arch villain, the recurrent nightmares had become so familiar they were like old friends, paying their obligatory visits. *Bam! Pow!* Seph and her villains duked it out night after sleepless night. The villains usually won. Friend or foe, she couldn't wait for them to leave with the morning light. At least she didn't scream out loud anymore.

In their absence, Seph awoke refreshed and hungry. She ignored her grumbling stomach and took a moment to try her mother, but the cell service was down. She frowned when her phone signaled a missed call and text. *Call home, Mom*. Weird. Her mother didn't own a cell phone, and Seph was fairly certain her mother didn't know how to text. The message was sent from her sister's cell, which meant Grace had at least made it home to Philly.

Seph squelched a pang of anxiety, stuffed the phone into her backpack, and strolled to the kitchen area where Alice and Lew were already seated for dinner. "May I join you?"

"Of course, Doctor," Alice replied. She unfolded a paper napkin and positioned it on her lap.

Selma swung by and plopped a tray on the table before Seph's butt hit her seat. Seph's appetite wilted. A peanut butter and jelly sandwich and an apple. With no running water, their options were limited. She should've brought more candy. Selma shrugged at the disappointment on Seph's face and smiled an apology. She zipped on to the next table, balancing multiple trays in each hand.

"Yum." Seph polished the apple on her shirt sleeve. "Everybody sleep well?"

Lew shook his head. "Not really." He rolled his shoulders in giant circles and twisted his neck until it cracked. "Those eensy-weensy cots are not a good fit for a big boy like me. I'm tighter than a rookie quarterback's ass. Chief's gotta feel even worse. Dude's built like a linebacker." He grimaced as he massaged a particularly bothersome knot in his neck. "I'll get over it."

Alice gifted Lew with one of her serene half-smiles. "I'm sure you will. I, for one, slept fine, thank you." She sliced her sandwich into tiny, perfect squares and wiped the residual red jam off her knife with a clean napkin. "He's looking good, isn't he?" She stabbed her fork in the air toward Joaquin. "Better than last night."

Employees and evacuees, gathered for their evening meal, crammed the surrounding tables. Joaquin sat to their right, chatting with a group of other nurses and acting his normal, amiable self.

Carol sulked by herself at the far end. Her eyes darted around the room as she furtively slipped an extra apple into her pocket. She, too, displayed no ill effects from the prior night's drama save an ugly crimson streak on the right side of her nostril where the tube had been.

An attractive young woman rested atop another nearby table, dangling her leg over the edge and flirting with Thad and Delmas. Further down, Father Barney gawked, mesmerized by her yellow stiletto as it swung back and forth like a canary on a perch.

Lew directed Seph and Alice's attention to Father Barney. "You see that? I think our chaplain's got a serious foot fetish, if you ask me."

"No way!" Seph's hand flew to the cross around her neck, as if it could somehow stave off evil thoughts and images. "Lew, that's kind of—I don't know—unfair, I guess. I mean, how would you know, anyway? Aren't priests supposed to anoint the feet of the poor and all that jazz?"

Lew wasn't dissuaded in the least. "If you're implying his interest is purely professional, then you should've seen him washing Carol's feet after you went to bed. The look on his face . . .well, you can call it religious ecstasy if you want, but, man, I don't think so."

"And *I* don't think I want to hear any more of this nonsense," Alice said. She removed the napkin from her lap, tossed it on her empty dinner tray, and huffed away.

Lew chuckled. "Alice can slap my wrists if she wants, but I call 'em as I see 'em." He stretched his arms overhead until his shoulders popped. "Ahhh . . .much better."

Before Seph could comment, Dr. Parrish strode into the center of the dining area and rapped a chair against the floor. All eyes turned toward hers—even Father Barney's. "Night shifters, I need a moment of your time. Gather around."

"She forgot to say 'please,'" Lew whispered to Seph, with a conspiratorial wink. Seph wrinkled her nose but declined to respond.

Dr. Parrish, scratching names off her mental list, studied the faces of the assembling crowd. "If anyone failed to check in for duty with Lew . . ." She pointed at him, and he raised two fingers in a mock salute. ". . . Please do so now."

Lew coughed at Dr. Parrish's unexpected—and perfectly timed—social pleasantry. Seph stifled a giggle.

If their boss noticed, she gave no visible sign. "I received my final update from central command. The eye of the storm is approximately fifteen miles to our east, and it's moving slowly. We can expect the hurricane-force winds and rain to continue for at least another day, maybe two. I say 'final update' because shortly thereafter, we lost cell service."

Several members of the crowd, doubting her words, pulled out their phones. She tapped her clipboard against her upper thigh and waited until she'd regained their full attention before continuing.

"Anyone experiencing symptoms of withdrawal yet? No? Good. The bottom line—we're locking the doors. We could have downed power lines, falling debris—hazards of every variety lurking in the darkness. No one goes outside the shelter for any reason without my approval. And if you ask, you'd better have a damned good reason. Nicotine withdrawal does not count."

Dr. Parrish frowned at the restless employees, her gaze lingering a tad too long on Joaquin as she added, "Here's to a quiet night. Alice?"

Alice glided forward.

"Are you ready to start rounds?"

"Whenever you are, Doctor."

"Excellent. Follow me." Dr. Parrish marched off, leaving Alice to scurry behind.

The crowd buzzed for a few moments before dispersing on its own. Chief Bishop caught Seph's eye and meandered over to chat.

"Annie's a real charmer, isn't she?"

"Annie? What—you're on a first-name basis now?"

"Yeah, well, I caved. What can I say? She's very . . .persistent. And since she's taken to calling me 'Shane' without my express written consent, I figured I could at least return the favor."

"I suppose." Seph eyed Dr. Parrish as she wove between the cots, Alice in tow. "I'm not there yet."

"Trust me. She'll wear you down eventually. But the real reason I graced you with my presence was to beg you to take the first Joaquin check at seven-thirty. You get to carry this sweet radio." He dangled the receiver in front of her as if it were a chocolate bar.

"Anything for you, Chief." Seph extended both hands like a bowl, and he dropped the walkie in. "Although you're far too imposing a figure to have to beg. Not to mention you're wearing a gun."

She inspected the radio's buttons. "I've never used one of these before. I'm assuming they're idiot-proof. Just push here and speak when I lay eyes on Joaquin, right?" Seph pressed the largest button, and the radio sputtered to life.

"Yep, and afterwards I'll instruct you to pass the walkie on to the next idiot—I mean, employee." The chief grinned. "He or she will be responsible for the seven forty-five check."

"Don't you think this is ridiculous? I'm sure Joaquin has made the appropriate adjustments. He's *not* an idiot, and I'm certain he, more than anyone, doesn't want his sugar bottoming out again. I heard he was mortified about what happened. It's overkill."

The chief shrugged. "This is the way Annie wants to handle it, and she's the boss. You saw him last night, Seph. Another fifteen minutes, and Joaquin would've been toast."

"Fine." Seph clipped the walkie to her waistband. "Whatever 'Annie' wants."

Chief Bishop chuckled. "See? That wasn't so hard, was it?"

Seph longed to stick out her tongue, but professionalism prevailed. Instead, she arched her eyebrows and stalked away. First, she'd check in with Delmas and Thad. Next would be Carol, then whoever else might need her assistance. She'd throw in a Joaquin check somewhere in between. Seph agreed with Annie on one thing and one thing only: They both hoped it was a quiet night.

Seph found Thad and Delmas at their cots, playing the same card game as the night before. This time, instead of aces, Delmas held a pair of red queens, and this time, unlike the last, both he and Thad acknowledged Seph's presence immediately. She took it as a good sign. She was making progress.

"Everything going okay for you two gentlemen?" Seph focused her attention on Thad's eyes. They were far less disconcerting than Delmas's.

Thad nodded. "I heard what happened to my nurse. Will he be back to change my dressing this evening? He did a good job yesterday—before he went psycho on me, of course." Thad emitted a low, gurgling growl—the closest approximation to a laugh his weak throat muscles could produce.

"His name is Joaquin, and I imagine he will be," Seph replied. "As a matter of fact, here he comes now."

Joaquin arrived toting his collection of wound care supplies. Seph wasn't sure how much he remembered from last night, but judging by the way he avoided her gaze, he remembered enough to be embarrassed.

"I'd offer to give you a hand, Joaquin, but wounds are definitely not my thing." Seph adopted a bright and breezy tone she hoped would diffuse his discomfort. "Which is one of many solid reasons I chose to study psychology and not nursing."

"I'm good. Thanks anyway." Joaquin kept his head bowed as he meticulously unfolded a long role of gauze.

"Alrighty, then. I'll check back with you guys when Joaquin's done, maybe around seven-thirty? Does fifteen minutes give you enough time?" Joaquin's interruption afforded her a legitimate excuse to scope him out at her assigned time.

"Should be." Joaquin steadfastly refused to look up from his supplies.

"Great. I'll see you soon." Seph drifted away in search of the next patient on her list—Carol.

She heard Carol cursing from a dozen rows away. Seph peeked around the corner of a rolling barrier and found the feisty patient in the midst of having her follow up medical exam with Dr. Parrish. Based on Annie's peeved expression and Carol's obvious displeasure at being poked and prodded, Seph opted against an interruption. She backed out of sight and, feeling useless, decided to park herself at one of the dining tables in the center of the shelter and look available. She'd only lingered for a few minutes before Selma, patrolling her home turf, toddled by.

"Can I get you anything, hun? Maybe a leftover apple or a granola bar? We don't have much to nosh on, I'm afraid, but

I always keep a little something squirreled away for my favorite chickies." Selma, clucking with motherly concern, hovered around Seph. "I know dinner wasn't especially filling—not enough to get you through a busy all-nighter, anyway."

"Dinner was just fine, Selma, thank you. After all, we're not exactly at the Ritz, are we?" Seph smiled and patted the chair next to hers, inviting Selma to join her. "How are you holding up?"

Selma hesitated briefly before settling her considerable heft into the seat next to Seph. "I'm doing fine, given the circumstances. I hate to admit it, but I'm getting too old for this kind of thing." She chuckled and patted both knees. "The concrete floor is murder on my creaky ol' joints, and we don't even wanna talk about my back! But this should be my last shelter. I'm set to retire the end of this year. Three more months to go for a full government pension."

"Selma, that's fantastic! Congratulations. You must be so excited. Do you have anything special planned for your retirement?"

Selma's face clouded over. "I did, but they've kind of gone by the wayside."

"Oh." Seph waited, inviting Selma to fill the silence with her story.

Selma sighed. "My husband and I had planned to travel out west in our RV. We had it all worked out—stops in Mount Rushmore and the Grand Canyon and a party in Las Vegas for our fortieth wedding anniversary. Then he up and died on me in March from a sudden heart attack. The RV's sittin' in my driveway growing rust, but I'm sure as heck not gonna drive cross-country by myself. I'll probably end up selling it and spending my time with the grandbabies. That's what my daughter wants me to do."

"Selma, I'm so sorry."

"I know you are, hun. I know." Selma twisted a tissue through her stubby fingers. "Life goes on, I guess. We don't have much say in the matter, do we?" She fluttered her hands in the air, and the crumpled Kleenex dropped to the floor.

Seph bent to retrieve it. "Do you have baby pictures?" She deftly steered the conversation toward a cheerier subject.

"Honey, you *know* I do!" Selma's face brightened as she pulled a locket from around her neck. It opened to reveal four tiny faces. Soon Seph had heard everything she needed to know and then some about Selma's bundles of joy. They both jumped when, a good while later, the walkie on Seph's hip crackled.

"Oh, crap!" Seph leapt from her chair. "I was supposed to check on Joaquin at seven-thirty." Seph glanced at her watch. She was only five minutes late. "We'll finish this discussion later tonight, I promise." Seph shot Selma a parting smile as she hustled off to rendezvous with Thad, Delmas, and, hopefully, Joaquin.

When Seph arrived, Thad's wound was already dressed, and Joaquin was long gone. Delmas grinned as Seph, breathless from rushing, approached his cot. "I wondered if you were coming back. You seemed like a woman of her word." He stood, his broad shoulders filling the narrow gap between the aisles. By accident or intent, his thigh brushed against hers.

Seph stepped out of reach. "Which way did Joaquin go?"

Delmas rolled his eyes toward Thad. "Snappish. Guess we don't count for nothing, huh?" They snickered.

"Sorry, but I have other priorities right now. I was assigned to keep tabs on Joaquin because of what happened last night, and . . ." Seph's eyes scanned the surrounding area. ". . . I've obviously failed in my duties. Don't you worry—I'll be back to chat if you'd like." She scowled to cover her distress. "I'd hate to hurt your tender feelings."

He shrugged. "Whatever, sweetheart. He went that way." Delmas pointed toward the vast sea of cots to his right. "For what it's worth, he seemed fine when he left. Not like before."

"Thanks." Seph raced through the congested aisles, mumbling apologies as she tripped over protruding limbs and errant baggage. By the time she reached the final row, it was eight o'clock, and Joaquin was nowhere to be found. Defeated, Seph moved to a conspicuous spot in the center of the shelter and unclipped the radio from her belt. She took a deep breath and pressed the call button.

"Chief, um, this is Seph." Her voice trembled. She berated herself and started over. "Chief, I can't find Joaquin. Do you copy? Over."

A voice boomed from behind. "I'm right here."

Seph twirled around. Chief Bishop was less than twenty feet away and closing fast. His expression was dour. "I saw you running around and figured something was wrong. What's going on?"

"Nothing. I mean, I can't find Joaquin, like I said. I last saw him at approximately seven-ten as he was changing Thad's dressing. Then I lost track of him. But honestly, Chief, I don't think anything's wrong. Delmas said Joaquin was acting normally when he finished with the wound about seven-thirty. I hunted for him, but it's such a huge place, and . . ."

Seph's tongue stumbled over her lame excuses, and she flushed from a sudden spurt of anger directed not at herself or Joaquin, but at Annie. "You know, it would've been much more efficient to give Joaquin a walkie and have *him* check in every fifteen minutes rather than have *us* flapping around like a flock of pigeons in a park trying to find him. Screw his fragile male ego!"

Chief Bishop ignored her fit of pique and grabbed his radio. "This is an all call to the members of the search team. We need eyes on Joaquin. We'll convene in the dining area at eight-thirty. First one to find him is to call me ASAP." He holstered his handset and pointed at Seph. "You stay put."

"But aren't I supposed to be searching with you? You know, the buddy system and all that?"

The chief smiled, but his demeanor remained cool. "You're fired. I can handle it from here. I'll see you at eight." He strode away, leaving Seph sputtering at his back.

"Shit!" Seph swore aloud and to no one in particular. At least Lew wasn't around to razz her about cursing. She heard his voice agitating inside her head, and that was bad enough. *Such language, Doc! From "holy moly" to "shit" in less than two days. Told you you're in hell.*

Rule #3: Always stay on the good side of the shelter police. She'd royally screwed up, and she knew it. Now she needed to figure out how to make it right.

Seph's head ached from the tension, and she massaged the bridge of her nose. A subtle "ahem" nudged her back to the moment. She realized how silly she must look—head down, tottering around in circles, spewing profanity. She'd attracted the attention of Father Barney. The quizzical look on his face indicated he'd been watching her long enough to have heard her swear. She blushed at the thought.

"Something bothering you, Dr. Smith?"

"No, thank you, Father." Her brain flashed an image of Father Barney rubbing Carol's feet, and Seph's color deepened. She stumbled over her intended words. "I, ah, I . . . well, I let the chief down, that's all."

The priest waved his hands nonchalantly. "None of us are perfect."

"I know that." She bit her tongue and cursed again, silently this time, ashamed of her surly response. Snarling at a priest? She really *was* going to hell, if she wasn't there already.

"Yes, I suppose it is your job to help people understand their human nature, with its host of glorious imperfections. It's part of my occupation, as well. We may use different methods to assist them in overcoming their flaws, but the intended result is the same."

Father Barney leaned forward and touched her shoulder. "I've witnessed your kindness, seen how you've treated Carol and those troubled young men. Have mercy on yourself, Seph, as you do for them. We are imperfect beings . . ." He swept his arms in a grand circle. ". . . In a far from perfect world."

Seph choked back another acerbic response to his blithe reassurances. She lowered her gaze to the floor and willed him to leave. Father Barney, satisfied that his message had been received, patted Seph's cheek and strolled away to mingle with a group of young women lounging around the nurses' station.

Seph had only been on duty for an hour, and she'd already been fired by the chief of police and sermonized by the chaplain. *What could possibly make her night complete?* She scanned around, seeking inspiration for her next, best course of action. "Staying put," as the chief had instructed, was not a viable option. Her anxiety demanded a distraction. If anything happened to Joaquin, she would feel forever guilty.

Seph walked the perimeter of the shelter, this time searching for Selma instead of Joaquin. She had unfinished conversations with Delmas and Selma, and of the two, the matronly cook was definitely the nicer option. But Selma was not in any of her usual haunts.

Which left Thad and Delmas. Seph dragged herself toward their cots, steeling herself for another one of Delmas's discomfiting full body scans. She was surprised (and relieved) to find Delmas absent from his customary position at Thad's side. Thad, for his part, was sound asleep, curled into as much of a fetal position as his malformations would allow and snoring away.

Curious as to Delmas's whereabouts, Seph lingered for a few minutes, expecting him to reappear. But when the lights dimmed at eight, she was forced to leave in order to reconvene with the team. She'd already disappointed the chief once; she didn't need to piss him off as well by being late. Seph had some serious sucking up to do, and she sucked at sucking up. It would require considerable effort.

The search party was already assembled and seated when Seph arrived. Annie filled her in. "We found Joaquin. He said he got pulled to the other side of the shelter to check a leg wound. I reminded him he should've checked with me first prior to leaving the area, but he said he got busy and forgot."

She paused to remove her glasses and ran a weary hand over her forehead. "I don't believe he truly forgot. I think he's being passive-aggressive. Joaquin knows what we're up to, and he's getting frustrated with being treated like an invalid. I can't say I blame him, but I don't know what else to do. We can't send him home now, can we?" Annie jammed her glasses back onto her nose.

"I don't know about that, Doc," Lew replied. "When I was deployed to Hurricane Katrina, we had this surgeon from Miami who thought he was a real hot-shot. Wore his Rolex into a disaster zone. You know the type—lily-white knight galloping in on a mighty steed to save the day. Well, let's just say the accommodations were not up to his standards. We were housed in these RVs in a state park, eight of us in one RV, with no electricity. It was a hundred degrees outside with one hundred percent humidity. You ever tried sleeping in an oven? Add some love bugs crawling in the sheets, throw in a handful of fire ants and the occasional hungry gator, and you get the picture. The doctor got assigned a top bunk and had a full-blown panic attack. Sir Lancelot turned into a babbling loon overnight. Almost drowned in his own drool. They shipped his ass out the next day. It can be done."

"I'm sure it can be done, but your situation was different. You didn't deploy to Katrina until *after* the hurricane went through, right? When you were in clean-up mode?"

Lew nodded.

"Then you had the ability to move people and supplies. It was tough, but you could do it." Annie motioned toward the metal hangar door, rattling ferociously in the wind. "We're in no position to safely send anybody in or out for another two days, maybe more. Hell, we couldn't call for a transport even if we wanted to—the phones are down, remember? We're *all* stuck, not just Joaquin."

"Then Joaquin will have to learn to deal with it." Seph, relieved to hear of Joaquin's safety but anxious to move on, hijacked the conversation. Her comment earned her several startled looks. "What? Is there a problem?"

"You're the psychologist here. Aren't you supposed to be the touchy-feely one? You know, the compassionate soul and all that happy crap?" Chief Bishop said what everyone else what thinking. "Besides, I thought you disagreed with the way we were handling the situation."

The chief's eyes shifted back and forth from Annie to Seph. "You mentioned asking Joaquin to report in every fifteen minutes rather than us hounding him."

Seph shrugged, striving to avoid any further conflict. "I don't mean to sound unsympathetic, but facts are facts. We're in a disaster zone. We came here expecting an uncomfortable environment, and we got one. Joaquin will get over it once he's back home and has time to realize we were only concerned for his welfare. With distance comes perspective."

Seph's next words were meant for her boss. "And as far as how we go about tracking him, I defer to Annie. She's in charge."

Dr. Parrish's smug smile spoke volumes. Whether through the use of Annie's given name or via the public vote of confidence, Seph was back in the commander's good graces. *One down, one to go. If she could only do the same with Chief Bishop . . .*

"Thank you, Seph. I concur." Annie stood, signaling the end of their meeting. "We'll do another Joaquin check at nine o'clock before lights out. Then . . ."

A loud noise whooshed from two tables over, drowning out her words. An elderly man wearing a driving cap had lugged an accordion from its velvet-lined case. He compressed the bellows and fiddled with the bass buttons, producing an oompah-pah rhythm deep enough to vibrate the breastbone of anyone within a ten-foot radius.

A few shy children approached and asked to touch the instrument's glossy surface, which the man happily obliged. "It's Italian. From Castelfidardo." He stroked the ivory keys as if they were his mistress. "All the best ones are."

The accordion was a thing of beauty, with its pearlized blue finish, chrome accents, and customized detailing, but Dr. Parrish was unmoved. "So you're evacuating your home in an emergency. You grab what you can, those few precious things you need to survive, and you decide to bring an accordion. Makes sense to me."

Lew grinned. "C'mon, Doc, lighten up! You heard the man. She's *Eye*-talian, and my Lordy, she's a sweet one!"

The man began to play one of those old, familiar tunes from the 1950s, a melody which conjured up vague, melancholic images of a Venetian café at dusk. A group of children, entranced by both the music and the strange sight of the moving bellows, clamored to watch. Mindful of his growing audience, the accordionist skillfully segued into a zippier Tejano style, knowing it would be more popular with his new fan base. He strolled among the dancing children, playing them like a pro and feeding off their exuberance.

The accordion is not a subtle instrument in any environment, but when surrounded by four steel walls and a sheet metal roof, it raged with a lusty passion. The notes blared, the chords soared, and the music echoed off every surface, resonating into a feverish pitch and filling the metal cathedral with a heady energy.

The adults gathered in a circle, beckoned to church by the handheld organ. The pedophile tapped his crocodile boots, watching his pied piper play. The prostitute giggled and twirled à la Marilyn Monroe, allowing any ogler within five feet a peep at her underwear. A man Seph recognized as one of the bus drivers picked up three apples and began to juggle, weaving in, out, and around the accordion player. Father Barnabas stood at the altar of a nearby table. He clasped his hands in front of his chest in delight and beamed his approval over the entire congregation.

Seph hung on the outside of the circle next to Lew, unsure if she should be enraptured or frightened by the carnival of the absurd unfolding before her.

"Looks like the circus has come to Hell," Lew said, dodging an errant apple. "All we need is a creepy clown and a knife thrower."

"Don't give them any ideas." Carol's gravelly voice registered inches from Seph's left ear, and she twitched in surprise.

The din had masked Carol's approach. She had a smoker's voice, always rough, but Seph detected a hint of something more than tobacco in the way Carol rasped her words. Something sinister. Seph's finely tuned alarms sounded a warning. She tore her eyes away from the surreal spectacle and gasped at her patient's disheveled appearance.

Carol glistened with sweat. Her pupils were dilated, and she fidgeted with her pocket watch at breakneck speed, in and out, in and out of her pants pocket, never pausing to glance at the dial. A dancing toddler tripped at her feet, and Carol growled, the noise barely audible over the bellowing of the accordion, but enough for the child to dash away in terror.

"You all right, Carol?" Seph tried and failed to make eye contact. The accordion disgorged an exceptionally discordant blast, and they both flinched.

"I don't like this kind of hoopla. I don't like it at all." Carol swiped at a lock of frizzy, gray hair sticking to her damp forehead. Her hand shook with the fine tremor commonly seen in people on prescriptions such as hers.

"I'm with you, sistah," Lew said. "It's nice to have a distraction, but getting people too wound up in a place like this . . .nothing good ever comes of it. Bad things bound to happen. Like a pressure cooker, building up steam. When the lid blows off, someone always gets burned." Lew covered his ears and stomped away, heading for whatever part of the shelter was farthest from the noise.

"Did you take your evening medications yet, Carol?" Seph asked.

Carol opened her mouth to answer but was interrupted by a noise emanating from the back of the shelter. The shrill scream pierced the cacophonous bubble around them, and the crowd expelled a collective gasp. Carol bolted for refuge.

Chapter Five

The music and the screaming stopped simultaneously, leaving the stunned shelter to cower in silence. A child began to wail, and the sound shattered the spell. The chief lurched into action. He sprinted, flashlight in one hand and radio in the other, toward the back of the shelter in the direction of the scream.

Annie pointed at Father Barney and Seph. "You two—take care of them." She waved her hands toward the flock of evacuees, many still frozen in place, mid-pirouette. She hurried after the chief, with Alice at her heels.

Seph dove into the crowd, firing consolations and platitudes at a rapid clip, while urging people back to their cots to hunker down for the night. Father Barney offered prayers in place of platitudes, and between the two of them, they successfully dispersed the crowd and calmed frazzled nerves.

Seph paced the now-empty dining area, hands on her hips, as she gauged the feeling in the room. "I think we're okay now," she said to Father Barney, who was toddling along beside her.

"Yes, I think we're okay." Father Barney echoed her words. He licked his lips and clutched a small Bible in his hands. His palms stamped sweaty prints on the cheap, red pleather. "What do you think is going on back there?"

"I have no idea. In a place like this, anything is possible. Maybe somebody saw a spider." Seph's smile lacked humor.

Alice burst from behind the rolling barriers cordoning off the dark side of the shelter. She pushed the flimsy partition out of her path, sending it skittering across the concrete floor.

"Do you think that's all it was—a spider? Or a mouse, maybe?" Father Barney squeezed his Bible tighter as Alice, her faced etched with distress, closed the gap between them.

"No. No, I do not." Seph stared at the vulgar splotches of blood on Alice's scrub top. "Last night it was Joaquin and Carol. Tonight, it . . ."

"Selma! It's Selma." Alice's voice sliced through the dank, heavy air. "She's asking for you, Father." Alice grasped the chaplain's forearm with an unsteady hand. "You have to hurry."

The determined nurse dragged him along with a strength disproportionate to her tiny size, forcing him to accompany her to the rear of the shelter. Seph followed behind, ready to add a sharp kick to the reluctant priest's derrière should he decide to balk.

"Why? What's happened? Tell me!" Father Barney panted for air as he labored to match her frantic pace.

Alice, her composure as ravaged as her scrubs, didn't respond. Seph spared her the trauma. She'd surmised the situation the minute she saw Alice's distraught face and bloodied shirt. "Selma's dying. She needs her last rites." Father Barney blanched and pressed his Bible to his chest.

Selma lay gasping for breath when they arrived. Like a fish viciously torn from the water, she pursed her lips in a vain attempt to drag more oxygen into her aching lungs. Her terror and suffering caused Seph's own chest to ache, and her throat constricted as she matched Selma's labored breathing.

Breath by torturous breath, Seph felt Selma's life slipping away as if it were her own. Her hands and feet turned to ice, and Seph shivered. Her vision narrowed until only a dark tunnel, lit by the faintest of lights, lay ahead. She reeled, grasping for even a sliver of the many coping mechanisms she'd learned throughout the years, but they failed her. Her skills had never been tested by a situation so brutal or extreme.

Battling for self-preservation, Seph fought to sever her agonizing connection to Selma by shifting her empathetic focus elsewhere. Annie, with her smoldering temper, was an easy target. Seph absorbed her anger, and its power sustained her.

Annie crouched over Selma and placed two fingers on her neck, feeling for the carotid pulse. She shook her head. "I can't help her. Not here. Not with what I have to work with." Father Barney tapped her on the shoulder, and she shuffled out of the way to allow him to kneel at Selma's side.

Father Barney clasped one bloodied hand in his. His sonorous voice trembled as he recited the Sacrament of the Anointing of the Sick, halting several times to regain his composure. Selma's eyes remained fixed, staring into the darkness above, but her face relaxed ever so slightly when he gently touched her forehead, tracing the Sign of the Cross with his thumb. She claimed one last shuddering breath before her glassy eyes closed, and her chest movement stopped.

The blood gushing from Selma's multiple stab wounds slowed to a trickle and dripped drop by drop into an expanding pool on the concrete floor. Father Barney finished his ritual and attempted to stand, but the clotting blood, sticky in some places and slippery in others, grabbed at his knees, and he fought to maintain his balance without putting a hand onto the contaminated cement.

Annie offered Father Barney no assistance. She watched, silent and inscrutable to everyone but Seph, who held her breath and waited for the volcano to blow. Unlike Alice's distress, Father Barney's compassion, or her own sorrow, Annie seethed with rage. Someone finally had the audacity to die on her shift.

"Do we have any idea who did this?" Annie asked. Her steady voice belied all emotion.

"None." The chief emerged from the shadows, and Seph jerked in surprise. She'd been so absorbed with watching—feeling—Selma die, she'd failed to notice his presence. A timid woman about Selma's age, her cheeks puffy and damp with tears, quivered beside him.

Chief Bishop touched the woman's arm. "Lois worked with Selma in the kitchen. She got worried when Selma didn't return from break, and instead of notifying me, she went searching for Selma herself. Thought maybe Selma got caught up in the crowd watching the accordion player. Then she saw Selma's necklace on the floor near the back barrier."

He dangled an evidence bag overhead. The locket's gold chain, twisted and torn in two, winked from the bottom corner. "When Lois went to pick it up, she found Selma like this. Whoever did it was already long gone. Lois said the last time she saw Selma, she was talking to you, Seph. Is that correct?"

"Yes." Seph's voice cracked when she spoke. She cleared her throat and tried again. "Yes. That's right. She and I were chatting about her grandchildren. Their pictures are in the locket." Seph's eyes filled with tears as she recalled Selma discussing her retirement plans. She blinked them back vigorously, hoping no one had noticed.

The chief pressed her for more details. "Did she talk about being afraid of anyone in the shelter or mention any arguments with other employees or evacuees?"

"No, not at all. She was so easygoing, so sweet. I can't imagine why . . ." Seph stuttered, swallowed, and started anew. "Alice, you . . . you spoke to Selma, didn't you? You said she asked for Father Barney. Did she say anything else, give any hints as to who did this to her?"

Annie held up a hand to stave off Alice's response. "Selma didn't really ask for the chaplain. She couldn't speak, or of course we would've questioned her about her assailant."

The chief's stern expression indicated Annie's brusque explanation was not sufficient. She softened her tone and added, "She drew on the floor with her own blood. It looked like a cross with a partial circle or a 'C' around it. From that, we inferred she wanted Father Barney. We knew she was a devout Catholic."

Annie examined the bloody floor, caked and smeared by footprints and Father Barney's knees. "You can't see it anymore."

The chief frowned. "This is going to require a thorough investigation, but in the meantime, do we have any body bags?"

Four pairs of eyes gawked at him, shocked by the mundane nature of his question. His scowl deepened. "Hey, it's a legitimate concern. And while we're at it, what are we going to do with her? We don't have a refrigerator unit large enough to hold a body, and from an infection control standpoint, we sure as hell can't leave her lying out and about."

"I, um, I do think we have a few body bags stashed somewhere," Annie said, looking at Alice for concurrence. Alice nodded. "And as for where to put her, I guess we'll have to turn one of these rear storage rooms into a makeshift morgue. The only other option is outside, but with the rain, wind, and any critters that might be lurking around . . ."

Lois, who unbeknownst to everyone was still standing in the background, gasped and began to wail. Seph shot Annie and the chief a disapproving glare. "I'm going to walk her out front. And Father Barney, too. He needs to change his clothes."

Father Barney, stunned by the morbid conversation, glanced at his pants, which were soaked from the knees down with Selma's blood. "Yes, I think that would be a good idea." He wobbled over to Seph, who grabbed him by one elbow and Lois by the other and headed toward the light.

Seph spent the better part of an hour calming poor Lois down. By the time Lois stopped sobbing, Annie and Chief

Bishop had finished their grisly business and were on their way back to the main part of the shelter. Seph and Father Barney, clad in clean pants and a pair of borrowed shoes, waited for them in the central dining area, otherwise vacant due to the nine p.m. lights-out announcement.

"I'm calling a huddle to brief the entire staff on the Selma incident. I hate telling the same story twice." Annie stormed past Seph and the chaplain without so much as a break in her stride.

Chief Bishop did stop, and he offered a conciliatory smile. "I think what she meant to say was, 'How are you, Father, and is Lois okay?'"

Father Barney stared vacantly at the arms of his chair. "Yes, I'm sure that's what she meant." He rocked forward in his seat. "What's happening here, Chief? To us?"

The chief dodged his question. "You'll hear it soon enough from Annie, after she calls her 'huddle.' I'm beginning to hate that word." He turned his attention to Seph. "How's Lois?"

"As well as can be expected. She'll develop classic short-term PTSD symptoms, I'm sure, but she'll be okay eventually."

"And you?"

"Me? I'm fine." Seph sounded surprised because she was. Not because the chief had asked about her well-being, but because she was, in actuality, fine.

With her hypersensitivity to the feelings of others, Seph always assumed she'd be extra squeamish around blood, guts, and gore, and she'd spent her entire life assiduously avoiding possible triggers—disturbing TV shows, the evening news, and even cheesy slasher flicks. Selma was her first significant direct exposure. And Seph was fine. True, she'd felt some distress while Selma was struggling with her last breaths, but once Selma died, it was as if a door had slammed shut. No more emotional connection to Selma.

Instead, Seph's brain was focused on connecting to Selma's murderer, reaching out via wispy tendrils of energy into the nooks and crannies of the shelter and probing the minds of every person who happened to walk by. A new door had opened, and her heightened senses throbbed in unfamiliar ways, flooding Seph with information previously restricted to just a single, intense connection with one individual.

Seph inhaled through her nose and honed in. The sensation felt simultaneously weird, foreign, and exhilarating. The pedophile strolled by, and Seph aimed her attention at his face, which seemed to glimmer and warp like a mirage in the desert, eventually splitting into two distinct images. Flustered, she blinked, and the second face disappeared. She pursed her lips and exhaled slowly. Lew was right. This shelter was a circus, and she'd become one of its freaks.

"Earth to Persephone." Chief Bishop waved his hand mere inches from her nose, breaking her reverie. "Really? You're fine? Because you're not acting fine."

"I want to help find Selma's killer." She rushed to fortify her bald—and bold—request. "I'm a good judge of people and an expert at separating the bullshitters from the psychos. You have to be to work in my field, just like in yours."

Seph scrutinized the sea of green cots. Most were filled with fitfully sleeping evacuees, but the ones that weren't—the ones which lay empty—those cots belonged to some familiar faces. "Besides, I've already spoken to all the creepy ones anyway, and I'd bet they hold the top five slots on your suspect list."

"True." The chief paused, and Seph knew why.

"I let you down earlier by losing Joaquin, but I promise you, I can do this. I know I can."

The chief debated for what seemed like forever before conceding with a lopsided grin. "All right, Doc. But interrogating a suspected criminal is way different than interviewing a patient, no matter how much of a mental train wreck he or she might be. With criminals, it's not what they say; it's what they *don't* say. You want to keep them talking, hoping that somewhere along the line, they slip up. You, on the other hand, need to keep your mouth shut as much as possible. You don't want to reveal anything about the investigation. In other words, you don't want them to know what you know."

"Got it. So, what do we know?"

"We don't know jack shit except Selma was stabbed to death."

"So the last part should be easy."

The chief paused again. "Right. Let's get started, then."

They were forced to temper their enthusiasm until Annie finished her all-important huddle. Annie's well-honed executive skills served her well, enabling her to provide the night shifters with the minimum amount of necessary information about Selma's murder while simultaneously strangling rumors. Her presentation contained the perfect ratio of authoritative reassurance to understated sorrow, with a dollop of false piety thrown in for good measure. By the time she'd finished, Seph was ready to barf.

Annie ended her speech with a warm hand off not to Chief Bishop, but to Father Barney, who, though not fully recovered, managed to stumble through an invocation. Hands clasped, he begged for peace for Selma's departed soul and pleaded for the protection of everyone else's. The chief fumed while the priest prayed. After the last "amen" faded away, Chief Bishop claimed the floor. He scowled as he surveyed the crowd of employee-cum-suspects, and he kept his words brief.

"The investigation is ongoing. At this time, I have nothing to add. Remember what I said earlier about traveling in pairs. No lone stragglers. Be safe."

The night shifters dissipated, leaving only Seph, the chief, Annie, and Alice. Joaquin and Lew walked over to join them.

"What's the plan?" Joaquin asked. "Do we even have one? Maybe we should do fifteen minute checks on everyone in the shelter. Whatcha think, Lew?" He elbowed his new best friend.

Chief Bishop parried Joaquin's smart-assed comment with a withering look. "The *plan* is for Dr. Smith and myself to interrogate the obvious suspects and for the rest of you to go about your normal business. You can do me a favor by keeping your eyes and ears open for anything unusual."

"Unusual? Here?" Lew crouched and peered over both shoulders in mock alarm. "Hey, no problem, Chief. We got no problem with that, right Joaquin?" Though smiling, Lew's voice resonated with an unaccustomed edge. He, as the person accountable for the shelter's personnel, had to be more upset by Selma's death than he was letting on.

Joaquin, scarred by his own devastating foray into the back of the shelter, remained silent.

Chief Bishop did not rise to Lew's bait. "Does anyone have anything more constructive to add?"

This time, Lew was smart enough to stay quiet.

"Hearing none..." The chief brandished a list of names he'd scrawled on a sheet of paper. "I'll start with the kitchen employees and move on to the other staff from there."

He handed Seph the slip of paper. "Doc, you take care of the people here." He pointed to Annie, Alice, Lew and Joaquin. "Get them cleared and out of the way first so they can return to work. Then you can start with the known criminals."

Annie interjected. “I’m not sure I like how you said ‘known’ criminals.”

“Yeah? Well, suck it up, buttercup.”

Seph gasped, and Lew pursed his lips in a silent whistle. Like it or not, Annie was still the boss and wouldn’t tolerate such public insubordination. Joaquin grinned and took a broad step backwards. They waited for the fireworks to start.

The chief stuck out his square chin, crossed his burly arms, and asserted his authority. “You’ve already created an unacceptable delay in my investigation. This is now a federal crime scene, which puts me in charge of anything related to the murder, including the interrogations. Everyone’s a suspect until they’re not.”

Annie’s face hardened. “Is that so? You wanna know what I think? I think you’re awfully young to be leading such an investigation, aren’t you, Shane? Tell me—how many of these have you done?”

“Enough to tell you to back the hell off. The Bronx is known to have a violent crime every now and again. Besides, it’s not the age; it’s the experience. You should know. How many of these have *you* done, Annie?” He spat her name like a curse.

Annie matched his stance by crossing her own arms, and the stare-down began.

The chief raked a hand over his close-cropped hair and heaved a heavy sigh. “Look, I get it. You’re standing up for your staff. Admirable. But if you don’t let me do my job, I’ll be forced to document in my official report that you refused to allow certain employees and yourself to be interviewed. You’ll have a load of explaining to do when you return home to Boston. Now, how would you like to proceed?”

Their silent duel lasted a full minute before Annie’s stare finally faltered. “All right, Shane. You win.” She raised both hands in mock surrender. "You heard the man. Who wants to go first?"

"I will." Lew stepped forward. "Doc and I are overdue for a chat."

Lew and Seph separated themselves from the group and sat opposite each other at one of the folding tables. Seph pulled a pen from her pocket and rummaged for a paper napkin in case she needed to take notes. She hoped she didn't appear as awkward as she felt. They made this look so much easier on TV.

Lew offered Seph a piece of nicotine gum, which she declined. "You don't happen to have one of those little airplane bottles of tequila stashed anywhere, do ya?" she asked with a smile.

"I wish. If you're feeling jittery, there's a guy in row twelve with a giant bottle of mouthwash. Stuff is twenty percent alcohol, you know. Me—I'll take a bottle of Jack over Listerine any day." Lew popped the gum in his mouth and chomped away while Seph fidgeted.

Seph struggled to find a tactful way to begin questioning her colleague—and new friend. The uneasy silence stretched onward until Lew threw her a line. "Nothing like a little, ol' murder to get the blood boiling, huh? So, whose team are you on, Doc—Team Parrish or Team Bishop?"

"I'm not on anybody's team."

"Liar, liar, pants on fire." Lew grinned. "You're with the chief. For now, anyhow. Things got a funny way of changing depending on which way the wind blows and the blood flows. You gonna ask me some questions, or what?"

Seph pressed both palms flat against the table. "Did you kill Selma?"

"That's it? That's what your gonna ask everybody?" Lew shook his head in disbelief. "Okay, I confess. I did it. You backed me into a corner."

"C'mon, Lew."

"C'mon, what?" He spat the gum into his palm and patted his breast pocket. A pack of cigarettes crinkled under his hand. "Man, I would kill for a smoke right now." He chuckled at Seph's shocked expression. "Sorry. Poor choice of words."

"Holy crow, Lew!"

"Yeah, holy crow, Doc. Selma's been murdered and that's the best you can do?" Lew snatched the empty pack from his pocket and tapped out an imaginary cigarette. He crumpled the pack in his fist and hurled it across the room. It bounced off an adjacent table and onto the floor.

Seph remained silent, delaying, gathering her thoughts to start over. She remembered what the chief said about getting people to talk, just talk, about anything at all. Lew had nothing to do with Selma's murder, of that she was certain. But she needed the practice, and he was a good test subject. She took a deep breath and tried again.

"I hate crows. Sneaky little bastards. Smart, too."

Lew's shoulders relaxed as he played along. "Sounds like you've got yourself a phobia."

"I don't have a phobia. I just don't like them, that's all."

"Sounds like a phobia to me."

"Lew, I know phobias, okay? I'm a fricking psychologist, remember? I don't like ricotta cheese either, but that doesn't mean I've got a phobia about it!"

Lew surrendered with a disinterested shrug. "I guess not." He took a drag on his imaginary cigarette. "You know I'm from Detroit, right?"

"Yeah, so?"

"Detroit had a tough couple of years. Lotta crime, lotta rough characters, even in my own neighborhood, and mine was considered middle class. I learned something then. People kill for what they want or what they think they need—money, food, sex, power, whatever. Or they kill for emotions like jealousy. They don't kill for no reason at all. Even serial killers are choosy. They have a type. Way I see it, no one had any reason to kill Selma. She wasn't raped, was she?"

Seph winced and shook her head. "Not that I know of."

"Didn't think so. It actually would've been better for us if she had. At least there would've been a reason."

"Lew!" Seph dropped her pen. "My God!"

"I'm sorry—Lord have mercy on my soul—but it's true. Don't you see? Why kill Selma?" Lew leaned forward in his chair so only Seph could hear. "I'll tell you why. Someone killed Selma because they wanted to. Just because they could. That's what I think. And it scares the shit out of me. It should scare you, too."

Little beads of sweat glistened like copper pennies on Lew's clean-shaven head. "How many deployments did you say you've done?"

"This is my third."

"It's my fifth, and let me tell you, this one is different somehow. I can *feel* it. Something's not right here, but I don't know what it is. It's like I fell down the rabbit hole, you understand what I'm sayin'?" Lew picked up Seph's blank napkin and began tearing it into tiny bits of confetti.

"No. I'm sorry, but I don't know what you mean. These deployments—they're *all* different. Chalk it up to Rule #5."

"Say what?"

"It's this mental thing I do. I started making up rules after my first deployment because it was such a royal cluster."

"Fuck. Say it, Doc. You can do it. Cluster. Fuck."

Seph ignored him. "I vowed to be better prepared for the next time. For example, my Rule #1 is: 'Always keep an emergency kit packed and ready at all times.' Rule #2 is . . ."

"I get the concept." Lew waved his hand, and the pile of confetti flew to the floor.

"Rule #5: 'Adjust, adapt, and overcome. No two situations are ever the same.' I stole it from one of my soldier patients—it's a military slogan—but it works for civilian deployments, too. The point is, Lew, you're upset, as is everyone else in the shelter, because of what happened to Selma, and things appear darker and more frightening than usual right now. The storm will pass."

"But what will it leave in its wake?" Lew staggered to his feet, causing Seph to jump from her chair in alarm.

"You feeling okay?" She reached for his shoulder.

He waved her off and wiped the sweat from his forehead with an unsteady hand. "I hope you're right about everything, Doc. I really do. For all our sakes." Lew managed a sickly grin. "Man, I could really use that smoke!"

After her disturbing discussion with Lew, Seph chose to speak to Alice next. Since Alice never strayed far from the nurses' station without Dr. Parrish by her side, Seph quickly ruled her out as a suspect but made sure to mention Lew's wan appearance. Alice drifted away in search of her new patient.

After Alice came Joaquin, who was even easier to eliminate given he was never out of sight for more than fifteen minutes at a time.

Annie was more difficult, mostly because she was Annie and enjoyed being difficult, but Seph finally completed interviewing her share of the shelter's employees. She was anxious to move on to what she hoped would be the more interesting part of the process: Chief Bishop's list of known criminals. At the top of the list were the two gangbangers, Delmas and Thad.

Seph interrogated Thad first even though it was obvious he wasn't physically capable of committing a murder on his own. "Simply being thorough," she told him, when in fact the only reason she interviewed him was because Chief Bishop indicated it would be disrespectful not to. So she stroked Thad's ego and wasted her time in the process.

Thad, to his credit, answered her questions dutifully, although he made no effort to hide his boredom. The knifing of a kitchen worker was of no interest to him.

Delmas, on the other hand, took full advantage of the opportunity to swagger through the story of his only score: "the only one the pigs know about, anyway." He'd hunted down and blown away a nursing assistant for pilfering drugs from Thad's stockpile. When Delmas wouldn't share the recovered bounty, his girlfriend turned him in.

"Bitch didn't even come visit me in prison. Amazing, huh? Some people." He fluttered his long lashes and feigned surprise. "I went looking for her after I was sprung, but she'd disappeared and disappeared good. She knew what would a happened if I'd a found her."

"What would've happened?" Seph asked.

As was his habit, Delmas leaned back in his chair until he was balanced on the rear two legs. He stretched his muscular arms overhead and played coy while he considered his words. Then he suddenly rocked forward, smacking the chair's front legs onto the concrete floor with a bang and thrusting his upper body over the table until his eyes, more grey than blue in the low light, were inches from her own.

"Lemme put it this way: If I had three days left to live, she would have two."

His words hung in the heavy air before sinking to the floor like a mountain collapsing into the stormy sea. He laughed in a delayed attempt to pass off his threatening comment as some kind of morbid joke, but it was too late. Seph's hackles were up, and her emotional connection to Delmas told her he meant every word he said.

"Anything else, Mr. Duchenne?"

He sneered at her frosty response. "I think I've said enough already." He stood to leave. "Whoever your murderer is, you let me know first. Especially if it's one of the niggers or towel heads."

Seph flinched at his vitriol, and to her surprise, he responded by shifting his gaze to his feet and softening his tone. "Selma was a nice lady. Treated me with respect, y'know? She didn't deserve what happened to her."

A radio crackled, signaling someone's approach. Delmas sauntered away. He eyed the chief as they passed within a few feet from each other and cocked a cool nod in his general direction.

Chief Bishop pulled up a chair and plopped next to Seph. He peered over her shoulder at her handwritten notes. "What do you think? Is he a homicidal maniac?"

"Homicidal, yes. A maniac, no. Delmas's homicidal tendencies are directed toward one specific person, and luckily, she's not here. Otherwise I'm sure we'd have a problem." Seph dropped her pen and rubbed her eyes. The dim light was getting to her. "And speaking of problems, what were you thinking when you called Annie a 'buttercup'? Have you lost your mind?"

"Not yet." The chief flashed a pair of boyish dimples. "I have my reasons. Had to send a strong message for the benefit of my other officers, who have a tough job to do. Annie may be in charge, but she still needs to play nice. Otherwise, I might have to arrest her for obstruction of justice."

"You wouldn't."

"Try me."

"I'll pass, thank you very much."

"Smart move. Now, what can you tell me about Marlboro Man?"

The chief gestured toward the pedophile who, with his multicolored cowboy boots crossed at the ankles, leaned against a nearby wall. He wore his shirt unbuttoned, revealing an orange, fake tan and a waxed chest replete with heavy gold chains. An unlit cigarette dangled from the corner of his mouth, presumably in an attempt to look cool. Instead, he looked like a pimp. Or a walking punchline. Or possibly both.

Seph wrinkled her nose in distaste. "I haven't formally interrogated him. He's next on the list. However, from my brief interactions with him to date, I would say he's totally icky but not murderous. I'm a hundred percent certain I haven't interviewed the murderer yet."

"A hundred percent, huh? I like those odds." The chief blessed her with another of his crooked smiles. "You know what, Doc? You've got good observation skills, you're not overly squeamish, and you're a quick learner. In other words, you're damned good at this kind of thing, for a newbie. Ever thought about changing gears and becoming a criminal psychologist?"

"Not particularly, but I appreciate the vote of confidence." Seph batted her dark lashes at him. "You taught me everything I know."

The chief chuckled. "Then I guess you shouldn't quit your day job quite yet. But, seriously, I know potential when I see it."

Seph shook her head. "Nah. I like helping people too much."

"Criminal psychologists help people, too. Just sometimes those people are already dead."

"Sounds like a hoot. Sign me up."

"As if listening to people piss and moan all day long is a load of laughs?"

The chief's attitude changed in a flash, and he hunched forward, suddenly intense. "You help the living, too, sometimes, by putting a sorry-assed criminal behind bars before he hurts someone else, someone you might love. Someone who doesn't even know she needs protecting yet. That's why I do what I do. An ounce of prevention, as they say."

His pained expression vanished as swiftly as it had appeared. "You should think about it, that's all. On the plane ride home, maybe. Despite what you see on TV, there aren't enough good criminal profilers around. It's a tough job. You could handle it."

"I'll give it due consideration."

The chief raised his eyebrows. "You're blowing me off."

"No, I mean it. I will. But for now, back to work. I want to keep chugging along. Makes the night go faster. Who's next on your list for me to chat up?"

"I gave the list to you."

"Oh, yeah." Seph dragged the rumpled piece of paper from her pants pocket and crossed Delmas off the top. She read the next name aloud. "Angel Giallo."

The chief pointed across the room to a woman with long, black hair dancing around Thad and Delmas. "Multiple arrests for petty crime and prostitution."

Seph rolled her eyes. "*Giallo* is Italian for yellow, which makes her our yellow angel." A sudden wave of homesickness crashed over her, and Seph stroked the cross around her neck.

Today was Sunday. She hadn't missed Sunday Mass with her mother since her last deployment a year-and-a-half ago.

The chief snorted. "I don't know about the angelic part, but maybe that explains those ugly yellow shoes."

Seph sniffled. "I'm surprised you noticed. Most men don't pay attention to such things."

"Hard not to, the way she prances around in them. I think that's the point. She doesn't strike me as a murderer, though. See what you can find out. If you uncover a lead, come find me. Otherwise, I'll see you at the morning huddle."

Seph finished interrogating those with criminal records shortly after five a.m., and by then, everyone else she'd hoped to speak with was already asleep. She wandered over to the nurses' station to see how Alice and Annie were doing after completing their four-hour long rounds. The night was almost over, and so far, their team was two-for-two. They'd had medical emergencies with Joaquin and Carol on night one and a murder on night two. Which was sort of a medical emergency, depending on how you chose to look at it.

Luckily, Annie and Alice had little to report. Alice was back to her sedate self. Annie grilled Seph on how the investigation was progressing; Seph questioned Annie on how some of the more mentally fragile residents were doing. The whole team met for sign-out at seven, and soon Seph found herself standing at the foot of her cot, staring at its superfluous wool blanket. The shelter, closed tighter than a steel oil drum, never cooled off overnight. It was currently eighty degrees and sticky.

Would she be able to sleep? The rattling roof answered her question. The storm had them surrounded. The wind and the rain raged in its search-and-destroy mission, intent on exploiting any holes in the shelter's metal armor. A homicidal maniac, identity unknown, roamed the battlefield. With her eyes toward the sky and hands clasped at her waist, Seph murmured her bedtime prayers.

In twelve hours, by the time of her next shift, the storm should have passed, and the roof would be quiet again. Maybe Annie would allow them to open the shelter doors and get some fresh air. The thought cheered her. Lew and the other smokers would be ecstatic, for sure.

Seph pictured Lew, sweaty and jittery from nicotine withdrawal. Now *there* was a dude who could use a good night's rest. Seph smiled at the thought and crawled into bed. Murderer or no murderer, she needed to sleep. No harm in trying.

Chapter Six

The Third Night

Last night I dreamt I went to Manderley again. Seph awoke with the first line of Daphne du Maurier's *Rebecca* playing over and over in her head. Except she hadn't dreamt of Manderley at all. Instead, she'd spent the night drowning in the murky depths of a recurring nightmare.

Her brain adapted to the persistent torment long ago. As the terrifying climax of each nightmare approached, Seph's brain always lobbed her a lifeline—a phrase from a familiar book or the tune of a favorite song. This distress signal flashed on the monitor of her unconscious mind and triggered a game-saving reboot. Manderley was nothing more than a favored kill switch. When she dreamt of Manderley these days, though, it was more in the context of Stephen King's *Bag of Bones* than it was of *Rebecca*.

Seph threw on a pair of rumpled scrubs and reported to the main dining area for sign-in. She hoped to hear that day shift had made a dazzling breakthrough in Selma's murder. The subdued vibe signaled otherwise. The teams intermingled as usual, but the buzz was gone. Their cocktail hour had become a wake.

Annie ran through her daily checklist followed by a brief rah-rah speech, but her monotone was devoid of enthusiasm, and she made no real eye contact with anyone in the crowd.

Seph knew why. She could feel it. Annie was anxious about the upcoming shift, and the fact that Annie was nervous made

Seph nervous, too. Selma's murderer was still on the loose, and Annie expected him to strike again. She indicated as much, though not in those exact words. Instead, she spouted something along the more politically correct lines of ". . . Chief Bishop and his crew are doing everything they can to identify and prevent any future catastrophes, blah, blah, blah . . ."

But no matter how eloquently Annie phrased it, the bottom line remained the same: A killer would be prowling again tonight. Annie—night shift's foundation, the rock upon which their church was built—was on edge. If Annie crumbled, the whole team might as well say their prayers.

Seph searched for Chief Bishop, whom Annie had conspicuously not asked to speak. She located him near the nurses' station, huddled with a group of police officers from day shift, comparing notes on the investigation of Selma's murder.

Seph watched and waited for him to finish, occupying herself by attempting to decode his hand signals and deduce the gist of the conversation. Out of the corner of her eye, she noticed Carol lurking nearby, fidgeting on her feet and fingering her pocket watch as usual. Seph hadn't spoken to her since Selma's murder; in fact, she'd barely spoken to Carol at all since her overdose. Awash with guilt, Seph donned her best, fake smile and beamed it at her patient.

"Do you hear that?" Carol pounced as soon as Seph made eye contact.

"Hear what, Carol?"

Carol hoisted her arms overhead and tipped her head back to stare at the shelter's ceiling. Seph paused to listen. Nothing.

"I'm sorry, Carol, but I don't hear a thing."

"Damn right ya don't. You know why? Because the storm's over, that's why. Things . . . they should be better, but they're not. They're worse." Carol traced random, squiggly lines on the concrete floor with the tip of one cheap and badly weathered flip flop, which disintegrated into tar-black bits of rubber.

"How so?"

Carol peeked over both shoulders. She shuffled next to Seph and lowered her voice to a hoarse whisper. "I've lived in the hurricane belt my whole life, except for Nam. Been in lots of shelters, all kinds of shelters. But this one is different. I can feel it right here."

Carol tapped the middle of her forehead. "Somethin's not right here, or else I'm not right. I dunno which. I just dunno." She pressed her palms against her eyes and shook her head violently back and forth.

Seph eyed Carol suspiciously. "Have you been talking to Lew?"

"Who's Lew?" Carol peeped at Seph from between her nail-bitten fingers.

"You know, the big guy from Detroit. With the clipboard. He checks people in and out for their work shifts. Walks around here singing. You must have heard him, at least."

"I don't know no one named 'Lew.' Why?" She dropped her hands, and for a moment the two women stared at each other with equivalent levels of paranoia.

"Because he said the same things you just said. I mean, almost the exact same things, word for word."

"See! He knows. Your Lew is a wise man. Maybe you'll listen to him since you won't listen to me." Carol turned to stalk away, but Seph intervened.

"Wait. Carol, I *am* listening to you. Tell me more. Tell me about Harry and why he gave you his watch. I want to believe you, but I need to know you better first."

Carol spun around in a fury, spitting her words through teeth clenched in rage. "You touched my watch!"

"It fell out of your pants while you were being treated for your overdose. I picked it up and put it back in your pocket so it wouldn't get lost. I checked it out first, though, to make sure it hadn't been damaged in the fall. I'm afraid it was, because it wasn't ticking. That's when I noticed the writing."

Seph uttered a silent prayer for forgiveness and made a mental note to tell Alice about her little white lie in case Carol asked around.

Carol's eyes grew distant. "It hasn't worked in years." Her jaw relaxed, and her gruff voice softened. "Harry was my old man, and the watch was a gift from his commanding officer in World War II. Considered it his good luck charm. Said it saved his ass on more than one occasion, and he hoped it would save mine, too. He gave it to me when I shipped to Vietnam."

"Did it work?"

"What do you think?"

"I don't know what to think. It's your story."

"A pocket watch in the jungle? No. It did not work. And it ain't doing much for me here in hell, either." Carol's eyes regained their angry glint, and she stormed away, leaving Seph with more questions than answers.

To Seph's chagrin, the chief had left the nurses' station while she was talking to Carol. Annie and Alice sat in his place, reviewing the list of patients in preparation for their evening medical rounds. Seph meandered over, brow furrowed as she puzzled over her conversation with Carol.

"Before you begin rounds, I was wondering if either of you've noticed any unusual behaviors among the patients?"

"Like what?" As usual, Annie answered for both of them.

"I don't know. Like excessive agitation or paranoia, maybe. Carol's got herself pretty worked up again. She's fretting up a storm—no pun intended."

"Carol? Worked up? Mercy—I can't imagine." Annie, the undisputed queen of sarcasm, dismissed Seph's concerns with a haughty sniff.

"It's not only Carol. Lew seems out of sorts, too. At least, he did last night. I haven't talked to him yet today."

"Really? He was spewing rainbows and unicorns a short while ago when I let him go outside for a smoke. He practically danced out the door."

Annie all but patted Seph on the head. "This happens when the weather breaks, Seph. You'd think people would relax once the hurricane passes, but instead, as soon as they take a look outside, they start to think about going home. Then they see the damage and wonder if there's anything left to go home to. They get anxious and impatient. This is par for the course."

Seph, tired of being patronized, let it go. "It makes sense. I just never noticed it being this bad on my prior deployments."

Annie's words made Seph feel better on a superficial level, but the psychologist in her remained uneasy. Perhaps Lew and Carol's paranoid perceptions of this shelter's uniquely nefarious nature was beginning to rub off.

She longed see Lew's broad smile. Hopefully he'd returned to his jovial self now that he'd had his cigarette. Seph scanned the common areas, where she could usually spy his bald head standing tall above the shoulders of the other employees. "I haven't seen Lew since check-in. Any idea where he went after his smoke? He must be lying low for the night."

Annie, intent on starting her rounds, rounded the corner of the desk. "No. He went out right after the change of shift. It's a good thing he took advantage of the opportunity, too, because I'm locking the doors again for the night. Shane didn't want the added burden of tracking people traipsing in and out of the shelter after dark. Besides, the roads are washed out—completely impassable—and the ground is soaked, so even though the storm is over, we're not going anywhere for a few more days."

A patient from a dozen rows over moaned as if he'd heard her. Annie sighed, tucked a pen behind her ear, and searched for his name on her clipboard. "Right on time. I'd swear he has a stopwatch telling him when he's eligible for his next dose of morphine. On the brighter side, cell service should be restored by tomorrow, which'll help improve the attitude around here. I predict we'll be able to start moving people out, either home or to temporary housing, within three to five days. By that time, this place will be a frickin' zoo."

Annie frowned as Delmas pranced by with the giggling Angel riding on his back like a horse. Her sullen boyfriend followed behind. "I mean, seriously, is this kind of thing really necessary?"

Delmas released Angel's ankle long enough to throw Seph a quick salute before he and Angel galloped away. Annie and Alice gawked at Seph, who smothered a grin. "I think now's a good time for me to go find Lew."

Seph circled the shelter slowly, stopping several times to counsel evacuees still shaken from the events of last night. She'd almost completed her lap when she spotted a group of night shifters having an animated discussion with Chief Bishop. Curious, she strolled their way, catching bits and pieces of the conversation as she drew near. Joaquin had disappeared again; she discerned that much. But there seemed to be something more. By the time she'd closed the gap, the group had already dispersed into two-person teams to go in search of Joaquin.

"Good morning, Chief. Or good evening, as the case may be."

"Seph." He offered nothing more.

"We're doing the first name thing now, too, huh?"

Not even a blink. Seph cut the niceties. "I gather Joaquin's gone again for, what . . . the third time now?"

"Yep." Judging by the chief's stony expression, he was either preoccupied or playing it close to the chest.

"Who had the last Joaquin check?"

"Lew." The chief avoided Seph's inquisitive gaze.

"Did you question him yet?"

"He's missing too."

Silence ensued as Seph digested the unpalatable morsel of information. *He knows. Your Lew is a wise man. Maybe you'll listen to him* . . . Her ears rang with the echo of her recent conversation with Carol. Something was undeniably wrong. Seph's stomach cramped as she imaged what that something might be.

Seph ignored the acid churning in her gut and matched the chief's flat demeanor and controlled, clipped speech. "Do you think he went AWOL? Annie told me she opened the doors. Lew went out to smoke. Maybe he never came back."

"That's one theory, although I had a guard at the door checking people in and out, and I posted an officer outside."

"Can I help search?"

"You're welcome to look on your own if you want, but only in the lighted areas. I handed out all my walkies, so you'll have to stay in the main part of the shelter."

"I can do that."

The chief had no knowledge of Seph's prior conversations with Carol and Lew and their macabre predictions of danger yet to come. But his distant façade cracked for a fleeting second, and the gravity of his expression gave him away. He already knew.

"I mean it, Doc. No going into the back of the hangar. And if you do happen to find Joaquin or Lew, follow the instructions Annie and I gave on day one."

"Which were?"

"Scream loudly."

Seph wandered aimlessly through the patient care area of the shelter, questioning anyone who was still awake if they had seen Lew or Joaquin. An hour turned into two, and she realized she was wasting her time. She plopped into a dejected heap at the nurses' station, nearly toppling the cheap folding chair. Her approach needed to be narrower, more analytical. She closed her eyes and took a deep breath in through her mouth, exhaling slowly through her nose. *Focus.*

Seph wasn't familiar with Joaquin on a personal level, but she'd gotten to know Lew well. If she wanted to find him, she needed to think like him. Seph pictured Lew in her mind, mentally replaying every discussion they'd had and reviewing every fact he'd revealed about his existence outside the fish tank in which they currently swam.

Lew hailed from Detroit. He wore a wedding ring. He was easygoing, yet conscientious about his work for the VA. He hummed and sometimes sang classic Motown while checking people in for their shifts. He smoked. Despite being a seasoned disaster worker with four previous deployments under his belt, he was inexplicably anxious about this shelter. He had the last Joaquin check.

Seph opened her eyes. If Lew lost sight of Joaquin, as she had done, he might have assumed Joaquin would wander into the back of the shelter like before. Prior to alerting the chief and admitting he'd been derelict in his duties, Lew would've tried to find Joaquin himself first. But Lew was frightened by the dark side of the shelter. For him to have crossed what Seph jokingly referred to as the "DMZ"—the demarcation between the lighted and dark sections of the hangar—alone and against orders, he must have seen or heard something urgent. Something, or someone, couldn't wait for him to run for help.

Convinced she'd tapped into Lew's thought process, Seph borrowed a flashlight from the nurses' station and marched past the employee cots to the far-right edge of the DMZ. She skirted along its haphazard line of rolling barriers and empty shipping crates and combed the area for anything out of the ordinary. Seph flashed the light into the darkness beyond, hoping to illuminate some kind of clue. She'd almost reached the mid-point of the shelter when she heard it.

Beep. The faint noise sounded muffled, as if it were emanating from beneath a mound of pillows.

Beep. Seph followed the high-pitched tone to a wooden shipping crate sitting a few feet within the DMZ. She pressed her ear against the box and waited.

Beep. Louder this time. The crate was huge, roughly eight-foot square, so Seph pushed a series of smaller boxes next to it and climbed them like a flight of stairs to reach the lid.

Beep. Seph used the lip of her flashlight like a crowbar, but it's short length gave her little leverage. She struggled, but finally managed to pry the top off the crate and send it flying to the floor below. She paused to say a silent prayer. She readied herself and shone her light into the bottom of the box.

Beep. Joaquin's insulin pump, its battery dying a slow and solitary death from hours of sounding the alarm, flashed forlornly within its wooden coffin. The box was otherwise empty.

Confused, Seph jumped down and debated her next move. She couldn't retrieve the pump, not without getting stuck in the bottom of the crate, and she wasn't sure it was necessary to do so. What mattered was Joaquin had lost his pump. Joaquin was dependent on insulin to survive and would've never willingly removed it, much less thrown it in the bottom of a box.

Beep. So who did?

As she stood puzzling over the latest bizarre development, Seph became aware of another noise, a hushed, melodic warbling masked by the shrill shriek of Joaquin's pump. Seph strained to determine its origin until a single, sustained note revealed its identity. Someone was singing.

Like a swimmer wading into the moonlit sea, Seph stepped cautiously into the depths of the forbidden zone. A precipitous drop in light lay ahead. Her dinged-up flashlight flickered, and she rapped it against her leg, berating herself for having used it as crowbar. Now was not a good time to have it go on the fritz. It rallied and bounced a concentrated beam off the white fabric of a rolling barrier directly in front of her. Behind the barrier, a half-dozen others had been subtly rearranged around a single large crate, creating a triangle-shaped area of walled-off space, easily overlooked by the casual observer.

"Lew?" She recognized his tremulous falsetto. The first time she'd heard him sing, she was shocked. She'd expected such a big man to possess a deep, velvety baritone à la Barry White. Instead, Lew's voice was high-pitched, delicate, and perfect for riffing from his hometown heroes, Stevie Wonder and Smokey Robinson.

"The man you know's been blown away,
Blinded by the storm . . ."

"Lew?" Seph tried again, firmer, louder. "I can hear you, Lew. C'mon, answer me. Everyone's worried about you."

"But don't pity me,
At least I'm free . . ."

The singing continued without so much as a quaver of acknowledgement.

Seph hesitated and glanced behind her at the main part of the shelter. By the time she located a police officer, Lew may have disappeared, and the search would have to start all over again.

Screw it. Her decision made, Seph dove into the darkness and covered the few feet separating her from the triangular area as quickly as possible. She tugged on one of the barriers, pushing it aside, and flashed her light into the exposed space.

"For God's sake, Lew . . . Oh my God!" Seph staggered backward and covered her mouth with one hand. "Lewis." Her voice was nothing more than a whisper. "What have you done?"

Lew, his face a mask of intense concentration, sat by Joaquin's dead body, threading the corpse's small intestines through his fingers. He raised his head at the sound of Seph's voice, and although his face showed no real expression, she knew her presence was unwelcome. A chill of terror raced down her spine. Lew was calm, but it was an otherworldly calm—a psychotic stillness Seph had previously observed only in her most insane patients. Any semblance to the amicable man who'd first helped her off the bus had been erased. But by what?

Lew stopped singing and meticulously tucked the string of entrails into place within Joaquin's abdominal cavity, where they quivered with residual peristaltic activity. He staggered to his feet, not bothering to wipe the gore from his hands. Blood dripped from his fingertips, and for a moment, he simply stared, unblinking and without a flicker of recognition, into Seph's horror-stricken eyes.

Seph willed herself to remain perfectly motionless, afraid any sudden movement might trigger an attack. She reached out with her mind, probing his emotions in a desperate attempt to connect to the man she hoped still existed beneath the crazed exterior.

But her attempts were blocked by a wall of confusion and pain. Her flashlight sputtered, and Lew's face seemed to change in the splintering light, transforming into someone paler, colder, and unfamiliar. She blinked, and his brown eyes faded to an icy blue. She blinked again, and his face returned to normal. The flashlight dimmed to a faint glow, and Seph knew she had to act before the bulb died and plunged her into lethal darkness.

"Lew, I'm going to go get some help, okay?" She took one small, tentative step backward. "You stay here. I'll be right back." Another step, a little bigger this time.

Perhaps it twinkled in the wavering rays of her flashlight, or maybe her movement caused it to stir from its nest at the base of her throat—Seph didn't know for sure—but something about Seph's gold cross caught Lew's attention, and he lowered his eyes to focus on the crucifix dangling around her neck.

Inadvertently, Seph raised her left hand to finger the necklace, and the innocent gesture caused him to snap. His lips twisted into a subhuman snarl, and with a low, guttural growl,

Lew lunged forward, his blood-encrusted hands reaching for Seph's neck.

Bob, weave. Scream loudly.

Seph dodged hard right and released a war whoop that hit the metal ceiling and echoed throughout the shelter. Lew's slippery fingers grasped her necklace, and she cried out in pain as the chain bit into her neck before giving way. She swung around with a high right hook, the heavy Maglite clamped in her hand. The punch caught Lew square across the temple, and he crumpled to the floor, clutching her necklace in his hands. He curled into the fetal position, moaned, and was still.

Shaking with adrenaline, Seph turned to run, only to see Chief Bishop, Annie, and an entire herd of people heading her way. She forced herself to stay put, inching just out of reach should Lew decide to awaken. Her right hand cramped from clenching the flashlight, but Seph couldn't convince her fingers to relax their death grip, so instead she concentrated on slowing her racing heart. By the time the chief and Annie arrived on scene, Seph had her game face back in place.

Annie took one look at Joaquin's gaping torso and launched into damage control mode, spreading her arms wide to block the approaching horde from coming any further.

"Everybody back!" She cordoned off the area like a human shield. "You, too, Alice." Annie lowered her voice so only Alice could hear. "You don't need to see this, and neither do they." She searched the crowd. "Father Barney?"

The priest hobbled forward, huffing and puffing from his sprint to the back of the shelter. He pulled a rosary from his pocket.

"Yes, Dr. Parrish." He didn't ask what she wanted. With the image of Selma's painful demise fresh in his mind, he appeared resigned and ready to administer last rites for the second time in two days.

Annie shook her head. "Not this time, Father. It's too late, I'm afraid. Can you manage the crowd for me? Get them back to the main part of the shelter, and keep them calm until we're done here, okay?"

Father Barney sighed in relief. "Of course, Dr. Parrish." He went to work tending the flock, shepherding them away from the grisly scene.

As soon as they were out of earshot, the chief turned on Seph. "What the hell happened here? Did I not make myself explicitly clear? How many times have I told you to stay out of this part of the shelter?"

Seph opened her mouth to explain, but, to her surprise, Annie intervened on her behalf. "Later, Shane. First things first. Are you hurt?" Annie performed a quick, visual scan of Seph's entire body, scoping for obvious injuries.

"What? No. Why?" The room began to spin.

"Because you have blood on your neck." Annie leaned forward and traced a line with one finger along the left side of Seph's neck. She tugged gently on the skin. "I don't see a laceration, though."

"It's not mine. I mean, I don't think it is." Seph's knees wobbled, and she resisted the juvenile urge to swat Annie's hand away. "It might be from my necklace. Lew, he . . ."

Seph bit her lip as an unexpected surge of tears burned her eyes and constricted the back of her throat. ". . . He tore it off."

Annie released Seph's neck and shifted her focus to the two men lying on the floor. "Well, you don't need a medical degree to know Joaquin is dead." She squatted to palpate his carotid artery. "Lew, however, is very much alive." She gasped as Lew, jolted awake by her touch, rolled over and grabbed her wrist in one fluid motion.

He sat up halfway, wild-eyed and confused, knocking Annie backward in the process. The chief pulled his weapon, but Lew's assault faded as rapidly as it had started. He slumped back to the concrete floor, and his tongue wandered around his mouth as if he wanted to speak but could not.

Rattled, Annie scrambled to her feet and rubbed her bruised wrist. "What . . ."

Before she could finish, Lew let out a long moan. His eyes rolled back until only the whites remained, his fists clenched, and his entire body quaked, followed by synchronous jerking of his arms and legs. Finally, his back arched, and Lew began to seize, banging his head against the concrete floor over and over again until Seph couldn't bear the noise any longer. She dropped the heavy flashlight with a clang and clasped both hands over her ears in a futile attempt to block the sickening sound.

"Seph, get out of the way! Alice!" Annie pushed Seph aside and crouched next to Lew's head, cradling it between her arms to prevent further trauma.

Alice sat on her knees opposite Annie and opened the emergency kit, rifling through the contents until she found what she wanted—a syringe filled with a clear gel, which she held up for Annie's inspection.

Annie nodded. "Perfect. See if you can find another one. We're gonna need it. Shane, I need you to roll Lew onto his side and pull his pants down so I can administer the rectal Valium."

The chief raised one eyebrow but complied without comment. After two syringes and what felt like hours—in reality, only a few minutes—the seizures stopped. Lew, blood oozing from his nose and left ear, lay motionless, his breathing steady and calm.

Annie took a deep breath and rocked back on her heels. "Well, that was fun. We should move him to the medical ward

ASAP. The Valium may not hold the seizures for long, and our bag of tricks is spent." She patted the emergency kit.

The chief radioed for a stretcher. Annie and Alice stood to stretch their legs, and Annie whistled at Seph, who was swaying on her feet with her eyes scrunched shut and hands white-knuckled by her sides.

"Are you okay?"

Seph's eyes fluttered open to stare at Lew's unconscious form.

"Did I do that?" Her voice was flat, dead.

"What do you mean?"

"Did I make Lew seize? I hit him with the flashlight. Really hard. See?" Seph pointed to the purple, swollen area above Lew's left ear. "I didn't mean to hit him that hard. I was just so scared. I . . . I don't know what I was thinking. I wasn't thinking, I guess."

Annie choose her words with surgical precision. "I don't believe you damaged Lew's brain, Seph. You may have fractured his skull—from the looks of things, you probably *did* fracture his skull—but as far as brain damage . . .no. While it's theoretically possible your blow caused internal bleeding which in turn triggered a seizure, such an event occurs several hours after an injury, not right away."

"Then what did?" Seph remained unconvinced. She judged herself guilty until proven innocent. Two male nurses arrived with the stretcher, and she watched as Alice assisted them with strapping Lew to each side.

"Seph . . ." Annie's short list of virtues did not include patience. ". . . I don't know the details of what transpired here, so how am I supposed to have a viable theory? Like I said to Chief Bishop: first things first. Let me finish stabilizing Lew. When I'm done, we'll have a group huddle, get our facts straight, and try to figure out what's going on, okay?"

Seph nodded.

"Good." Annie gave the trio of nurses the green light. "Ready? Let's move."

Seph and the chief watched as the caravan receded into the distance. An awkward silence replaced the chaos. Seph focused on her feet. The chief cleared his throat.

"Seph . . ."

Fearing a lecture, Seph cut him off. "What do we do with him?" She gestured toward Joaquin.

"Same thing we did with Selma. Wrap him in a blanket, and lock him in the supply closet-slash-morgue."

It suddenly seemed darker. Seph stooped to retrieve her fallen flashlight, brandishing it like a sword to hold the surge of claustrophobia at bay.

Bleeerp. Without the background clamor of the medical team, Joaquin's pump alarm reasserted its presence. It gasped out a terminal wheeze before switching off, its battery drained.

The chief looked around, as perplexed as Seph had been when she'd first heard the unfamiliar noise.

"What the hell was that?"

Seph pointed to the box a few paces ahead. "Joaquin's insulin pump is in the bottom of the crate. That's how I found him. I heard it first. Then I heard Lew singing."

"Lew was singing? Was that before or after he gutted Joaquin like a fish?"

Seph shuddered and launched into a detailed explanation of what she'd seen and heard, walking the chief from one location to the next so he could better envision the scene. They finished back at the large crate. Between the two of them, they managed to retrieve Joaquin's defunct pump from the bottom of the deep container. The exercise was as therapeutic as it was productive.

The chief flipped the pump over and over in his gloved hands, inspecting it for blood, damage, or other clues and finding none. He pulled a plastic evidence bag out of his back pocket and dropped the device inside.

"You have a fingerprint kit here in the shelter?" Seph asked.

"No, but we have baby powder and a camera." Seph's eyes lit up with interest, and the chief grinned. "Watch and learn, Doc. Watch and learn."

The chief circumnavigated the entire scene a second time, opening every crate and checking around each barrier. Seph followed alongside, studying his actions and filing them away for future reference. When he'd finished, she pressed him for answers.

"Why do you think Lew killed Joaquin in the first place?"

"I'm not sure he did."

"What do you mean? Need I remind you I saw him playing with Joaquin's bowels?"

"Did you witness the actual murder?"

"No."

The chief spread his arms wide. "And where's the murder weapon?"

Seph frowned. "Good question."

"You bet it is. I find it difficult to believe Lew was able to fillet Joaquin open, run off to hide the knife, and return to sing him a lullaby—all without being seen by any of the search teams."

"I see your point." Seph mulled the situation over in her head. "What do you think happened, then? Someone else killed Joaquin, and when Lew found the body, he went insane?"

The chief shrugged. "It's possible. Insanity is your area of expertise, not mine. I'm merely saying we shouldn't jump to conclusions. We know Lew didn't murder Selma. He had an airtight alibi. We've either got two killers, or the same person killed both, and Lew happened to find Joaquin first, as you said. Hopefully Lew will recover enough to give us an accurate rendition of what actually occurred."

Seph pictured Lew repeatedly slamming the back of his head against the concrete floor, and she winced. "Even if he recovers physically, I'm not sure he'll recover mentally. Not after the seizure and the traumatic brain injury he sustained."

"We can only hope." The chief made a final visual sweep of the area. "We're done here. Let's head up front and get an update from Annie."

"Okay." Seph moved to take one final look at Joaquin, but the chief grabbed her by both shoulders and forced her body straight ahead.

"No. If you're going to survive in this business, you need to remember one thing: Leave the dead behind. Never carry them with you."

Seph had a new rule.

They arrived at the nurses' station just in time to watch Lew die. He was still lying on his right side in what Alice referred to as the "recovery position," sporting an IV in his right arm and a blood pressure cuff on the left. As Seph rounded the corner, Lew's eyelids fluttered open, as if he'd been awaiting her presence. His eyes, clouded with confusion, sought her face, and for an instant, they flickered with recognition. Then his lids sagged shut, and Lew was gone.

Annie started CPR. Alice pushed every drug the pharmacy had available through his IV in a futile attempt to restart his heart. After a half hour of pounding on Lew's chest, Annie called it quits.

Seph pressed her palm over her mouth to stifle her sobs as Alice and the other nurses removed Lew's IV and cleared away the empty medicine vials. Exhausted, Annie leaned against the table. Her arms trembled from thirty minutes of administering chest compressions, and she stared at Lew's bruised face, her own a mask of controlled emotion.

After the nurses drifted away, the chief broke the silence. "The morgue is getting full."

Annie snorted and cupped her right hand over her chin but did not otherwise respond. She furrowed her brow in preoccupation. The chief eyeballed Seph as if to say, "It's *your* turn."

Seph sniffled and rubbed her puffy eyes before directing Annie's attention to the chairs at the nurses' station. "Maybe this would be a good time for us to sit and review what happened. You said we would once Lew was . . .stable."

Annie exhaled with a loud hiss. "Yeah, he's stable all right. As stable as anyone can be."

"You need the rest anyway." Seph touched Annie's shoulder; she jerked herself out of reach.

"Not now."

"Why not?"

"I'm thinking."

"About what?"

"I'm thinking Lew's pupils were blown, and I don't know why."

Seph's eyes welled with tears. "Is that important?"

"Yes."

The chief interjected. "Then maybe you should interpret for us non-medical folk. And make sure you dumb it down a notch."

"It means both his pupils were extremely dilated and unresponsive even before he began seizing, which is strange. Bilaterally blown pupils are found in patients who are fully brain dead or in cases of massive head trauma—something much more significant than getting whacked in the temple with a flashlight. Lew's presentation was anomalous. I know of no disease process consistent with what I just saw. Something's not right here."

I told you so! Seph counted to ten and kept her childish retort to herself. Instead, she donned a wry smile.

"If I hear that phrase one more time I'm going to scream. Don't you remember, Annie? I talked to you earlier today about how several people in the shelter seemed out of sorts, Lew being one of them. They used those exact same words. I wholeheartedly agree. Something *isn't* right here. We're deployments pros, yet I'm willing to bet none of us has had one, much less three, people die during any of our previous deployments. If we continue at our current rate, we could hit double digits by the time we pack things up."

Annie scowled at the thought of such a malignant statistic. "I think it's pretty obvious what's going on. We've got our very own Jack the Ripper running around, and he's making people nervous. Understandably so, given they're trapped in a shelter with nowhere else to go."

Annie crossed her arms over her chest. The gesture was Annie's "tell" and indicated she'd traversed the line from chronically testy to frankly irritated. "When we talked about this earlier, I told you I didn't see anything unusual, given the extenuating circumstances. Despite Lew and his blown pupils, I still believe that. I'm sure there's a perfectly reasonable medical explanation. So, what exactly are you suggesting?"

"I'm not sure, but I do think there's more to it than typical shelter shock. A lot of people—evacuees as well as seasoned employees, who have no reason to develop shelter shock—are doing weird things. We've got the murderer, whoever he or she may be; Carol with her overdose, Lew, and even Joaquin with his wandering off. You can blame it on stress, insulin, or pre-existing mental instability if you want, but I'm not buying it. We should search for commonalities. Did they eat the same foods? Take the same medications? Those are the kinds of things we need to question."

"You sound like a detective."

"Psychology is a type of detective work, or so the chief's been telling me." Seph looked over her shoulder at Chief Bishop, begging for validation, and he nodded his support. "When you think about it, what do therapists do? We dig around a patient's brain for clues. We use our words to poke underneath the grey layers of protective spackle, attempting to deduce the cause of his neurosis—what is it that makes him sad or angry or afraid."

It's the storm, Doc. Sergeant Bradley's words burst into her mind like a flash of lightening. *It's as if it's alive, crawling into your eyes and lungs like a parasite until you're so disoriented . . .*

"Maybe it has something to do with the storm itself," Seph said, thinking out loud.

Annie stared at her blankly. "As in . . ."

"You told me you saw Lew smoking in the rain hours before he went missing. He worked outside unloading the buses up until the very end, when the storm got so bad he was forced to come in. I saw Carol outside smoking when I first arrived at the shelter. She was soaked. Selma was too, come to think of it. Maybe the rain was poisonous, or perhaps the hurricane winds carried some kind of toxic fumes."

"That's just nuts, Seph."

"What? You've never heard of acid rain before?"

Annie rolled her eyes.

"If you've got a better idea, let's hear it." Seph stuck out her chin and matched Annie's defensive posture.

"I already told you my theory, and you didn't *want* to hear it!"

Annie's simmering temper threatened to boil over. She smoothed her face into a bland mask, transforming into practiced doctor mode. "Look, you've had a traumatic couple of hours. Go meditate somewhere or something. We'll talk about it more later. I need to chart Lew's death, and Alice and I have yet to finish rounds. I'm too far behind to relive *The X-Files.*" Annie stalked off before Seph could think of a smart response.

"For what it's worth, I agree with you. And with her. You sounded like a total nut job."

Seph spun around to glare at the chief, who stood behind her grinning from ear-to-ear. "Nice. I suppose I should've worked through the details before I spoke. Have you come up with any new theories of your own?"

The chief's grin vanished, and he shook his head. "No, 'fraid not. But Lew didn't strike me as the type of guy who would totally wig out over one dead body. And he sure as hell didn't fit the profile of a serial killer. He was as solid as they come."

The chief scanned the shelter. Despite the late hour, the stagnant air buzzed with an invisible force, a restless energy powerful enough to make bellies cramp and hairs stand on end.

"There are as many possibilities as there are loonies in this bin," he said. "For example, someone, maybe even our murderer, could be slipping people hallucinogenic drugs just for shits and giggles. I'm sure plenty of pills are changing hands here in the shelter. Or perhaps the environment itself is toxic, like you said. It would be nice to know why the base was decommissioned and left to rot. For all we know, we could be sitting on top of a chemical landmine."

He lowered his head toward hers before continuing. "Annie will continue to insist this is all due to shelter shock, because the truth is, as the team leader, she's responsible for anything else that happens. She can't prevent shelter shock, but if people are dying because the food's contaminated or the HVAC is malfunctioning, it'll be 'off with her head!'" The chief drew a line across his throat for emphasis. "Even the boss has a boss to report to. Dr. Parrish is no longer impartial; you understand what I'm saying?"

Seph nodded.

"Good. And another thing. Should a cover up become necessary, I have absolutely no doubt she'd throw us under the bus without a second thought. Which means from now on, we keep things between the two of us. Besides, she thinks you're flippin' nuts."

Seph grimaced. "Lovely. What's our next move?"

"Have you talked to Delmas and Thad lately?"

"No, why?"

"Those bad boys seem to know everything about everything going down in this joint. If there's a pot boiling, their fingers are in it."

"Okay, I'll scope them out."

"Don't sound so happy about it." The chief's shrewd gaze missed little.

"Delmas makes me nervous."

"He makes me nervous, too, but not in the same way as you, I'm sure. You'll get over it."

Seph threw him a withering look. "And what exactly are you going to do?"

"I'm going to fingerprint Joaquin's pump so when the phones and internet are up and running again tomorrow, I can hopefully get some answers as to the identity of our killer."

"You wanna switch jobs?"

"Not a chance."

Seph wandered toward Delmas and Thad's cots, hoping they'd be asleep but doubting she could be so lucky. She wasn't. She found them in their usual positions, propped on pillows and playing cards. Delmas held aces again, and Thad clutched a pair of eights. This time, Seph didn't wait for them to acknowledge her presence; she barged right in.

"Hey."

They both looked up from their cards.

"Hey," Delmas replied.

"You hear about Joaquin and Lew?"

"Yeah." Delmas lowered his eyes back to his aces. "Shame about Joaquin. He was a good nurse—for a Spic. Did a great job with Thad's wounds." Thad nodded his assent.

"You know anything about it?"

"What you're really asking is if we had anything to do with it." Delmas's sardonic jab hit close to the truth, and Seph felt herself blush.

"No, I know you didn't." She caught Delmas off guard, and he stared at her face. Her color deepened under his scrutiny, and she rushed to explain. "You'd have to be a pretty stupid Aryan to commit a hate crime in a place with such a limited pool of suspects, and I know you're not stupid. Why would you risk going back to jail for someone like Joaquin? He wasn't worth it to you. In fact, you found him helpful. Killing him wouldn't make sense."

"Glad to hear you've got it all figured out." Delmas sneered at her sincerity. "I heard the nigger did it."

Seph choked as if she'd been punched in the throat. "You . . .you *asshole*. Who are you referring to? Are you talking about Lew? Is that it?"

The words tumbled out of Seph's mouth as her raw sorrow morphed into white-hot rage. She pictured Lew—the beautiful man who'd welcomed her to the shelter, who'd entertained her with his vault of useless movie trivia and delicate singing voice, who'd razzed her about her reluctance to curse—slamming his head against the unforgiving floor. She pictured the desperation and fear in his tawny brown eyes as he drew his last breath, and her whole body shook with uncontrolled fury.

"Lew was a good man, a better man than you'll ever be."

Delmas, unimpressed by her wrath, shrugged. "You don't know that. I'm a good man . . .in certain ways. In others, not so much. You'll find most people are like that. It all depends on the circumstances . . .and how you define 'good.' From what I heard, your good man Lew did a very bad thing."

"Chief doesn't think so."

"Chief Bishop couldn't find his ass with both hands. He's in way over his head. Goddamned federal police officer. Spends his days patrolling the VA, patting veterans on the head and thinks he's hot shit." Delmas's lip curled in contempt. "He ain't even old enough to be called a pig. He's a piglet—that's what he is."

Thad chortled with glee. "Piglet." He grunted and gasped from the effort.

Delmas grinned. "I'd bet my left nut your chief has never worked a homicide case before. Probably hasn't even seen one up close."

"Yeah? He loves you, too. I think you're underestimating him, but hey—what do I know? The bottom line: Right now, he's what we've got, and he doesn't believe Lew had anything to do with Joaquin's murder. So, tell me what *you* think—who do we need to watch?"

Delmas placed his cards face down and uncoiled from his cot, rising in one lithe motion to confront Seph face-to-face. "What I don't understand, baby girl, is why you give a shit *what* we think."

"Because you keep your eyes and ears open, and you've got street smarts, which is something I don't have. Not yet, anyway. I'm learning." Seph's honest reply elicited a rare response from Thad, who usually let Delmas do the talking.

"You'd better learn quick." Thad's thin voice trembled, weakened by the same muscle wasting that ravaged his arms and legs.

"What do you mean? Are you . . .threatening me, Thad?"

Delmas and Thad exchanged cryptic looks. Delmas invaded her personal space, leaning in until Seph felt his breath on her cheek. She fought her natural inclination to run away.

"I know what you want me to say." Delmas deepened his voice, accentuating his slow, Southern drawl. "But I don't know who your murderer is or what kind of game he's playing. For all I know, there could be more than one." He circled her body with his own, his breath in her ear, then her hair, then back to her cheek.

"Something is spreading, like a disease. Maybe it started with Selma's murder, or maybe it started with the storm itself. I knew we were in trouble the minute the queen closed and locked the shelter doors. Can't you feel it building? That off-kilter feeling, like you're in a fun house at the country fair?"

Seph swallowed, struggling to focus as the intensity of Delmas's words provoked and overloaded her sensitive system. She clenched her fist over her stomach and swayed on her feet, as nauseated as if she were indeed stumbling around a fun house with its psychedelic hall of mirrors.

Delmas smirked at her obvious discomfort. "You've heard of mass hysteria?"

"Of course," Seph whispered. Collective hysteria, hysterical contagion, and the entire family of herd mentality disorders had fascinated Seph since grad school. The only requirement for an outbreak was a triggering incident and a group of people ready to fall into a shared delusion.

Delmas stepped back, granting Seph a reprieve. "I've seen it occur in prison. Something ugly goes down, and before you know it, everyone's foaming at the mouth like a pack of rabid dogs. Inmate, guard—it don't matter. The paranoia's so intense, it makes their skin crawl. Strike first instead of strike back—that's what they do. Now, instead of one murderer, you've got an entire pigpen full of potential murderers. It's happening here. No one is safe. Not me, not you . . ." Delmas reached out to stroke a strand of Seph's long, dark hair before abruptly returning to his cot. "Sit back, and wait for the anarchy to begin."

"Dr. Parrish will not allow the shelter to degenerate into chaos. She has everything under control." Her words sounded hollow even to herself. Seph strained to hide her horror at the appalling scenario Delmas depicted.

Delmas sneered at her lack of conviction. "The Red Queen? How do you know she's not a murderer, too?" Delmas retrieved his aces from where they lay, signaling an end to the conversation. "Protect yourself, Persephone Smith. I've seen how scenes like this play out. The nice people always die first."

Go meditate somewhere. Seph, desperate to escape from the disturbing images Delmas had planted in her mind, followed orders and slipped into the non-medical half of the shelter. Hoping to find some anonymous quiet time to recover from the trauma of the last few hours, she removed her orange armband and melded into a corner behind a group of swarthy men gambling with dice. Despite the hour, a significant portion of the seven hundred or so healthy evacuees were awake, which kept the staff hopping and allowed Seph to linger unnoticed while she collected her thoughts.

She watched the men toss the dice high into the air and their eager faces as they watched the dice fall. The dice bounced and rolled over the concrete before churning to a halt, accompanied by the muted cheers of those who'd placed the winning bets and the groans of those who had not. The men were oblivious to Thad and Delmas's dire warning, and after careful deliberation, Seph decided their words were indeed a warning and not a threat, though she wasn't sure the chief would feel the same. She opted to keep the details of their unsettling conversation to herself.

One of the men noticed her attention and motioned for her to join them. She declined with a smile and drifted away, waiting until she was out of sight to reattach her armband and sneak back to the medical unit to complete her shift.

She met the chief in the dining area prior to the seven a.m. change of duty and before Annie gave her report. They huddled together, exchanging information in rushed undertones like guilty lovers trying not to get caught in a tête-a-tête.

"What did you learn from Delmas?" he asked.

"He's an honest-to-God asshole."

"We knew that already. I meant about Joaquin's murder."

"He doesn't know anything."

"And you believe him?"

"Yes."

"What about Thad?"

"Thad knows what Delmas knows." Seph shushed the chief from asking anything more as the crowd parted, indicating Annie's arrival.

Annie, a paragon of grim professionalism, stepped into the center of the room, and it fell silent. Unlike her glossy presentation after Selma's demise, this time she made no attempt to spare the crowd from the blunt force trauma of her words.

"By now, every single one of you is aware Joaquin Acosta was murdered, and Lewis Liddell died from a massive seizure. I've appointed Lorina Pleasance as the new head of personnel." Annie motioned toward the mousy woman standing to her left. Lorina raised her hand in a meek wave. "From now on, you will check in and out with her."

Annie referred to the scrawled reminders on her clipboard before continuing. "On a happier note, we anticipate restoration of telecommunications tomorrow, which includes cell service. Should your cell phones happen to work when you awaken tonight, do not discuss the deceased with anyone from home. The next of kin have not yet been notified, and we have an active criminal investigation which must not be compromised. Please be discreet, for the sake of their families. Chief, do you have anything to add?"

"No, ma'am."

"Good. I'm not accepting questions tonight because I have no further details to offer. Rest assured, we're taking your safety seriously and are doing everything we can to keep this situation under control. I appreciate your ongoing cooperation. Stay calm, and perform your duties." Annie peered over the rim of her glasses at the crowd, drooping from physical and emotional fatigue. "Go get some rest."

Chapter Seven

The Fourth Night

Seph programmed the alarm on her phone for twenty minutes earlier than usual on the slight chance she would be able to call home and check on her mother. She shouldn't have bothered. *No service.* Seph stared at the words on the screen and gave her phone a brisk shake, as if it were a Magic 8-Ball capable of predicting her future. The words on the screen did not change.

Seph tossed the phone onto her cot and stalked away. After a few feet, she stopped to reconsider. She had a long shift ahead of her. Maybe things would change overnight. She returned to her cot, retrieved the phone, and crammed it into her back pocket.

Seph fumed as she waited in line to check in with a frantic-appearing Lorina, who Seph learned was a ward clerk in real life and ill-prepared to handle Lew's job. The delay evaporated Seph's early arrival, and she hustled to the dining area to join the other night shifters in their huddle. She found Chief Bishop sitting by himself, staring into the glass-enclosed telecom room where they'd first met Annie.

"Sorry I'm late. Lousy day so far, and it's only just begun. Can't wait for the rest." Seph followed his gaze to where Annie and Peter Dodgson, the team leader for day shift, were having what appeared to be a heated conversation. "What's going on?"

"See the guy sitting in the corner, trying to stay out of the line of fire?"

"Yeah. Who is he?" Seph grabbed an apple off the nearest table and took a bite.

"Henry. He's our one and only tech geek. He was assigned to day shift, but Annie declared Henry is now to remain in the telecom room 24/7. Even moved his cot in there. Dr. Dodgson appears to disagree."

"Why? And, so what?" Seph failed to see the significance despite the chief's obvious concern.

"Do you have cell service yet?"

"No, and thanks for reminding me. I got up early for nothing."

The chief ignored Seph's peevish reply. "No one has service. No one except Annie, that is."

Seph stopped mid-bite. "What are you saying?"

Chief Bishop did not respond.

Seph persisted. "Are you saying she's blocking our cell signal on purpose? Can she do that?"

"I think she can—with Henry's help, of course. And keep your voice down. This is between us, remember?"

"Why would she do such a thing?" Seph's mind caromed from theory to theory. The whole idea seemed preposterous.

"I'm assuming to give herself time to better cover up the murders."

"That makes no sense whatsoever. She can't hide them. Everyone here knows what happened."

"Okay—maybe 'cover up' wasn't the right phrase. 'Explain away,' 'deflect blame' . . .I'm grasping at straws here."

"Obviously, and you may be catching a case of the shelter paranoia, too. It's running rampant, as you may have noticed."

The chief nodded, still distracted by the conversation taking place behind the glass walls.

"Look, Chief, Annie wants to shut this place down and go home as much as any of us. We need phone service to arrange temporary housing and begin moving people out of the shelter. Without outside contact, we could be stuck here for weeks. Annie understands this better than anyone."

"Your point's valid, but can you come up with any other reason why Annie would want to keep us on radio silence?"

"No." Seph slowly chewed on what remained of her apple as she considered his question. "Although she did mention she didn't want the next of kin to find out second hand."

"Or the media, I'm sure. But neither of those is adequate justification. Not when you consider the major boost in morale the staff would get from being able to call home. There has to be something more, something big for Annie to crush the hopes she raised last night when she led everyone to believe we'd have cell service today. Something changed while we were sleeping, and only they know what it was. Whatever she's thinking, Dr. Dodgson is clearly not on board with her plan."

Seph flinched as Annie slammed her hand on the plastic table, sending a flurry of papers scattering to the floor.

The chief scowled. "I've been watching them argue for the better part of an hour. I got up early to investigate some of the daytime employees. Annie has a satellite phone hidden somewhere in the control room. I saw her talking on it a while ago, when she thought all of us night shifters were still asleep. I'm sure she and Dr. Dodgson think they have the only one."

"Don't they?"

The chief tapped his empty belt clip. "Nope. I've got one, too. I decided to put it away for safe keeping." He put a finger to his lips in a shushing motion.

The door to the telecommunications room opened, and the two team leaders stormed out. The chief lowered his voice even further.

"The phone has crappy reception inside the shelter, though. I suspect the metal walls and ceiling interfere with the signal, send it bouncing it around. I'll have to sneak outside to use it. If I can get through to my central command, I'm hoping they'll be able to clue me in as to what's going on with Annie. If not, I can at least inform them of recent events, so they can start an accurate paper trail and send reinforcements once the roads are clear. Can you distract Annie for me?"

"I'm sure I can think of something."

"Good. Not yet, though. Let's wait until the lights turn off at nine, okay?"

"Roger that." Seph snapped him a two-fingered salute. "Do you think it's safe going outside alone after dark?"

"Can't be any worse than it is in here."

A stone-faced Dr. Dodgson accompanied Annie to the center of the shelter before he split off to head to his cot. Annie presented her usual start-of-shift briefing to the crowd.

"The good news: Our pregnant evacuee delivered a healthy baby girl today. Both mother and child are doing fine. The bad news: I know you were looking forward to having phone and internet service tonight, but I'm sorry to say I've received word that the damage to the cell towers was more extensive than originally thought."

A collective groan echoed through the shelter.

"I know, I know. It's disappointing. The devastation to the infrastructure has been severe, with widespread power outages and roads blocked by debris. The road crews have to do their work before the telecom people can start theirs."

"Any idea when service will be restored?" Father Barney asked.

"I'm afraid not. I do have one satellite phone, which I use to stay in touch with central command at FEMA. I can allow personal use only in an emergency. I need to keep the line open in case any new, important information becomes available. If you must send an urgent message home, see me, and I'll try to work something out."

One of the maintenance workers raised his hand. "Does this mean we'll be here longer than usual?"

Annie frowned. "I don't think so. Dr. Dodgson and I were just debating how we could keep things moving forward. We decided to grant the social workers limited access to the satellite phone during normal business hours so they can begin to coordinate housing and transfer arrangements for the evacuees. That should help some, but I can't make any promises."

Once again, Annie cut things short. "I have sick patients to see." She spoke over her shoulder. "If anyone has further questions, come find me during rounds." She disappeared into the maze of cots beside the nurses' station.

"And that's the end of that." Seph said as she watched Annie hurry away. "The length of these huddles is inversely related to the level of insanity around here."

"Yep," the chief replied, eyeing the door to the shelter. "Remember—nine o'clock."

Seph drifted into her own rounds, chatting blithely with employees and evacuees alike and generally attempting to appear blasé. When the lights dimmed at eight, her brain kicked into high gear, creating and discarding an assortment of machinations with which to distract Annie during the chief's escape through the shelter's squeaky front door.

Angel twirled by, holding her boyfriend's hand. Her presence reminded Seph of the accordion player. His raucous music would make a perfect diversion if only it weren't so closely associated with the memory of Selma and her gurgling last breaths. No, she didn't want to get everyone in the shelter keyed up right before bed. She needed a subtler plan.

By a few minutes before nine, Alice and Annie had progressed to the last row of the medical beds, near the employee cots. They were as far from the front doors as one could go without entering the DMZ, and Seph was still sans plan. It was now or never. She'd have to improvise.

Seph sauntered up, the theme from *Mission: Impossible* running through her head. Alice and Annie were engrossed in a patient's chart, and, as Seph waited, her imagined music grew louder. *Da, da-dah . . . da, da-dah . . .* She put her hands in her pockets. She took them out and crossed her arms. She uncrossed her arms and clasped her hands behind her back. Lord almighty, she was worse than Carol. Was it possible to fidget casually? By the time Annie lowered the clipboard and glanced her way, Seph's palms were damp with sweat. She decided she'd make a lousy spy.

"Did you need something?" Annie hung the patient's chart on the end of his cot and turned Seph's way.

"Yes. If now's a good time, I'd like to discuss something with you." Seph sent Alice a pointed look, leaving no doubt the conversation was personal.

"All right. We're done here anyway." Annie nodded, and Alice glided out of earshot.

Seph took a deep breath and launched headfirst into her smokescreen, making it up as she went along.

"I wouldn't be doing my job as a psychologist if I didn't ask how you're holding up. I've noticed you've seemed tense the last day or so. Are you doing okay?"

The overhead lights clicked off, and Seph heard a faint, metallic screech emanating from the front of the shelter. The hangar door had opened. Luckily, Annie didn't seem to notice.

"I'm fine. Thank you for asking." Annie's voice was even—too even, for someone of her temperament.

Seph dragged the conversation onward, keeping one ear cocked as she waited to hear the door squeak shut again. "Are you sure? There's nothing wrong with asking for a little help. I know, as the team leader, you're expected to maintain a calm façade, but sometimes leaders need emotional support, too. God knows, with everything that's happened here lately . . ."

"I said I'm fine, Seph." Annie's curt response was accompanied by a dismissive wave of her hand and, more significantly, a move toward the main part of the shelter. Seph grabbed her by the elbow and resorted to provocation.

"What's happened since last night? What aren't you telling us? Either you're hiding something, or you're ready to crack—I don't know which—but your whole demeanor has changed. Don't think I haven't noticed."

"I am not cracking!" Annie yanked her elbow out of Seph's grasp.

"Then you're hiding something." Seph's placid expression met Annie's glower. The standoff dragged on while Annie struggled with how to best respond to, or at least deflect, Seph's accusation. While Annie hemmed and hawed, Seph heard the front door creak shut. *Finally.*

Annie employed her routine tactical maneuvers, crossing her arms and flattening her tone and expression. "Listen, Seph. There are some . . .unusual things happening outside this shelter. I'm not at liberty to discuss them further, but let's just say that right now, as hard as it is to believe, this shelter may be the safest place for us to be. I don't want widespread panic, so I'm keeping a lid on things until the situation is better delineated."

"I won't panic. Did the government drop a nuclear warhead or something?"

"I know you won't, and no, they didn't."

"The zombie apocalypse, then?"

"No, Seph! Stop." Annie raised a hand to her forehead and tried again. "I know you won't panic," she repeated, "but I can't take the chance you might tell others who would. Now more than ever, we need to trust each other. It's difficult, I know. Stay in your lane, and let me drive. Trust me when I say I have the best interest of every single person in this shelter at heart. I'll fill you in as the details unfold."

Seph nodded and lowered her eyes, awash with guilt over her deception. They walked together toward the middle of the shelter until Annie located Alice at the nurses' station and split off. Seph spied Chief Bishop leaning oh-so-casually against the door to the telecommunications room. She continued to the dining area and pretended to grab a snack. The chief moved to join her.

"Was the mission a success?" Seph opened a bottle of water and sat at the closest table.

"You might say that. Any problems with her?" He nodded toward Annie.

"No. She didn't suspect a thing. She hinted about strange events outside the shelter, but she wouldn't give details. She didn't come right out and say she was blocking cellular communications, but she implied it. Said if people knew what was happening, they'd panic."

"She's right." The chief's expression was grim. "Apparently, we're not the only ones having problems with acutely paranoid schizos running around murdering people. All along the east coast of Texas, any place that got hit with the brunt of the hurricane, rescue workers are reporting an abnormal number of violent individuals. Normal, average human beings with no prior history of mental illness are going totally nutso. The

CDC is scrambling to determine the cause. Right now, every possibility is on the table: toxic exposure, infectious disease, even terrorism." He paused. "Until they get a handle on it, they've quarantined eastern Texas."

Seph choked on her water, coughing and hacking until tears rolled down her cheeks. "As in?"

"As in, we're not going anywhere until the authorities are absolutely convinced we won't spread something lethal to the four corners of the United States."

They sat without speaking, absorbing the unnerving implications of this latest development. Seph sipped her water. Chief Bishop drummed his fingers on the plastic table. Seph offered the first round of observations.

"You won't be able to physically restrain people from leaving once they hear the news. You don't have enough officers to maintain that level of control. The parking lot is filled with a fleet of buses. People will find a way out. Hell, they'll walk if they think they have to. You'd have to shoot them."

The chief stopped drumming and curled his fingers into a fist. "I don't think I have to worry about it. Someone else has already been assigned that particular pleasure."

"I don't understand."

"While I was outside in the dark talking on my phone, I noticed what looked like headlights and smaller lanterns—flashlights, maybe—twinkling in the distance. There had to be at least a dozen, if not more. They were arranged in a ring formation, as if they were encircling the entire compound. My source back home told me the governor deployed the National Guard to enforce the quarantine, and the soldiers were given orders to shoot on sight. 'No runners,' he said. They're serious about this, Seph. No one leaves until they say so."

"Holy Mother of God!" Seph's voice began to rise. "We're talking about martial law here. You really think we're surrounded? No wonder Annie doesn't want anyone to know. What are they going to do—let us go crazy and kill each other? The last one standing gets to go home?"

"I don't think they know what they're doing yet. Knee-jerk reaction. You know how the government works. And keep your voice down." The chief's feeble attempt at reassurance failed miserably.

"We're like contestants on *Survivor*, or at least we will be once the food starts running out. We only have enough supplies for a few weeks."

I won't panic. Seph's earlier conversation with Annie returned to mock her. "I'm not panicking, by the way."

The chief examined her as if she'd lost her mind. "Um, I didn't say you were."

"I'm just making myself perfectly clear."

"Got it."

They lapsed into an uncomfortable silence.

"What do we do now?" Seph asked, when the quiet became unbearable.

Chief Bishop shrugged. "Not much we can do except watch it play out, like everyone else. We still have a murderer to catch, as well as our regular duties to perform. We'll protect each other. That's what we're here for."

"You make it sound so easy." Seph sighed. "Have you ever had to shoot someone?"

"Yes. I didn't always work at the VA. And I'm from the Bronx, remember?"

"But I read somewhere that most police officers retire without having had to pull their guns from their holsters."

"Yeah? In Boise, maybe. Not in Hunts Point, where I'm from."

"Did you always want to be a police officer?"

"No. I wanted to be a psychologist." He laughed at her startled expression. "Kidding. Jesus, you're gullible. Why the sudden inquisition? Have I joined the list of suspects?"

"No, of course not. Self-therapy, I guess. Performing habitual activities has the ability to calm agitated minds. My habit is to ask questions."

"And you do it very well. It's funny, you know? We go about our work in different ways, but you and I serve essentially the same function here—to keep the peace. And both our jobs are gonna get a lot harder over the new few weeks. Annie won't be able to stall the truth forever. Let's hope no one gets shot in the process."

As if on cue, a squabble erupted in the first row of cots. The chief jumped to his feet. "Go soothe some souls, okay?" He took a few steps, then turned around to add, "And whatever you do, for God's sake, don't panic!"

Seph hurled her empty water bottle at his head. He dodged it with athletic grace and an easy grin.

As the chief hustled away, Seph took a minute to gather her thoughts. *Go soothe some souls.* Easier said than done considering it was late, and most normal souls were settled into bed. The creatures of the night would be prowling, of course—Marlboro Man, Angel, Delmas, Carol, and maybe even Father Barnabas. Seph didn't want to talk to any of them. She retrieved her water bottle from the floor and pitched it in the garbage. She'd wander around and leave it to chance. The needy would find her.

To her surprise, Seph ran into Delmas, carrying Thad on his shoulders like a backpack, first. She'd only seen Thad out of bed at mealtime.

"Good evening, gentlemen. No cards tonight?" Seph plastered a smile on her face.

"You sound like a hooker at a truck stop casino." Delmas eyed her standard-issue polo shirt and scrub bottoms. "Shame you don't dress like one."

Seph's smile evaporated into a cloud of steam. "That wasn't very nice."

"No, but it was funny, wasn't it, Thad? Did I hurt your itty-bitty feelings?"

Thad peeped over Delmas's shoulder at Seph and giggled. Delmas grinned. "Thad's tired of sitting around. Doesn't help his ulcer, either. You found your murderer yet?"

"No."

"What about the ape-shit lady? You seen her recently?"

"The ape-shit lady? Do you think you could be more specific?"

"You know who I mean. The one with the pocket watch."

"Carol? No, as a matter of fact, I haven't. Not tonight, anyway. Not yet."

"You should. She looks nasty, worse than the night she popped her pills. Carried on like a crazy mofo all day today, from what I heard. Day shift stuffed her full of sedatives, enough dope to drop an elephant, but Thad and I just walked by the nurses' station, and she ain't anywhere near her cot."

Seph frowned. The image of Carol running amok was not a pretty picture. "I'm sure the nurses are already aware, but thanks for the info. I'll let Dr. Parrish know."

Delmas snorted. "You'd be better off telling your pig pal instead. At least he's got a gun. You two seem nice and simpatico lately. Something going down, or did you just find yourself a pretty boy to take home?"

He knows! Seph's brain screamed in a panic, but she managed a casual shrug. "We're hunting a murderer, remember? We spend a lot of time comparing notes. Besides, I already have a 'pretty boy' back home."

Seph mentally crossed her fingers. Delmas didn't need to know Steve was an ex-boyfriend. She put her hands on her hips. "Who do you think you are, anyway—my father?"

Delmas smiled, and her heart skipped a beat. Delmas, he of the shaved head and multiple tattoos, was quite attractive when he smiled—a genuine, unguarded smile as opposed to his usual smirk. It was the first one Seph had seen, and she marveled at how such a small thing could change his entire appearance.

"Definitely not." He grinned again, but this one was sly, winking. "But don't let me catch the two of you slipping outside after dark, young lady." Thad chortled in appreciation, and the two of them strutted away, leaving a stunned Seph behind.

Once she'd recovered her wits, Seph made a beeline for Carol's cot, only to find that both it and the nurse's station were abandoned. She spied the nurses across the room, gathered around an old man in respiratory distress. Several steps away, crumpled on the floor like a tattered rag, was Carol's plaid shirt, the one she'd worn on her first night in the shelter. Seph walked over, and as she bent to retrieve it, she noticed another piece of clothing thrown a few more feet in the distance—a lilac T-shirt, embellished with the faded decal of a wide-eyed cat and the words "I am purr-fectly calm." Seph recognized it as the one Carol had worn on the night of her overdose—a random, yet ironic choice of apparel.

A shoe here, a pair of shorts there . . . Carol's personal effects lay scattered like a trail of breadcrumbs leading into the depths of the DMZ. At the edge of the darkness, a faint glint of gold reflected off the most distant of the discarded articles. Carol's watch. It had to be. Yet Seph knew Carol would never, under normal circumstances, leave her most precious possession behind.

Seph ran along the trail, gathering the clothing as she went. She reached the final item, a pair of nondescript black leggings with matching holes in the knees. The gold pocket watch lay on the floor beside them, its crystal face shattered into sharp, angular pieces. Seph dropped the clothes into a heap. She picked up the watch with two fingers, and as she held it in her hand like a bird with a broken wing, a familiar, gruff voice beckoned from beyond. "You're late, Doctor Smith. It's past time."

✚

Seph stepped over the line and into the darkness to face Carol, stripped naked and grinning from ear-to-ear. She curtsied to a make-believe audience and performed an odd little jig, hopping back and forth with her left hand tucked behind her back and her right waving a butcher knife overhead. Right foot, left foot, slash, slash, slash. She danced to the rhythm of a tune only she could hear.

Seph struggled to stay calm despite the expression in Carol's eyes, the same psychotic stare Seph had seen on Lew's face less than twenty-four hours ago. In a sudden and horrific flash of insight, Seph realized the knife Carol clutched was likely the same one used to kill Selma and Joaquin. Poor Lew may have lost his mind, but he was no murderer. That role belonged to Carol.

Seph took a deep breath and adopted the same calm, soothing voice a kindergarten teacher would use to address a hyperactive toddler. "Carol, how about we put your clothes back on, and go see Dr. Parrish? I'm sure she'd love to see you. Put down the knife, and get dressed for me, okay?"

"Uh-uh. I don't wanna." Carol pouted like a crazed two-year old.

"Okay, Carol. What *do* you want to do?"

Carol slashed and jabbed the air with her knife.

"Carol, did you hurt Selma?"

Carol ignored the question. She thrust her left hand forward, opening her fist to dangle Seph's gold cross from her twiddling fingers.

"Where did you get that?" Seph resisted the urge to reach forward and snatch her necklace out of Carol's hand.

"Suddenly so serious, Per-seph-phone-ee." Carol mocked Seph with a sing-song incantation. She stopped hopping and crouched on her heels, with the knife clenched in her right fist. Every fiber in Seph's body twitched with anxiety, and she shuffled backwards.

A slow, wide smile spread across Carol's face, and she rocked forward, closing the gap Seph had tried to create. "I told you the first night. God doesn't bless people like me." She lowered her voice to a conspiratorial whisper. "Turns out, he doesn't like you much either."

The dim light behind her jumped and flickered like a candle sputtering in a cold breeze, casting shadows which danced across Carol's leathery face. Seph watched in horror as that face twisted and contorted, morphing into something, someone, altogether different.

Carol's next words were spoken in a voice which was not her own. "We're all mad here. I'm mad. You're mad. Carol is certainly mad. Isn't that right, Dr. Smith?"

"Luna?" The menacing hiss was unmistakable. Seph, shocked beyond reasonable thought, whispered her secretary's name.

"Tick!" Carol-Luna turned her face toward the ceiling and crowed with a triumphant grin, as if she'd just won a bet with the devil himself. She sprang off her heels and onto her haunches, bending forward like a football player ready to tackle.

Seph was in trouble, and she knew it. The knife-wielding creature in front of her could not be talked down from its psychotic state. The most she could hope for was to distract it long enough for her to make her escape.

"Luna!" Seph, in a last-ditch attempt to gain control of the situation, shouted her secretary's name like a reprimand.

But Carol-Luna was undeterred.

"Tick. Tock." She swayed back and forth, still dangling Seph's cross from one fist. "Luna ticks, tock. Luna ticks." She lunged forward and raised the knife overhead, ready to strike. "Lunatics!"

Seph's terrified screams echoed off the hangar's high metal ceiling. *Duck, cover, bob, weave!* She might have gotten away had she not tripped over the orange pylon behind her left leg. Instead, Seph went sprawling face-first onto the cement, arms and legs flailing as she rolled to avoid the knife plunging toward her back.

Bam! Something warm and sticky sprayed onto her neck, and she instinctively curled into a tight ball, eyes closed, hands over her ears to protect against the deafening reverberations of the gunshot.

Thud. Someone landed hard on the floor next to her. When Seph opened her eyes, she found herself staring into the face of Carol-Luna, still grinning despite the bullet hole in her forehead. Seph blinked, and the monstrous visage melted away. Carol became Carol again. The stillness of death erased any aberrancies.

Seph willed herself to roll onto her back. She was met by not one, but two sets of eyes. Delmas stood over her, gun in hand, with Thad clinging to his shoulders.

"Are you hurt?" Delmas asked.

"No," she whispered, gingerly touching her neck. Her stomach churned at the sight of her blood-smeared fingers. Seph swallowed and tried again with a little more force. "No, I'm not."

"Drop your weapon!" The chief's demand was accompanied by the thunderous sound of footsteps as the whole shelter, it seemed, descended upon their location.

In a split second, Seph imagined how the scene must look—her lying on the floor covered in bits of gore, Carol dead beside her, and Delmas towering menacingly overhead, gun raised and at the ready.

"Wait! Chief, wait!" Seph raised a bloody palm into the air and struggled to sit upright, slipping and sliding in the maroon puddles on the floor.

Thad, startled, chose that moment to lose his weak grip. He plummeted to the cement, his bones breaking with a sickening crack. The sudden shift in weight caused Delmas's torso to jerk forward. Seph closed her eyes as the shot rang out, unwilling to bear witness to a second death in the span of a minute's time. Another body hit the ground with a thud. Her horrorstricken brain revolted, and Seph's muscles went limp as she slipped into blackness.

Seph floated above the scene, a distant observer of both her own feelings and those of the concerned faces swarming around her. Chief Bishop crouched beside her unconscious form, which meant Delmas, and not the chief, had lost the gunfight. Her detached self was surprised to note she was unrelieved. A rough hand grabbed her chin and tugged her out of the clouds.

"Hey, Seph, wake up. Are you okay?" The chief's grip hurt, and Seph mumbled her displeasure as she yanked her head away. She squinted, and the world around her came into focus.

"Give me a minute." She turned at the touch of Annie's fingers on her neck, checking her pulse. Seph attempted a weak grin. "Isn't that Alice's job?"

Alice, her forehead creased with worry, stepped out of the background to assist. Seph raised one arm. "No, Alice. Go check on Thad." The nurse paused but didn't leave Seph's side. "Alice, please. I'm fine. I need you to check on Thad."

Annie gave a subtle nod, and Alice glided off to where Thad lay in a twisted heap on the concrete floor.

The chief pushed himself off his knees and addressed the crowd. "All right, everyone. Thank you for responding, but the situation is now under control. Return to the main part of the shelter. Keep your radios close. I'll call for assistance when we're ready to move the dead."

Annie helped Seph into a sitting position. A few feet away, Delmas's lifeless body lay draped atop of Carol's, with a bullet hole to match. Blood oozed from the exit wound at the back of his head, mixing with chunks of grey matter and bits of blasted bone. Seph blinked back tears and pointed an accusatory finger at Chief Bishop.

"He saved me, you know. From Carol. Carol was the murderer, not him. You didn't have to kill him. You could've shot him in the arm, or something. It would've been the, the . . ." Seph, still foggy from fainting, strained to find the right word. ". . . The *decent* thing to do." She hoisted herself off the floor as she spoke, refusing the hand he proffered.

The chief waited until they were eye to eye before responding. "He had a nine pointed right at us, Seph, and his intentions weren't clear. If I would've shot a *decent* man, I'd be worried about it. But I didn't, so I'm not. No one in the shelter's sorry Delmas is dead, except maybe him."

The chief nodded at Thad, who was sprawled on the floor with Alice at his side. "You'd better harden up, Doc, or you won't last long in this line of work. Nice people drop first."

"You know what's funny, Chief? Delmas told me the exact same thing. Then he went and proved it."

"Get over it, Doc."

"Jesus, Shane, that's enough. The woman was almost hacked to death, for Christ's sake." Annie jumped to Seph's defense, just as she'd done the night of Lew's murder.

"Dr. Parrish." Alice's voice broadcasted over their squabble, and the trio fell silent. Alice never interrupted, so whatever she had to say must be urgent.

"I think Thad has a broken hip." Alice tried to turn him onto his side, and he moaned in agony.

"Don't move him, Alice." Annie ran her hands over Thad's limbs in a quick, but expert examination. "I agree." She pointed at the chief. "Call for a stretcher."

The chief radioed for a gurney, and Seph took the opportunity to bolt.

"I'm gonna go get cleaned up," she said to Annie, who nodded without taking her eyes off Thad. "Tell the chief I'll give him a full report later."

Seph pushed her way through the crowd and ran toward the light.

Chapter Eight

Seph managed to hide while Annie and Alice were stabilizing Thad and the chief dealt with the dead. She wiped the blood from her neck and changed her clothes, trying to do so without awakening the day shifter asleep in their shared space. A neighboring cot sat empty, tempting her to lie down and pretend that she, too, was asleep. Seph resisted its siren song. Annie and the chief would probably come and drag out her out of bed by her hair. At this point, Seph couldn't decide who she disliked more.

She loitered for an hour or more before composing herself enough to exit the employee rest area. She shuffled toward the nurses' station, predicting Alice would be there monitoring Thad. She was correct. The team had moved him to the same prime piece of real estate once occupied by Carol, Joaquin, and Lew—the cot directly in front of the station. Thad lay moaning and cursing as two male nurses propped his broken left hip on a stack of pillows, twisting his already contorted torso into an abstract, geometric form no human should be able to attain.

Alice used a needle and syringe to suction a colorless liquid from a miniature, glass vial. Seph watched as Alice stuck the needle into Thad's IV port and depressed the plunger on the syringe, gradually pushing the liquid into his veins. Within seconds, Thad's moaning stopped, and his quivering muscles relaxed.

"Morphine," she said, before Seph could ask. "If you want to talk to him, you'd better do it now. You've got about fifteen minutes before this reaches full effect—give or take." She plucked his clipboard from the foot of the cot and headed to her makeshift desk to document the injection.

Seph touched Thad on the shoulder and waited for him to acknowledge her presence, but he did not. "May I sit down?" she said, gesturing to the stool Alice had situated next to his cot.

"Suit yourself." Thad's eyes were, for the moment, bright, and though his thin voice quavered, it sounded no different from any of their prior conversations. Seph searched his tone for any nuance of grief and his expression for any sign of mourning. She found none.

Seph perched on the edge of the backless stool and interlaced her fingers in her lap. "I'm sorry for your loss," she said. "Delmas didn't deserve what happened."

"Sure he did." Thad smiled at Seph's shocked expression. "Delmas was no saint. Never claimed to be. A sinner's debts gotta be paid someday, somehow."

So much for trite condolences. "Are you saying Delmas saved me to repay his debt to society? As some kind of bizarre penance? Ridiculous. Even if it were true, I don't understand why he would choose me."

"I don't know why he did either. Stupid-assed thing to do, if you ask me. I wouldn't of, I can tell you that, for sure."

Seph raised her eyebrows.

"Nothing personal, sweetheart. Think about it—would you risk your life for me? I don't think so."

"I don't have a debt to repay."

"Don't kid yourself. We all owe something to somebody. It's just a matter of to who and how much they're gonna make you bleed. Payback's a bitch, ain't that what they say? Or maybe you're the one who's the bitch?" Thad's words were beginning to slur.

Seph ignored his drunken ramblings. "What are you going to do without him? Who'll help you once you're discharged from the shelter?"

Delmas did everything for Thad. He functioned as his nurse, his personal assistant, and his Sherpa. Thad couldn't survive on his own—not with any modicum of independence.

"You my social worker now?" Thad's thin shoulders twitched with silent laughter. "I have others I can mobilize once I get outta here. No big deal."

Seph shook her head in disbelief. *No big deal. The man who's carried you around on his back and wiped your ass for God knows how long was shot dead today. No big deal.* Since she'd first seen Delmas carrying Thad into the shelter on his broad shoulders, Seph had harbored a preconceived notion of how they'd first met. Hers was a sweeping epic of brotherly devotion and true kinship, and Thad decimated it in three casual words. Now she wanted to know the truth. She decided to take advantage of his intoxication and put her curiosity to rest. "Tell me your story, Thad. I want to know everything."

As it turned out, their kinship was real. The gangbangers were half-brothers. Thad related his life story in a stream of boozy, tangential fragments which Seph stitched into a semi-straight line.

Thadeus James Becker was born first, to a crackhead prostitute whose greatest gift to Thad was her fatal overdose on his fourteenth birthday. Delmas Duchenne was born to a Louisiana oil worker as abusive as he was paranoid. David Duchenne worked twelve-hour days on the offshore oil refinery, and while he ranted to his coworkers about how the Mexicans were plotting to steal his job, his wife ran around with the owner of the local Latino market. David ran around with prostitutes.

After Thad's mother died, Children and Youth Services placed him in foster care while they searched for his father, hoping to find him a permanent home. When the agency came calling, David took one look at the picture of his illegitimate son, wheelchair-bound with limbs already beginning to atrophy and curl, and responded with a sullen "no." His wife intervened, realizing what Thad represented—access to a plethora of social and, more importantly, financial support programs from the state and federal governments. She accepted her handicapped stepson with open arms and dollar signs blinking in her eyes.

Delmas was twelve when Thad rolled into his life. Scrawny and neglected, he couldn't fathom how Thad meant anything other than him having to share what little food and attention he received from his absentee parents. He was wrong.

At age fourteen and despite his physical weakness, Thad was as savvy and manipulative as any con on the planet, with a well-honed set of survival skills forged from having to fend for himself. Thad could con the pants off a priest, and he refined his talent during his frequent hospitalizations, playing the nurses and social workers as if the facility were his own private theater. The entire medical staff, enthralled by his rare condition and duped by his piteous appearance, was at his beck and call.

After his discharge, home nursing and home health aides provided a constant stream of attention and hot meals; but the hospital represented a safe haven, a respite from David Duchenne's relentless abuse. Thad simply had to cough or act out of sorts, and he and Delmas were whisked away for a night or two of inpatient monitoring. Thad took Delmas under his fragile wing and insisted Delmas be allowed to stay by his side at all times, professing a brotherly bond which, if broken, would cause Thad to degenerate into hysterical fits.

In return, Delmas was Thad's legs, his man on the street. He spent his nights roaming their neighborhood, and, over the course of the next four years, he grew into an imposing figure, known for quick fists and the ability to take a punch without so much as a flicker of pain.

Delmas quickly learned the power players from the posers, and Thad used his intel to decide that the Aryan Brotherhood offered the best opportunities for advancement. When Delmas turned sixteen, he and Thad signed on the tattooed line and submitted themselves to the hazing ritual. To spare Thad a beating, Delmas took two.

At first, the other Aryans dismissed Thad as some kind of weird pet, but they soon realized that, although disabled, their devious new member was not to be crossed. Thad studied the other players as if they were pawns in a chess game, staying two moves ahead and outmaneuvering them at every turn. He and Delmas shot up the ranks together, cornering the prescription drug market thanks to their steady stream of willing suppliers—contacts Thad had made during his many hospital stays.

Delmas functioned as Thad's knight, following orders without question and eliminating anyone who stood in their way. Their symbiotic relationship even survived Delmas's incarceration, which conveniently allowed Thad to move into the prison drug trade. By the time of Delmas's release, little Thad was the second most powerful Aryan in Texas.

"Now you know. Ain't nobody gonna miss him, just like nobody's gonna cry on my coffin when I go. They'll throw a fucking party, so they will." Thad's words were almost unintelligible as the morphine fully kicked in. "You think you're any better than me? You think anybody cares whether you live or die? Here's a hint: They don't."

"You're wrong. *I* will miss Delmas. He saved my life. I owe him that much, as do you." She stood to leave. "Would you believe I felt sorry for you? Worried about your welfare? Trust me when I say I won't make that mistake again." Seph stalked away, but Thad's taunting voice followed her.

"Even your sissy don't care."

Seph spun on her heels. "How do you know about Grace?"

Thad giggled, releasing a stream of drool that dribbled down his chin. "Didn't you pay attention? The moral of the story is: I know everything. People talk; Delmas listened." He closed his drooping lids and, before Seph could question him further, succumbed to a morphine-induced slumber.

She yearned to grab him by his slender shoulders and shake him awake, or at least until his teeth rattled, but mindful of Alice's vigilance, Seph restrained herself. *Drunken ramblings. Nothing more.* She gritted her teeth and stomped away. Two hours until change of shift. Two hours to seethe.

She plunked herself into a chair in the farthest corner of the dining area, where she struggled to clear her mind. *Breathe in, breathe out.* Despite her best efforts, her mind continued to drift to the events of the last twenty-four hours, starting with their quarantine and ending with Delmas's murder. She remembered the chief's words about the CDC investigating the potential etiologies of the acute psychosis and forced herself to review the day she'd arrived scene by scene, seeking commonalities between those who had exhibited mental status changes as opposed to those like herself who, so far, had not.

Her mind kept returning to the concrete patio outside the shelter's front door, where a dozen federal employees had stood smoking in the rain. Selma was there. Carol was too. Seph tried to remember the other workers, to picture their faces, but they'd been mostly obscured by the hoods of their rain ponchos and the clouds of smoke rising from their mouths. Some of them were day shifters, and Seph never learned their names.

She pictured Lew unloading the employee buses, until finally, soaked through and through, he'd ushered the last stragglers in and shut the door behind him. The more she thought about it, the more convinced Seph became. Her old patient, Sergeant Bradley, was right. It was the storm. Whatever was triggering the insanity had been born in the waters off the coast of Africa, where most hurricanes form. Ignatius had gathered the malefactor in his windy arms and carried it across the Atlantic Ocean to the United States.

She'd shared the fledgling idea with Annie immediately after Lew's death, and her boss deemed her crazy. But this time, as the overhead lights began to shine, signaling the start of another day, Seph had a fully developed theory and a plan of action. Now all she had to do was sell it to Annie.

Seph cornered Annie and Alice at the nurses' station as they prepped their patient roster for the morning sign-out. They looked up when she approached, and Seph dove in before Annie could speak.

"Annie, Alice, I thought a lot about our recent events, and I'm convinced that people who had high levels of exposure to the early, heavy rains have been contaminated by either an infectious or toxic water-borne agent. I believe this agent affects the brains of those exposed, causing psychosis, then seizures and ultimately, death. It can't be contagious or else we'd be seeing a more rapid bloom of cases, but I do think we should attempt to identify those who were exposed and quarantine them for observation in a supervised area of the shelter in case they become acutely psychotic and dangerous. We should notify the CDC of our situation so they can transport the exposed for evaluation and treatment, assuming a treatment exists."

Seph paused. Annie and Alice sat expressionless and unblinking, so Seph went for broke, completing her recommendations in two, long-winded sentences.

"I also feel you should perform basic autopsies on Carol and Lew and, at the minimum, dissect their brains looking for areas of necrosis or other findings. I know certain infections can cause masses in the brain, large enough to be seen with the naked eye, so if we identify something like that on autopsy, we'll at least know we're dealing with an infectious etiology, right?"

Blink. Alice and Annie's eyelids moved in unison, their faces otherwise frozen into identical masks.

"Can you excuse us, Alice?" Annie asked.

"Of course, Doctor." Alice cast Seph a worried look before hurrying away in search of the day shift nursing supervisor. Seph claimed her seat.

"Seph, if you have something loony tunes to say, say it to me alone, or else you'll be the first person I decide to quarantine for unstable behavior. I won't allow you to freak out Alice and the rest of the staff."

"They have a right to know what's going on, Annie. They have to be able to protect themselves."

"From whom and from what? Do you know, exactly?"

"Not *exactly,* but I've given you a good place to start."

"Based on what evidence? Some vague causality you've established, or think you've established, in your mind?" Annie lowered her voice. "Have you talked to the chief about this?"

"Not yet."

"Good. Don't. Otherwise, before you know it, he'll be herding people into corners like we're in some kind of concentration camp."

"Annie, we have to do something. We can't just mope around and hope this is going to burn itself out. If we wait for the cavalry to arrive . . ."

"Who's moping? Not me. I'm too busy trying to save lives and dial down the drama. You can help by not creating any. Face it, Seph. We don't have a freakin' clue as to what's actually happening here. Until we have some definitive answers—scientific answers, not your voodoo magic—I'm not twisting everyone's panties into knots. Two people went a little nutso, that's all. End of story."

"A little nutso?" The image of Lew kneeling next to Joaquin's disemboweled body flashed through Seph's mind.

"We've had five people die, and you're saying they went 'a little nutso'? Is it really so hard for you to admit that something environmental or infectious could've triggered their acute psychoses? Mercury exposure can do it—it's what made the Mad Hatter mad. Syphilis does it by gnawing away at the nervous system. There are brain-eating amoebas living in swimming holes, for Christ's sake! Those are three examples out of dozens. You have to acknowledge it's a possibility." Seph defended her case as if she were pleading for her life before an unsympathetic judge.

"I do, Seph! I do acknowledge it's a possibility." Annie's voice rose with her frustration level. "But I also know it's way more likely these people simply cracked under the stress of being stuck in a sweltering shelter for a week. Carol was already teetering on the edge of sanity when she came in. I don't see the hidden crisis here."

"Lew wasn't crazy."

Seph spoke softly, attempting to de-escalate the rising tension. She adopted her best psychotherapy voice. "When people have stress-related breakdowns, they cry, they overeat, they binge drink, they become catatonic or depressed. They do not sit on the floor and play cat's cradle with another person's small intestine."

"Yeah, right, thanks for the psychology lesson, Dr. Smith. I studied mental illness in medical school, too, you know."

"If you would just perform an autopsy, you might find . . ."

"No!" Annie threw both hands into the air and jumped out of her seat to hover over Seph. "There is no way in *hell* . . ."

Annie stopped and sputtered, realizing she had inadvertently used Lew's pet name for the shelter. ". . . There is no way I'm performing an autopsy on their brains. I don't know how, I'm not qualified, and I don't have the proper equipment to analyze the tissue or blood samples. All I'd manage to do is thoroughly muck up the bodies. Then, when a credentialed pathologist attempts a real autopsy, any evidence which might have been present would be contaminated and useless."

Marlboro Man, attracted by the drama, strolled by, his boots click-clacking on the cement floor. A snarling Annie made no attempt to be nice.

"Shouldn't you be in bed?"

He raised his eyebrows in amusement at her snappish remark before tipping his oversized hat and sauntering away.

Annie waited until he was out of earshot and evened her voice. "Seriously, Seph, what do you expect me to find? Do you think I'm going to cut into Lew's chest and an alien's going to pop out, like in the movies or something? Well, you're no Ripley, and this is not the *Nostromo*."

The hangar disagreed with a loud bang of one of its industrial-sized ducts. Seph and Annie jumped and stared into the darkness above. The hulking structure's exposed metal beams shrieked at random intervals in response to Ignatius and his howling winds. It could easily pass for a ship, isolated and floating in the blackness of space.

Annie shrugged. "I guess it wouldn't be too much of a stretch. It doesn't matter. An autopsy is not going to happen. I know my place and my limitations. You need to learn yours."

And you're a two-faced liar. Seph bit her tongue to keep the caustic words from escaping her lips. She knew what was happening in the world outside the shelter, and she longed to expose Annie's game. The crisis was real. They were ensnared in a disaster within a disaster, and Ignatius held the key.

Still, Seph was savvy enough to realize Annie was not just her boss but the shelter commander. As such, Annie held the only means of communication with the outside world. Or at least, she thought she did. She didn't know about the chief's satellite phone.

Seph remained silent, knowing she could say nothing without exposing the chief and his phone. If Annie wanted to label her a fringe conspiracy theorist, a troublemonger of the kookiest kind, then Seph would need to suck it up, play along, and find her own solution to their crisis. But first, salvage mode. Remember Rule #4?

Seph relaxed her shoulders and forced a wan smile. "You know what, Annie? You're right. I guess the last few days have made me sort of crazy, too. I apologize. You would think my prior deployments would've better prepared me for this kind of thing, but then again, nobody was murdered during my prior deployments. Big difference, huh? I'm going to turn this whole mess over to you and Chief Bishop and get back to my patients. As you said, that's my place. It's where I belong."

Annie flashed the evil stink eye. "I know when I'm being played, Seph."

"The apology is genuine."

"Bullshit." Annie crossed her arms. "Fine. Whatever. Sounds like a plan. Get some rest first. That's an order." She abruptly turned and clomped away.

"Yes, ma'am," Seph whispered at Annie's departing back, knowing she would do no such thing. Seph had a phone call to make.

Seph lingered around the employee rest area and casually chatted up the other night shifters as they headed to their cots. She blended into the crowd, trying to be as inconspicuous as possible as she waited for Chief Bishop to appear. The police officers had claimed the front row of beds closest to the main part of the shelter, which made sense in the event of a hurry-up emergency. It also made the chief easy to spot when he finally called it a day after another long night.

Seph watched as he unbuckled his belt and removed the gun from its holster, tucking the weapon underneath his pillow. He shoved the belt under the cot for safe keeping. The satellite phone was hidden in a multipurpose pouch on his belt, one which could've just as easily held pepper spray or handcuffs. She would have to pray the chief was a sound sleeper.

Seph went through the motions of going to bed, curling into the fetal position with her face toward the concrete wall on her right. The guy in the cot next to hers was snoring a discordant symphony, enough justification for her to have whipped out her trusty earplugs and eye mask. (Disaster

Rule #6: Never travel without high-quality earplugs and an eye mask.)

Instead, Seph set her cell phone alarm for nine a.m. in case she did, by some miracle, manage to doze off. She had three hours to listen to her neighbor snore and fart. By that time, the East Coast would be hopping, the chief should be asleep, and Seph could make her call.

Maybe I should just ask to borrow the phone? Seph stood at the foot of the chief's bed, doubting not so much the wisdom of her plan, but her ability to pull it off. Stealth was not one of her shining attributes.

If Seph knew for certain the chief would agree to her request, she'd lean right down and shake him awake, but they hadn't separated on good terms. Something to do with him fatally shooting Delmas for questionable reasons . . .

The image of Delmas, minus half his skull, lying on the blood-spattered floor set Seph's teeth on edge and stiffened her resolve. She crouched to grope under the chief's cot. She worked her way around the location where he'd placed his belt until her fingers touched leather. His belt held several pieces of gear with the potential to wake the dead should they hit any part of the cot's metal frame, so Seph attempted to open the accessory pouch while leaving the belt safely in place.

She cringed and held her breath when the snap released with a loud, well, snap. Like a kid caught with her hand in the cookie jar, she froze, waiting for the chief to leap out of bed with his gun in hand, ready to shoot first and ask questions later. He didn't. Seph allowed herself to exhale. She extracted the phone from its case and slid it into her pocket before slithering across the floor to return to her own bed.

Seph sat on her cot and faced the cement wall, using her back to shield the phone from view. She only lingered a few minutes, long enough to examine the satellite phone's functionality. No sense sneaking outside if she couldn't figure out how to use the damn thing. A cursory inspection reassured her she'd be okay—it appeared to operate like any other phone—so she hid it in her backpack along with her orange armband and slipped into the main part of the shelter.

Blending into the crowd of staff and evacuees was much easier during the day. Everyone was up and about, and the staff scurried to occupy the evacuees with silly games for the kids and exercise for the adults.

Seph stealthily merged into a confederation of power walkers doing laps around the shelter's perimeter, detaching herself when she reached the front door area. To her surprise, the heavy, metal door was propped wide open, allowing the cool morning air and a hint of sunshine into the shelter. A large woman in too-tight yellow leggings waddled by, carrying a pack of cigarettes in one hand and a lighter in the other.

Seph caught up and tapped her on the shoulder. "They letting people outside?" she asked.

"Honey, didn't you hear the announcement?" Annie had given her briefest speech to date during the seven a.m. change of shift, but Seph, intent on tracking Chief Bishop's movements, hadn't bothered to pay attention.

Seph shook her head and pointed toward a rambunctious group of children playing nearby. "My boy was screamin'. You know how it is."

"I heard that. Thank God mine are all growed up." The woman tapped a cigarette out of the pack and offered it to Seph. "You want one? We allowed outside as long as we stay in the parking lot. No more than ten at a time, and no more than fifteen minutes at a time. They got a policeman out there making sure. Don't know what they think we gonna do. Walk to Houston, maybe?"

Seph accepted the cigarette with a smile and followed the woman outside. After a long week of night shifts, the sunshine was a shock to her system. She shielded her eyes from the glare and watched as three lanky teens expended their pent-up energy by booting a soccer ball around the stadium-sized parking lot, while their parents lounged on the cement patio, smoking. Seph squinted into the distance, searching for evidence of the Guard unit the chief believed to be present. She saw nothing.

"You wanna sit by me?" The lady handed Seph her lighter and patted the folding chair next to hers.

"Thanks, but I think I'm gonna go for a stroll." Seph took a drag on the cigarette and released a puff of smoke. Perfect. A literal smoke screen.

She walked to the farthest edge of the parking lot, which gave her a good view of both the soggy field ahead and the shelter behind. The hurricane winds had shredded whole sections of the hangar's roof and damaged several vehicles, and chunks of spouting, glass, and the occasional tuft of upholstery lay scattered about. Lew's "Welcome to Hell" sign, which had been hanging by a rusty thread from the get-go, now pierced the windshield of a yellow school bus. The steering wheel held it upright like a billboard.

Seph made a big show of turning her face toward the horizon, puffing on her cigarette as if she were contemplating the fate of the universe itself. Every few minutes, a bright light flashed in the distance, glinting like sunshine reflecting off the metallic shards. Maybe the chief was right, and they were surrounded by soldiers after all. Or maybe it was just debris. She was about to find out.

Seph dragged the backpack off her shoulders and removed the pilfered phone, dropping the bag at her feet. She powered on the handset, setting it to speaker so she wouldn't have to hold it to her ear, and continued to puff away, engulfing herself in a protective haze. She glanced over her shoulder at the police sergeant, who tapped his watch, reminding her she was on a schedule. She waved her cigarette and nodded. Time to call in the cavalry.

Seph would never have predicted that her first phone call after days in a disaster shelter would not be to her mother or sister, but to Luna. Luna. Just saying the name conjured up images of Carol's distorted face, and Seph shuddered.

The phone rang six times before Luna deigned to answer. Seph didn't wait for her to speak. "Luna, I need to be transferred directly to the chief of staff. Tell him it's a true emergency."

"An emergency? At a disaster shelter? Go figure." Seph pictured Luna's smarmy smirk and responded with a snarl.

"*Now,* Luna." Her stern attitude made not one iota of difference.

"Hold, please." Click. Cue the elevator music. Luna disappeared from the line.

When she returned home from San Antonio, Seph vowed her first priority, her all-consuming mission, would be to have that woman fired. She took a long, jittery drag on the cigarette and peeped over her shoulder again at the police officer, who was busy rounding up the power walkers at the opposite end of the lot. By the time Uncle Chick accepted the call, Seph was ready to melt into a toxic puddle of stress hormones.

Thanks to the byzantine layers of middle management between the behavioral health department and the highest echelon of Chick's office, Seph had been able to keep her application to the Philadelphia VA a secret. She'd never forget the proud look on his face when, on her first day at work, she'd walked through his office door wearing her shiny new federal ID badge. He, more than anyone, had faith in her abilities. He would believe her; of that she had no doubt. The question was whether he had the power to help her.

Seph almost sobbed with relief when she heard Chick's warm, familiar voice on the other end.

"*Fiorellina,* I've been so worried. I've been praying every day for God to protect you. Are you safe?"

"So you know what's been happening?"

"I know there's been some sort of an outbreak in the hurricane-affected areas, as if the three inches of rain and one-hundred-fifty mile per hour winds weren't bad enough. Ignatius hit the coast as a category four. Galveston Island didn't weaken it a bit, and the damage was extensive. The CDC isn't allowing our deployed staff to return home until the situation's clear. The VA has the greatest number of employees of any of the federal agencies manning the shelter, so we chiefs have been meeting regularly with Washington on this."

"Well, let me tell ya, while Washington's having their pow-wows, we've had two people go postal and five violent deaths. The team leader's cut us off from outside communications, and the National Guard has us under quarantine. I think I know what's happening, Uncle Chick. Based on the profiles of those affected, I believe a biologic agent has contaminated the storm water, and it's infected certain people. Maybe they had a cut or open sore. Maybe they had the longest exposure, like the smokers, who were out in the rain until the very last. Either way, things are ugly, and I doubt they'll improve any time soon. Tell me the CDC's all over it, and, better yet, tell me they have a plan to get the rest of us out of here alive."

"The CDC's thinking the same way you are. They've done some autopsies, I'm told, and they've found huge brain cysts and other physical evidence pointing to a parasitic infection with *toxoplasma gondii.*"

"The parasite you catch from cat litter?" Seph had heard of it. Recent articles in the psychology literature suggested chronic infection with toxoplasma may be the hidden trigger for the development of schizophrenia and some neurodegenerative disorders.

"From the cat feces, not the litter, but, yes—same concept. The parasite burrows into the brain, eye, and muscle tissues, but the infection is usually a slow, chronic process with no symptoms whatsoever—after all, parasites have nothing to gain by killing their hosts. Typically, only those people with poor immune systems develop fulminant disease."

"This is not slow, and as far as I know, the victims were not immunocompromised in any way. When I say 'slow,' we're talking about only a few days between exposure and the onset of psychosis."

"Assuming the CDC is right, this would have to be a mutated form of toxoplasma—one not known to the States. Atlantic hurricanes form off the coast of Africa. God only knows what kind of weird variety might've developed in the jungles and been carried here by the wind and rain. Do you have running water in the shelter?"

"No. We've been drinking bottled water."

"Good. You don't think you've been exposed, do you?"

"No. But there were at least ten people standing outside in the rain before the shelter closed its doors. If every one of them goes berserk . . ."

Seph re-envisioned day one and the bevy of federal workers crammed shoulder to shoulder on the concrete patio.

Carol and Selma were there, standing next to a police officer or two. The rest of the faces remained a blur.

From the corner of her eye, Seph saw the sergeant trying to catch her attention. She ignored him, and he marched her way. "Look, I gotta go. If what you say is true, the disease is not spreadable from person-to-person, so there's no reason to keep us interred in a concentration camp. Promise me you'll get me out of here ASAP."

"I didn't realize things were so bad. Washington made it sound like you were well-stocked and comfy-cozy, as if the shelter were the safest place you could be right now, given the circumstances. Is it really that bad, Seph?" He sounded troubled.

Normally, Seph wouldn't have wanted to worry him, but she was way beyond spouting false reassurances. "Yes, it's that bad, and it's only going to get worse the longer we're trapped inside together. Paranoia is running rampant. You have my word; we are not comfy-cozy. If we were, I wouldn't have stolen a satellite phone and snuck outside to send you an SOS. I'm not counting on God to protect me anymore—I'm counting on *you*, Uncle Chick.

"Call our shelter commander, Dr. Anne Parrish. She knows some of what's going on, but not the details. Tell her everything you told me about the infection. Maybe she'll agree to separate the personnel who were exposed and contain them in their own part of the shelter until we're permitted to leave. It's the only way to keep everyone safe. I suggested this before when I told her my theory, but she didn't believe me. Maybe she'll believe you."

"Okay, I'll work on it." He paused. "You stole a phone?"

"Yes, and I'm about to get my ass kicked if I don't get inside and return it."

Chick chuckled. "You'd better go, then. I'll tell your mother you called—give her an update."

"Leave out the infected, crazed lunatic parts, okay? Oh, hey—did Grace make it home?"

"Yes." Chick's tone changed ever-so-subtly, but it was enough to activate Seph's internal radar. She hesitated, desperate to continue the conversation, but also acutely aware of the officer's proximity. Out of time, she cursed under her breath and disconnected the call.

She dropped her cigarette and ground it underfoot, leaning forward to give the sergeant a sublime view of her rear end. Her tush was nothing special, but hopefully it served as an adequate distraction. His footsteps faltered. She wiggled once or twice more for good measure and hurried to stuff the chief's phone inside her bag. Seph yanked the stubborn zipper shut and returned upright, throwing the backpack over her shoulder. With one hand on her hip and a seductive smile curving her lips, she slowly turned around.

"Sorry to hold you up, officer. Gorgeous out, isn't it? We deserve such a beautiful day, after everything we've been through." The shifting wind blew the cloud of cigarette smoke into her face, and her words degenerated into a hacking cough, totally ruining the *femme fatale* effect. Mata Hari she was not.

"Time to give someone else the chance to enjoy it." He raised his eyebrows as her wheezing continued. "Are you okay? Should I call a doctor?"

"Fine. No. I mean, yes, I'm fine. I don't usually sm . . ." Seph caught herself and cleared her throat to cover her incriminating faux pas. She smiled again in what she hoped was a beguiling fashion. "Kennel cough." She nodded toward the shelter. "You know how it is."

"If you say so." The young sergeant touched her upper

arm and guided her toward the entrance. "I haven't seen you before. Are you a night shifter?"

"Yeah. Usually. Couldn't sleep. My circadian rhythm's screwed up. Thought maybe some fresh air and sunshine would help."

"You're going to have a helluva night, then, after being up all day."

"Let's hope not." Seph tossed her hair. "I don't intend to stay up the entire day. Just this little bit. Gives me the chance to chat with nice people like yourself. You see, that's the problem with night shift. Most of the handsome guys work during the day."

He chuckled. "I'll be sure to tell the chief you said that."

"Don't you dare!"

Horrified, Seph groped for an appropriate way to dissuade him from following through with his innocent threat. She settled for something inappropriate.

"He might spank me."

The officer blushed and stuttered. They stepped inside and were instantly assimilated into a horde of people swarming around the doorway, anxious for their time in the sun. Seph took advantage of the chaos and bolted.

"G'night." She raised her hand and vanished into the crowd, weaving her way to the back of the shelter.

Seph paused to catch her breath when she reached the relative safety of the employee rest area, where she slipped into stealth mode and returned the satellite phone to the chief's belt without incident. Exhausted, she crumpled into bed, sagging into the flimsy fabric as she willed her tense muscles to relax. As nerve-racking as her subterfuge had been, she vowed to repeat the maneuver tomorrow night. Next time, she was calling Grace.

✚

Seph's daytime shenanigans had left her physically spent but emotionally too tightly wound to sleep. She groaned when the alarm sounded at seven p.m. and reluctantly rolled from her cot to join the others at dinner. Bleary-eyed from lack of sleep, she imagined her guilt was written on her face—along with the dark circles—for all to see. She grabbed a dinner tray from the cafeteria line and plopped at the nearest table, keeping her head low as she ate.

Her eyes darted around the room, searching for any aberrant behavior. They widened when she spotted Annie, along with Dr. Dodgson, the day shift supervisor, chatting up the young officer who'd been monitoring the courtyard during her morning escapades.

"Hey, Doc. You got a headache, or something?"

Chief Bishop buzzed up from behind and dropped his food tray next to hers with a clang.

Seph choked on her dinner roll, coughing and gagging until her cheeks burned.

"Sorry about that. Didn't mean to scare ya." The chief patted Seph on the back with questionable benefit. "Don't die on me, okay? You all right?"

"I'm fine." Her hacking ceased, and she dabbed at her wet face. "I was distracted, that's all. Didn't see you coming."

The chief followed Seph's line of vision across the room. "Two of those three people should be in bed."

"My thoughts exactly."

They watched until the conversation came to an end. The two men headed toward their cots. Annie moved to the center of the dining area and launched into her customary start of shift announcements.

"The roads have been cleared, and tomorrow the Army National Guard and DMAT—the Disaster Medical Assistance Team—will be stopping by the shelter to conduct some testing. It seems the storm carried with it an infection out of Africa, one we're not used to seeing here in the States. Some of you may have been exposed via the rain water." A nervous twitter ran through the crowd.

"The DMAT physicians will take a history and draw some blood from each of you. We might be forced to separate those with probable exposure until the results are back. The good news: The infection doesn't appear to be contagious. They've seen no person-to-person spread, so you don't need to wear masks or any other personal protective equipment. Please remain on duty for as long as it takes for you to have the mandatory testing. DMAT has agreed to evaluate night shifters first."

Annie's expression remained impassive, but her eyes shifted to Seph's face. "They will also be removing the dead for processing. Any questions?"

Father Barney raised his hand. "What happens if we test positive? Is a treatment available?"

"Yes, but I was told the medication is in short supply because the disease is so rare. The Feds are working on procuring enough for everybody. Anything else?"

Lois, the kitchen worker who'd discovered Selma, raised her hand. Her voice trembled as she asked, "Does this infection have anything to do with what happened to Selma?"

Annie paused before answering. "It might."

She examined the faces standing before her, some set in grim determination and others twitching with anxiety. "If you notice any atypical behaviors tonight, report them to myself or to the police. Otherwise, it's business as usual. Outbreaks are not rare at shelters. We work around them, because we still have a job to do. Dismissed."

Annie pointed to Chief Bishop. "Chief, a word, please. You too, Dr. Smith."

Seph and the chief exchanged expectant glances as they elbowed their way through the crowd toward Annie. Once they were within earshot, Annie wasted no time.

"Until today, I only knew that, throughout eastern Texas, people were exhibiting strange and violent behavior. The etiology was under investigation. This morning, Dr. Dodgson and I received an update." Annie put her hands on her hips. "Looks like you were right all along, Seph, about an infectious outbreak. Except this is no Montezuma's revenge. It's more like *Invasion of the Body Snatchers*."

That must've hurt. Seph arched her eyebrows but kept her mouth shut.

"What else were you told?" The chief's bald question caught Annie off guard, and she fumbled for an answer. "Annie, I need to brief my officers on what to expect. Let's cut to the chase, shall we? Are we in a 'shoot first, ask questions later' scenario or not?"

"No." Annie frowned. "This is a medical shelter, not a war zone. We will never be in a shoot first scenario."

Chief Bishop snorted. "Not true. Not by a long shot, if you'll pardon the bad pun. From where I'm standing, it depends on the math. If we end up with dozens of people foaming at the mouth at once, deadly force will be necessary. Double that if any of them turn out to be armed, like we experienced with our gangbanger."

"Delmas." Seph spoke through clenched teeth. "His name was 'Delmas.' In case you forgot."

Annie's frown became a scowl. "Maybe if you and your fellow officers had done their jobs and conducted a more thorough weapons search on day one, we wouldn't have to worry about such eventualities."

Chief Bishop's voice shook with controlled fury. "Maybe you can stick . . ."

Annie jabbed him in the chest with her finger. "You asked what else I was told. Well, here ya go: This thing is huge. Hundreds, if not thousands, of rabid people roaming the streets, committing atrocities. The military is stretched thin, sweeping town by town, trying to test and contain those who've been infected. None of the local hospitals have lockdown units capable of holding that many people, not to mention the staff to run them. They all evacuated. The Feds plan to deploy the USS Mercy and put the infected in the cargo bay, for Christ's sake! No treatment. There isn't enough, and it'll take weeks to make more. They plan to let them die, like dogs fighting in a cage."

Annie removed her finger from the chief's chest and paused to regain her composure. "Their only goals are to keep the non-infected safe and to limit the flow of information outside of Texas so the whole country doesn't panic. The rains carried onward through the Midwest, you know. But so far, Texas appears to be the only state affected. Or *in*fected, depending on how you look at it."

Seph shuddered. Uncle Chick had glossed over some heavy, sordid details. No wonder he thought the shelter was the safest place for her to be.

"So is the Guard here to keep us in or the crazies out?" Chief Bishop crossed his arms.

Annie ran a shaking hand through her short hair. "Both. I told you the Guard is here to test us for infection. Personally, I find their presence reassuring. It's nice to know someone's protecting our perimeter. Trust me—now that our bosses know the disease isn't contagious, they want us cleared and shipped out ASAP. They'll need our warm bodies if this develops into more than just a regional event. Unfortunately, the blood test takes seven to ten days to come back. We're stuck here until then."

"And the cell phones?" The chief refused to let Annie wriggle off the hook.

Annie fiddled with her clipboard. "Blocked, of course. I did what I had to do to maintain control of the situation."

"Yes, we know. You're a saint."

Annie's scowl returned. "Even with my *saintly* efforts, someone from inside this shelter managed to make at least one call." Annie surveyed the chief's utility belt with its array of clips and pouches. "Tell me, Shane, since we appear to be doing the full disclosure thing, what's in the pouches? You wouldn't happen to have a satellite phone, would you?"

"I do."

"And how do you know Chief of Staff Rizzo?"

The chief frowned. "I don't. From which VA?"

Annie shifted her gaze to Seph. "Philadelphia."

The chief's face hardened as he reached for his phone. "The only person I know from the city of Philadelphia is standing by my side."

"That's what I thought." Annie smirked. "Seph? Any comments?"

Seph had failed to develop a contingency plan for being busted. She averted her eyes as her brain floundered through a tangled mass of potential explanations. Meanwhile, the chief booted up his phone and accessed the call log.

"Someone placed a call which lasted just under ten minutes to a Philadelphia area code at nine this morning. The only problem is that I was sound asleep at nine a.m." The chief slammed his phone into its pouch and glared at Seph. "I guess we can add 'petty thievery' to your list of accomplishments, Doc."

"I didn't steal it. I borrowed it. You weren't taking me seriously. Neither of you were. And, as Father Barney would say, 'God helps those who help themselves.'"

"Save it for confession."

"I'll see you there. How many calls did *you* make, Chief?"

Annie's eyebrows shot skyward at Seph's accusation. "Do tell, Shane."

If looks could kill . . .Seph coolly withstood the chief's ferocious glare. He opened his mouth; she braced for a verbal lashing. But before he could utter a word, the shelter exploded in gunfire.

Chapter Nine

The Fifth Night

Seph lost count after the third gunshot. They burst forth in quick succession, and as their echoes faded into the rafters, they were replaced by the sound of a baby wailing.

She and Annie dropped to the ground with the first shot. When they dared to rise, the chief was already gone. They followed the first responders and raced across the dining area to the non-medical part of the shelter.

Chief Bishop and three of his officers formed a protective perimeter around a stunned woman clutching her crying newborn. Marlboro Man, riddled with bullets, lay face down in an expanding pool of his own blood, an unlit cigarette still dangling from his flaccid fingers. Inches away, a young sergeant held his gun, aimed at the dead man's back.

Seph gasped as she recognized his face. He was the same officer she'd flirted with outside the shelter earlier today. Only now, his bright eyes were dull and glassy, and his cheeks glowed pink with fever.

"He was staring at the baby. I had to save the baby." The sergeant's flat voice lacked emotion.

The chief shot the infant's mother a questioning look. She shook her head "no."

A man stepped out of the crowd. "I seen the whole thing." He scuffed his grungy sneaker on the concrete in the corpse's direction. "All that poor guy did was walk by. Nothin' more."

He spat at the sergeant's boots. "Pig was just lookin' for an excuse."

The chief signaled one of his officers, who grabbed the man by the elbow. As he was escorted from the scene, the witness swept Marlboro Man's fallen cowboy hat off the floor and placed it on his own head.

"Mighty fine hat. No sense lettin' it go to waste. Not a spot on it." He shrugged the officer's hand off his elbow and strutted away with a grin.

The sergeant's gaze never wavered from the bullet-riddled body on the floor. "I had to save the baby. I heard what the devil was thinking, what he wanted to do."

Chief Bishop took a step forward. "I know, Sergeant. You needed to save the baby. But she's fine now, so why don't you give me your gun while we sort this thing out?"

The sergeant tore his gaze away from the corpse. "You want me to hand over my weapon?" His shoulders sagged.

"You know how the protocol works, Sergeant. Any death warrants an investigation. It's standard operating procedure. Routine stuff."

The sergeant bobbed his head in erratic circles. "No. I will not surrender my weapon. Not here. You see all these crazy people?" He waved his gun wildly in the air, and the crowd gasped and shrank back in fear. "They're out to get me, and you, too, Chief. No way am I turning over my gun."

The sergeant gripped his pistol with both hands, squeezing until his knuckles turned white. Arms forward, elbows locked, he shuffled his feet like a boxer in a ring and aimed the barrel at random people in the crowd.

Chief Bishop's fellow officers whipped their weapons out of their holsters and readied them by their sides. The chief raised a hand. "Steady, boys. Sergeant, let's keep the crowd out of this, okay? Look at me. Only at me."

The sergeant's eyes glazed over, and his voice trembled. "Oh, my God. You're with them! What is this—some kind of conspiracy? A deal with the devil? Maybe *you're* the devil I heard talking, not him."

He viciously kicked the body at his feet. The cigarette dropped from Marlboro Man's limp fingers and landed in the pool of blood. Mesmerized, the sergeant watched as the white wrapper hungrily absorbed the crimson liquid, growing fat and red.

The sergeant stomped on the engorged cigarette and ground it beneath the heel of his boot. Blood, tobacco, and gunpowder—Seph gagged and raised her fist to her nose. Afraid to watch, she held her breath and tried to pray. But the words would not come.

The chief, holding both hands high in the air, inched closer. "Son, there are events at play here you don't understand, things that are messing with your mind. How about you and I head outside where it's quiet, and we'll talk about it man-to-man. We'll get through this together, I promise."

The sergeant stepped backward, leaving a bloody boot print in his wake. "No. I get it. I understand." He lifted the gun to his temple. "You can all burn in hell."

"No!" The chief lunged forward, arms outstretched.

Seph ducked and covered her ears as, for the second time in less than an hour, a gunshot reverberated off the metal roof and walls of the shelter.

She stayed down for a long time, expecting to hear the chief shout an all-clear. Instead, the ringing in her ears persisted, drowning out everything except the frantic beating of her heart. Confused, Seph stumbled to her feet. Engulfed by a wave of vertigo, she swayed as her surroundings spun in dizzying circles. She closed her eyes and waited for the nausea to pass. When her eyes reopened, Annie was in her face.

"We've got a dozen traumatized people who just witnessed a suicide, Counselor. Pull yourself together, and get to work. You should be used to this by now. Alice!" Annie bellowed her nurse's name even though Alice rarely drifted more than ten feet from her side.

"Here." Alice moved closer.

"First things first: You and I need to examine the baby—confirm the sergeant was indeed out of his mind and that nothing actually happened to her." Annie cursed under her breath. "Hopefully the kid won't grow up deaf from the noise exposure."

"Of course, Dr. Parrish." Alice moved to the bedside to exchange a few quiet words with the mother, who wept while her newborn screamed.

Father Barney touched Seph's elbow, jerking her into motion. "Same routine as before, my dear? Like after Selma?"

Seph, still disoriented, nodded.

"A shame, isn't it? That we've done this enough times to have developed a system, I mean." He shook his head and crossed himself. "May God bless us all."

Seph made her rounds on autopilot, ending up back where she'd started and in record time. The acrid smell of bleach assaulted her senses and triggered another bout of vertigo. Housekeeping had finished cleaning up the mess. Two men wrapped in makeshift hazmat suits—garbage bags and duct tape—waddled by, each carrying a bucket of gore. They'd made record time, too.

"Numbers six and seven," one said to the other, his voice muffled by his plastic shield. "Lucky number seven."

His companion snorted. "Yeah, lucky number seven. But who's counting, right?"

"Right."

Seph watched them slosh their way toward the temporary morgue, where Annie had dictated they were to stash the potentially infectious waste. *Seven*. Her knees threatened to buckle. Who *was* counting? Annie? The chief? God himself?

Seph raised a trembling hand and fumbled for her missing gold cross. Old habits died hard. Carol leered at her from within, and Seph flinched, dropping her hand to smack the plastic tabletop. The table teetered from the force of the blow, and she massaged her stinging palm. The pain made Carol disappear, and that was good enough. Her necklace was probably lying in the morgue with the rest of the dead and discarded.

"Are you okay, Dr. Smith? Another distressing night, I know." Father Barney had finished his own rounds and settled next to Seph, touching her hand as he spoke. She jerked it away as if she'd been burnt.

"God is not here, Father. He's not keeping count."

"Of course he is, child. God is everywhere."

"Was he here for Selma? Or Joaquin? Where was he just now, when the sergeant blew his brains out? I sure as hell didn't see him."

"God works in mysterious ways."

"Don't feed me that line of crap! How can you spout such garbage when the truth is obvious?" Seph jumped from her chair, toppling it on its back. "If there is a God, he's abandoned us, left us to the mercy of the storm and what came with it. What kind of god ignores his children is their darkest hours of need? Wouldn't it be better to believe there is no God than to believe in such a cruel and indifferent one?"

"You're being tested, Dr. Smith. It's normal to question your faith in moments of weakness."

"Weakness?" Seph jeered the chaplain's sanctimonious remarks. "Save it, Father. Save your prayers for someone who believes. Someone *stronger*." Seph turned to stumble across the shelter, running as far as the building would allow, horrified by what she'd said and done. But beneath the horror ran an undercurrent of relief, the same bizarre sensation she'd felt after Selma's murder. Another door had slammed shut, and this time, there was no going back. God would not save her now. She'd have to escape Hell on her own.

Chapter Ten

Wrapped in a thin blanket, Seph sat cross-legged on her cot until her feet tingled in protest. Head down, hunched forward, she kept her hands clamped over her mouth, as if to stave off any further damning outbursts. *See no evil, speak no evil.* The lights shut off at nine, and the darkness whispered in her ear, informing her she'd been rocking in place for at least an hour. But Seph didn't care. Her soul was as numb as her toes.

She heard him approach. The brisk cadence of his gait had become so familiar. He stopped a foot or two from the bottom of her cot. She forced herself to speak first.

"Chief."

"Seph."

"You talked to Father Barney?"

"Yes."

"What do you think?"

"About what?"

"Do you think I'm infected? Am I going crazy?"

"Why do you say that?"

"I renounced my religion."

"You might change your mind once you get back home."

"I doubt it." A solitary tear ran down her cheek and slipped between her cupped hands. She tasted the salt on her lips and compelled her stiff neck to straighten so she could meet the chief's unwavering gaze. "Promise me, if the time comes, you'll kill me rather than let me hurt someone else."

"Seph, seriously, that's *not* . . ."

"*Promise* me!" The snoozing day shifter in the bed next door grunted his displeasure at her outburst.

"You know I would."

Seph sniffled. A steadier stream of tears dripped onto the cot. "I thought I knew, but since I stole your phone . . ."

The chief sighed and crouched to address her at eye level. "Forget it. We're all going a little loco given the circumstances. It's hard to know who to trust. At least now everyone has the same information. We're on the same page, we know what to expect, and we know what to watch for."

"Yes, but what are we going to *do*?"

"We wait for the DMAT folks to run their tests. Then we wait for orders to demobilize, and we all go home. What else can we do?" He stood and swiped a weary hand over his face. "In a way, our mission hasn't changed. Provide medical care and protection to the evacuees. Watch out for the bad guys and the loons. There's just more of them this time, that's all."

"And some of them could be us."

"Possibly. Which means some of us won't be going home for a long time."

"If ever." Seph scrambled out of her cot and tripped in her haste, pitching forward. The chief caught her by the shoulders, and she used his proximity to whisper in his ear. "I might have another option. A way to speed things along."

He pushed her upright and frowned. "What do you mean?"

"I have to make another phone call first to determine if my plan is even feasible."

"I'm gonna need more than that."

"I don't believe the military plans to remove and quarantine the infected, Chief. You heard what Annie said—they don't have anywhere large enough to contain them. The part about using the USS Mercy was total bullshit. They fed her a story she wanted to hear, including the reassurance that our bosses want us mobilized ASAP."

"Why wouldn't they want us home? They're short-staffed, and we're valuable."

"Keep telling yourself that, Chief. You sound like Annie. Think about it. Let's say the military does magically produce a facility vast enough to detain thousands of sick, crazed individuals. The treatment, if one really exists, is in short supply. Who gets to live, and who dies? More significantly, who's got enough balls to make that decision? Not any bureaucrat I know. It's political suicide."

Seph glanced over her shoulder before continuing. "I think the plan is the exact opposite: Let us die in place. Contain us until the infected are dead and any threat of new cases developing has passed. Then, and only then, will they permit the survivors to go home. And that could take weeks."

"And you're basing this theory on what?"

"Because of something Uncle Chick said."

"Uncle Chick?"

"Sorry—Chief of Staff Rizzo from Philadelphia VA. He's a friend of the family."

"Let me get this straight: You didn't believe my report from when I called home, so you phoned 'Uncle Chick' to find out the honest-to-God truth. Because police chiefs are lying SOBs, but hospital administrators are paragons of virtue."

Seph had the decency to blush. "I called to beg for help, actually. Instead of offering assistance, though, he told me I was in the 'safest place I could be.' Annie was fed the same line by her superiors. I didn't think much about it at the time, but now it makes sense. Uncle Chick figured I was safe because I was in a place with police protection and medical care, as opposed to the general populace trying to survive on their own in zombie land. He knew I was stuck in Texas for the long haul."

"Nice. Some relative you've got there."

The chief scratched his stubbly chin. "Still doesn't make sense, though. Once the lab work is back, the military could ship the healthy out and leave the infected here to rot. Why bother testing if they don't plan to act on the results?"

"Research, public relations—any number of reasons. You're assuming the test is a hundred percent accurate. Think of the PR nightmare, not to mention mass panic, if they allow us to go home, only to have someone come down with the illness afterwards. Easier to leave us here, stall by pretending they're awaiting lab results, and, in the meantime, learn a thing or two in case of future outbreaks. Do you honestly think in this day and age an emergency blood test takes more than a week to come back? Quarantine, and let time figure it out. I'd bet my license it's their strategy for the entire Texas seaboard."

"I think you're being paranoid." The chief's words lacked conviction. Seph sensed his uncertainty and remained silent, allowing him to think the scenario through on his own.

"Who is it you need to call?"

"My sister. Grace is an officer in the Navy, and her job involves mobilizing staff for drill and disaster scenarios. If the Feds *were* considering using the USS Mercy as a floating morgue—which I sincerely doubt—Grace would've been briefed. Either way, she'll know what's going on, for sure. And she might be able to help us figure a way out."

"Seph, we can't let anyone leave, ourselves included, until we know who's infected."

"I know. We'll jump that hurdle if and when we get to it. But it can't hurt to explore our options."

The chief snorted. "Forgive my lack of optimism. This deployment has been a cluster since day one. If we're gonna do this, I suggest we leave Annie out. I know I said it's nice having everyone on the same page, but undermining her authority with a second outside phone call might be the final straw."

"Agreed. What's the plan?"

"You tell me. You're the pro at this."

"Right." Seph opted to ignore his sarcasm. "It'll be easier this time since I won't have to, uh, *borrow* your phone. That was the hardest part."

"I'll take your word for it. I'm assuming you went outside with the smokers?"

"Yes. If you walk out with me, you can chat up the guard while I make my call. Distracting him was the second hardest part."

Seph pictured herself flirting with the smiling young sergeant. The pleasant scene dissolved into an image of his trembling finger on the trigger. The resurgent smell of gunpowder and blood swamped her senses, and she shuddered.

The chief noticed her distress and misinterpreted its source. "Since you obviously didn't sleep much today, we'll go bright and early in the morning so you can hit the hay. We have ten full hours to kill first, though. Think you can hang in there?"

Seph nodded. "Of course. What makes you think otherwise?" She dabbed her nose with the back of her sleeve.

Chief Bishop raised his eyebrows. "Have you looked in a mirror lately?"

"I'm trying not to."

"Good idea. You're starting to resemble Carol. Some friendly advice: Straighten up, or DMAT's likely to lock you up with the crazies."

"That's not funny."

"It wasn't meant to be." He strode away.

Seph groped underneath her cot until she found her backpack. Her wallet held a sliver of a mirror, and she contorted the leather flap until she garnered enough light with which to see her reflection. *Ugh.* She snapped the wallet shut. The chief was right. With her swollen, bloodshot eyes, dark circles, and disheveled hair, she looked more like an escapee from the Arkham Asylum for the Criminally Insane than a psychologist.

She smoothed her long hair into a low ponytail and blotted her nose and eyes. Despite her outward appearance, Seph felt strangely calm, as if the drama had damaged, or at least deadened, her fragile nerves. The crying jag helped, as did having a plan. Whether or not Grace could pull strings was beside the point. Things weren't right at home. Seph sensed it the minute Uncle Chick dropped his subtle hint. She wanted—needed—to speak to Grace. Tomorrow, she hoped to gain some clarity. For tonight, hope was enough.

Somewhere between five and seven a.m. Seph realized their plan had a fatal flaw. DMAT was coming, accompanied by the National Guard. Soon, the shelter would be crawling with uniformed men and women carrying large weapons. No way would she and Chief Bishop be able to slip out of the shelter unnoticed.

She caught the chief's eye moments before the morning huddle. He sauntered over and pushed a Styrofoam cup of steaming black coffee into her shaking hands.

"Here. You look like you need this."

"Yeah. About the plan . . ."

"I know. I was thinking about it, too. Forgot about DMAT, didn't we? Your call will have to wait another day."

"Maybe we could get up an hour early and do it then." Seph sipped the turbid liquid and gagged. She handed the cup back to him. "I don't need the caffeine that badly, thank you very much. I'd have to be desperate. As in, marooned-on-a-desert-island desperate."

"What were you expecting? Starbucks?"

"No, but I was hoping for more than melted crayons. Something with a salty rim and a twist of lime would be especially nice." Seph missed Sammy, her favorite bartender, far more than was healthy. Her pounding head and clammy skin told her so.

The chief chuckled. "Embrace the suck, Doc. In my world, there's no such thing as bad caffeine. You'll learn." The chief tipped the cup and chugged its contents in one large gulp. "But to answer your question: No, we cannot get up an hour early and do it then. The sun starts to set by six, and my guys don't allow anybody out after dark."

"You make the orders. Can't you change them?" A jolt of anxiety surged through her, or maybe it was the caffeine. Either way, Seph had no intention of postponing her call to Grace.

"I would—if it wouldn't appear so flamingly suspicious. My guys aren't stupid, you know."

"Just give me the damned phone." Seph thrust out her hand. "I'll figure something out."

"Later." Chief Bishop nodded toward the shelter's main entrance, where Annie, day shift leader Dr. Dodgson, and Henry, the computer geek, were gathered. Annie had her hand on the door. "Looks like DMAT's early."

The chief and Seph watched as Annie opened the door and admitted two soldiers dressed in fatigues. After a short conversation, Annie handed them a fistful of papers from her clipboard. They studied the sheets intently, requesting clarification when necessary. The gesticulations and head nodding continued until the men appeared satisfied with Annie's explanations.

"What do you think's going on?" Seph asked.

"Annie was uncharacteristically quiet last night. If you hadn't been so preoccupied with your crisis of faith and petty thievery, you would've noticed. Instead of doing rounds with Alice, Annie spent most of the shift hunched over her clipboard. I suspect she was instructed to provide the commanding officers with a detailed list of anyone with possible exposure to, or exhibiting symptoms of, the disease. Knowing Annie, those notes contain the names of everyone in the shelter—color coded, cross-referenced, and ranked by the potential to commit homicide."

The chief's mouth twisted into a wry grin. "Wouldn't you love to know where we fall on the list?"

"Not really."

"Liar."

Seph conceded with a shrug. "Okay, maybe. I'm fairly sure I'm in the top ten."

Their conversation complete, the commanding officers propped the shelter's doors open, allowing a unit of armed soldiers and DMAT personnel, some pushing crates of medical supplies, to file in. Annie waved them through to the central dining area. All but two followed. They stood guard at the doors.

While the team unpacked and assembled their equipment, Annie addressed the night shifters.

"The testing procedure involves drawing a small blood sample. Please stay in this area until your name is called as the testing will not be done alphabetically. Afterwards, you'll be given a plastic wrist band to wear, signifying you've been tested. Do not remove it under any circumstances. Doing so will result in a formal reprimand, a second blood draw, and possible quarantine pending the results. After you get your wrist band, clear the area. No milling about. Go to your cots, and get some rest. Day shift will be tested next, followed by the evacuees. Questions?"

One of the pharmacy technicians, a tiny woman with long, blonde hair, raised her hand. "What if you, um, tend to faint with blood work?"

"We'll draw you lying down."

"I really don't like needles." The tech's voice quavered.

"Refusal is not an option." A deeper voice boomed from behind Annie's left shoulder.

Annie shifted out of the way. "Commander Pierce."

The commander stepped forward. A foot taller and twice as forbidding, he loomed large over Annie and the crowd.

"Don't make this more difficult than it already is. No one goes home without being tested. Period." He let the heaviness of his words sink in the dank air before pulling a list from his front pocket. "When I call your name, line up."

Seph closed her eyes while the commander rattled off the first five names. Neither she nor the chief was among them. She opened her eyes to see the chief, his face grim, surveying the frightened, silent crowd. He pushed his way to the front and grabbed Annie by the elbow, pulling her aside. "Was that really necessary?"

Annie shrugged and fluttered her clipboard. "He thought so. I don't like it either, but both commanders made it abundantly clear: I am no longer the highest authority here."

Annie, Seph, and the chief watched as the first of the five employees was led to a chair to have her blood drawn. A uniformed health tech wearing not only the usual gloves, but also a full face shield, strapped the woman's arm to the chair's metal frame and applied a tourniquet. A nearby printer surged to life, spewing out three labels—one for each tube of blood and one for the wrist band which the tech secured around the employee's wrist. One expert needle stick later, and she was done.

The pharmacy tech, her face green with fear, paced in line. A soldier motioned for her to move into place. Wild-eyed, she hesitated and turned toward Annie, desperately seeking a reprieve. Another soldier bumped her in the low back with his weapon, and she pitched forward, landing on all fours on the concrete floor. Together, the two soldiers dragged the crying woman to her feet and into the chair, holding her down as the tech strapped her arm into position.

"This is insane." Annie, outraged, crammed her clipboard into Alice's hands for safekeeping and charged toward the front. The chief intervened.

"Is something wrong, Dr. Parrish?" Commander Pierce dared her to challenge his authority.

Chief Bishop squeezed Annie's arm.

She spat her response through gritted teeth. "No." She winced at the chief's firm grip on her forearm, and her eyes narrowed into angry slits. "No," she repeated, in a more temperate tone.

"Good. Next."

The chief guided Annie and Seph to the far fringes of the crowd. "I know how you're feeling, Annie, but let's think about this for a minute. The Guard has to believe they have our complete cooperation; otherwise, we may be out of options."

"Options? Who's got options?" Annie's bitter tone implied she, at least, believed they had none.

"We might. Seph and I volleyed around some ideas. But we need you to be totally honest with us about what you know. Seph believes the Feds have no intention of letting any of us leave until the disease has run its course. In other words, this is all a sham, and the Guard is gathering blood for research purposes only. Is that true?"

Seph opened her mouth to protest and was rewarded with a glare. Ten hours ago, he'd wanted Annie excluded from their plan. Now he was recruiting her. Maybe. Unsure of his intent, Seph did the sensible thing and clamped her mouth back shut. Safest to let the chief do the talking.

In the front of the room, a centrifuge loaded with tubes of blood began to spin, its high-pitched whine drowning out further conversation. The commander shouted five more names. Seph was again spared. Annie was not. Her shocked expression suggested the commander had varied the order of her detailed list.

"I, uh, we'll finish this conversation in a few, okay? I need to get this over with." Annie set her mouth in a thin line and stalked across the room to stand inches from Commander Pierce. They exchanged a few heated words before she was lead to the chair.

Seph and the chief dropped even further toward the rear where the decibel level wasn't so high.

"What are you doing?" Seph hissed, as though Annie could somehow still hear her. "I thought we were keeping her out of this."

"That was before Commander Pierce pissed her off. Annie may be a by-the-book, chain-of-command type leader, but she's also shrewd. These guys have alienated her enough already to plant a seed of doubt in her mind, which in turn might make her open to your phone call with Grace. She'll be searching for options now, too. Whatever plan we devise, it'll be stronger with her in it. It's always better to have the team leader on your side."

"Rule number four," Seph muttered.

"What?"

"Never mind. Speaking of Grace, any ideas on how we can make that phone call actually happen? Today, I mean."

"One. It depends on when we get picked for our blood draws. But if we succeed in recruiting Annie, we won't need to sneak outside to use my satellite phone. We can use her cell and call from the telecom room. Easy peasy."

Seph's disposition brightened. "Excellent point. I didn't think about that."

Chief Bishop tapped the side of his head with one stubby finger. "Nothing escapes me. Like a steel trap." He laughed at her expression. "Don't ever play poker, Doc. You'll get fleeced. Anyway, if we get separated, we'll rendezvous at your cot. Got it?"

"Got it."

"Good."

Commander Pierce readied his list. The blood draws were getting quicker as the process gained efficiency. This time, instead of five names, the commander rattled off ten. Dr. Persephone Smith and Father Barnabas were numbers one and two.

"And you're off." The chief patted Seph on the shoulder. "Run along now, like a good little counselor. Time to talk to the vampires. Try not to faint."

"I'm not above knocking out a few of your perfect teeth. Make a note of it." Seph waved her hands in the air, and the commander checked her off his list. "And as for talking to the vampires, the chaplain and I are no longer on speaking terms, remember?"

"I doubt it'll last. After all, he is a priest. I'm sure he's already forgiven you a dozen times over. Probably spent the past ten hours praying for your tortured soul."

Seph rolled her eyes and trudged her way through the crowd. The commander herded her to the front of the line, and she fixed her eyes on the med tech ahead. Behind her, the other nine shuffled into place. As Chief Bishop predicted, Father Barney was inclined to talk.

Seph ignored his subtle cough and timid "ahem." He resorted to tapping her on the shoulder, and she had no choice but to turn around.

"Are you feeling any better now, Dr. Smith?"

"I'm fine, thank you." She expertly deflected his attention. "Just trying to help the others stay calm. I'm surprised at how many of them are afraid of having blood drawn. Are you afraid of needles?"

"Oh, heavens no!" The priest chuckled. "Once upon a time, I was an addict."

Seph's eyes widened.

"Surprising, isn't it? Seems like a million years ago now. A whole other life. Mine was the prototypical story. Rough childhood. Ran away more times than anyone cared to count. Joined the army fresh out of high school. Infantry, if you can imagine that. I was a hundred pounds lighter and hungry as hell. Picked up a heroin habit in Southeast Asia. Between the Viet Cong and the drugs, I was on the brink over a dozen times. The last overdose was my turning point. A miracle from God saved my life and my soul. I've trusted myself to Him ever since. Now I feed off the energy of my parishioners, not heroin."

"Sounds like a memoir in the making."

Despite their prior spat, the chaplain had piqued Seph's interest. She never could resist a good story. The med tech snapped a fresh pair of gloves into place, and the metal chair creaked as it was vacated.

"I'd be happy to share the details with you, if you'd like."

A soldier motioned for Seph to move forward.

"Some other time, maybe." She shuffled into place.

"I'll look forward to it." Father Barney beamed as if her soul was, in his mind, already saved.

Seph settled into the seat and offered her left arm.

"Name and social security number, please." The med tech hunched over her equipment, assiduously avoiding any eye contact.

Seph recited her information, and the printer sprang to life. She studied the tech, observing her appearance and body language before releasing the probes. "This must be pretty boring for you, huh?"

No response. The needle jabbed Seph's arm, and she flinched. Blood spurted into the tube. "Any idea when the results will be back?"

"No."

"Someone else told me a week."

"You'd have to ask Commander Pierce."

"Sure. He seems prone toward conversation. Definitely the chatty type."

The med tech finally made eye contact. "I'm sorry. I can't tell you anything."

Seph detected a hint of a smile. "I know. Didn't hurt to try, though."

The tech removed the tourniquet and slapped a Band-Aid on Seph's arm. "You're done."

"Let's hope not." Seph pointed toward Father Barney and winked. "Watch out for that one. He's a real badass." She strode away, leaving a puzzled Father Barney in her wake.

As per prior instructions, Seph made a beeline for her cot. Her trot slowed to a crawl when she caught sight of Annie and Chief Bishop huddled near the telecom room, their faces solemn. They were so engrossed in their conversation, the chief failed to hear his name called for the next round of blood testing. Two soldiers appeared to escort him to the front of the line. Along the way, the chief glanced back at Annie, and she nodded.

It was a subtle motion, but their silent interchange was so grave, so conspiratorial, it sent a chill racing down Seph's spine. *It's hard to know who to trust.* She heard the chief's prescient words again. Yesterday, he'd called her paranoid. Today, she almost believed him. *You're only paranoid if it's not true,* an inner voice whispered. Seph pressed her palms over both ears to drown out her thoughts. She had no choice; she had to trust the chief. She needed his phone. Plus, he had a gun. Annie did not.

Seph craned her neck but lost sight of him until she saw his broad shoulders weaving through the crowd on his way to her cot. His face relaxed when he found Seph waiting for him as advised.

"I didn't hear you scream," Seph said, as he rolled his sleeve down, buttoning it at the wrist.

He arched his eyebrows. "Takes more than that."

"I saw you talking to Annie."

"She's on board. And unlike my satellite phone, her phone works from inside the control room. Henry's able to ramp up the signal. You might have to sit on the floor because of the glass walls, but with her and me providing a screen, you should be able to make your phone call without being seen. We won't even have to wait until later. Now is a perfect time given the number of people standing around waiting to have their blood drawn. You ready?"

"Beyond ready."

"Then today's your lucky day."

Annie and Henry waited in the command center until precisely seven forty-five a.m.; then the show began. She flipped papers back and forth on her clipboard; Henry pointed at the laptop sitting before them. Annie removed her phone from her belt and handed it to Henry, pretending to compare its screen with the images on the laptop. When Henry shrugged, Annie tossed the phone in disgust. It skipped lightly across the table and slid out of sight onto the floor below. She pantomimed a heavy sigh, caught sight of Seph and the chief as they strolled by, and waved them in. The chief closed the door behind them.

"Henry will take it from here." Annie continued her dramatic performance by poking the chief in the chest with her pen and gesturing him out of the room. "I need to talk to you." They stepped outside the door and positioned themselves in front of the glass where they engaged in loud conversation.

Seph stood frozen next to Henry. He shuffled his feet, shrugged again, and mumbled, "Um, I think she meant for you to pick up the phone. Maybe pretend to be helpful, or something."

"Oh, right. Good idea." Seph forced a smile and pointed across the room. "Let me get that for you." She rounded the corner of the table and squatted below the edge of the glass to retrieve the phone. Luckily, it was intact. She cursed as her trembling fingers misdialed not once, but twice.

The call went to Grace's voice mail.

"Dammit!" Seph smacked her palm on the concrete floor. Of all times for Grace not to answer her phone. She always answered her phone.

Henry's voice floated over the table. "If the call dropped, I can boost the signal." He moved toward an array of monitors on the back wall.

"The signal was fine. I need to try someone else." Seph punched in her mother's number. Grace answered the phone.

"Grace—thank God! Listen up. I've only got a few minutes. I need your help getting me—us—out of here. And while you're at it, can you tell me what the hell is really going on?"

"What do you mean?" Grace's voice was cautious, flat.

"We're quarantined, Grace. Left here to die. First it was the storm. Now the Guard has us hemmed in. They've cut off communications. Don't you know? You always know. You have your finger on the pulse of the entire eastern half of the United States, for Christ's sake!"

The silence on the other end was chilling.

Seph's babble tapered to a whisper. "Why . . . Why don't you know, Grace?" Tears stung the corners of her eyes. "What's happening?"

"My commanding officer raped me. I've been on administrative leave of duty, pending the investigation."

"Wha . . ." Seph's lungs refused to allow her to finish. She rocked forward, gasping for breath. When Grace was a child, every negative event turned into a major drama, accompanied by tears followed by a prolonged period of withdrawal. Their mother blamed it on their father and his abandonment. Seph blamed it on attention-getting. She changed her tune when her enhanced empathy blossomed, and she herself entered counseling.

During her own treatment, Seph realized Grace was sensitive, too, but in a different way. Joining the military was Grace's atonement for her childhood behavior, her way of toughening up. For this to happen . . .

Grace continued to speak in the same flat voice with which she'd answered the phone. ". . . When I went to ask him for emergency leave to take care of Mom. 'Tit for tat,' he said. Clever, right? When I refused, he raped me. He thought I'd stay quiet—I got the feeling he's done this before—but when it was over, I left the base and drove straight to the nearest civilian ER. They took samples and . . ." Grace's voice broke, but she rallied quickly. ". . . And everything. Then I came home to Mom. I haven't been back to work since."

And everything. As if those two words could begin to summarize what her sister had gone through. "Grace, I'm . . ."

"So sorry, I know. That's why I turned my phone off. Word spreads fast, even with a military hush up. Everyone's so sorry."

"And Mom?"

"Taking it hard. I thought about trying to hide it, but she's like you. She always knows."

That's it, then. Game over. Grace was her last hope. Seph's mind swirled with a toxic mix of despair, fury, and guilt. "It's my fault. I asked you to sit with Mom."

"Don't start that. This was his fault. Not yours. Not mine. His." For the first time, Grace's voice held a spark of emotion.

Henry cleared his throat. "Dr. Smith, we're running out of time. Commander Pierce just announced the last round of names for blood testing. Night shift will be ordered to bed soon."

"I've got to go, Grace." Seph's throat tightened as she realized, depending on the results of her own test, she might never speak to her sister again. "I love you both, okay? You'll get through this."

"Seph, wait. You said you needed help. Uncle Chick told me a little bit, but not much. Trying to protect me, I suppose. What can I do?"

"I was hoping you could use your contacts to get us home. We're trapped with violently insane, sick people, and I believe the government has decided to cut their losses. If we survive, great. If not, oh well. But it would take someone pretty high up in the ranks to make it happen, so considering what occurred between you and your boss . . ."

"I still have friends, Seph. Lots of them and at all levels. I'll make some phone calls and find out what's happening. I can get you home."

"How?" Seph was surprised at her sister's conviction.

"Worst case scenario, I cut a deal."

"I'm not following you."

"I told you before. My commanding officer is the son of a Texas senator."

"No, you told me he was senator's son, but you didn't say from where."

"Well, he is. Big oil. Old money. Protective of the family name. If I agreed to drop the charges . . ."

"Grace, no. Don't you dare. I'd rather take my chances here than have you let that son of a bitch off the hook."

"He'll fly free anyway, Seph. You and I both know that. You have to come home." Grace's voice was calm, unwavering. "Mom needs you. I need you."

"You don't need me. Mom will help you like she always has. You two will take care of each other. And Mom—she's got enough strength for the three of us. She'd have to—she raised *us*, didn't she?"

"No mother is strong enough to outlive her daughter. Not and remain mentally intact, anyway. You're her baby girl. Sephie, I can do this. It's a small price to pay. Sit tight. You'll know what to do when the time comes."

"Grace? *Grace*?" The line was dead. Seph jumped to her feet and waved the phone in Henry's face. "You cut us off!"

"I didn't! She hung up. And play it cool, will you? We've got company." Henry snatched the phone out of Seph's hand and turned his back to the door as it swung open. Annie stuck her head through the doorway.

"Time's up. We need to haul our asses to bed with the rest of the night shifters before we attract any more attention."

Over Annie's shoulder, Seph spied Dr. Dodgson and Commander Pierce conversing. Dr. Dodgson motioned their way.

Seph brushed past Annie and rushed toward the employee rest area. Chief Bishop followed closely behind. Once they'd ducked behind the rolling dividers, they paused to wait for Annie.

"I'm guessing from your frenzied expression your sister can't help." The chief stepped aside as Annie rounded the barrier to join them.

"Wrong." Seph closed her eyes and fought to collect her thoughts. "She's helping us. I just don't know how."

"Explain." Annie punctuated her terse remark by whipping off her glasses and cramming them into the pocket of her scrubs. She rubbed her forehead with both hands. "And make it quick. I'm getting a migraine."

"Grace's commanding officer is the son of one of the Texas senators. She's going to cash in a favor, and they're going to figure us a way out of here. Call in the Rangers, or something. She said I'd know it when it happened."

"That's it?"

"We didn't exactly have enough time to hash out the details. My sister's word is good. If she says she'll get us out, she will. At least now we have some hope."

"Fuck hope—I want a *plan*, Seph!" Annie's voice echoed in the quiet rest area.

"Hey." The chief put a hand on Annie's shoulder. "Quiet down. You'll wake the neighbors."

Despite the attempted levity, his forehead wrinkled with concern. His eye darted to Seph's. "Seph is right. It's something to work with, but not anymore tonight. We've had an exceptionally long shift, and you have a headache, so let's get some rest. Okay?"

"Pfft." Annie waved one hand in the air. "What a waste." She stalked off in the direction of her cot.

Seph and Chief Bishop watched as Annie flopped on her bed, curled into the fetal position, and yanked the thin blanket over her chin.

"You think she's infected?" Seph whispered.

Chief Bishop grimaced. "Funny—she asked me the same thing about you earlier."

"I'm not surprised." They stood in silence for a few minutes, watching Annie as she tossed and turned, trying to get comfortable. "I know she does have migraines. She mentioned it a few days ago. Grace gets them, too. Says they're brutal."

"You gonna tell me what else Grace had to say? I told you once already—don't play poker if you can't hide your cards." He watched the emotions flit across her face. "I thought we weren't going to do that anymore."

"Yeah, well, old habits die hard."

The chief crossed his arms.

"Kidding," Seph muttered. "It's personal—a family issue. Has nothing to do with our current situation. Our mother is sick with cancer. They need me at home, which is why I have no doubt Grace will keep her word." *Was she still lying if what she said was true, but not the truth he was seeking?*

"I'm sorry to hear that. As if you need something more to worry about."

"Exactly. So if you don't mind, I'm going to take your advice and go get some rest. Hopefully, things will seem clearer in the morning."

"You mean in the evening. It's morning now." The chief grinned.

"Whatever. Damned night shift, anyhow. Good night."

Seph stumbled her way through the maze of cots until she reached her own. Emotionally spent and physically exhausted, she closed her eyes and prayed to no one in particular for the simple gift of a dreamless sleep.

Chapter Eleven

The Sixth Night

No nightmares. Bonus. Seph stretched, willing her cramped muscles to comply. She must've slept in the same position all night. After Grace's revelation, Seph expected her nocturnal demons to come a-calling, but instead they remained at bay. This deployment had turned everything on its head, including her nightmares. Normalcy was a faded dream.

The sleep had done her good. She felt alert and ready to face the music—whatever song Annie decided to sing. As if on cue, several long, drawn-out notes filled the humid air. The accordionist was playing for his supper. He tipped his hat as Seph scurried past to check in with Lorina.

Her brisk steps faltered at the sight of Annie, who stood waiting for the night shifters to assemble. Annie's olive skin glowed a sickly yellow in the fluorescent lighting, and her rumpled scrubs and the scowl on her face suggested her headache had not resolved overnight. She appeared both ill and ill-tempered, and, as the rest of the staff trickled in too slowly for her liking, Annie lifted the bullhorn to her lips.

"Night shifters, report to duty *now*!"

The accordion player screeched to a halt mid-tune.

"She's the only woman I know who can bellow louder than an accordion." Chief Bishop, coffee cup in hand, joined Seph at a table. "And that's saying something. I've met a lot of—shall I say—*loud* women in my day."

"I bet you have." Seph ripped open a bag of dried fruit and grimaced at the contents. "You seem in good spirits this morning."

"Why shouldn't I be? Sister Smith is coming to the rescue, right? Besides, the Guard is gone. Guess they only wanted our blood after all. And why not? This infection would make a hell of a biological weapon. I'm sure somebody smarter than me is already fleshing out the gory details."

He slurped his coffee, exhaling with a satisfied "ahhhh." "Anyway, I was worried they might leave a contingency behind. Under normal circumstances, I'd welcome the additional security presence, but we both know these circumstances are anything but normal."

Seph stopped munching and surveyed the area. Sure enough, the Guard *was* gone, and since the accordion player had cease-and-desisted, the place was as quiet as a disaster shelter could be. She'd been so focused on Annie's ghastly appearance she hadn't noticed.

"What about outside? Are they still patrolling the perimeter in case anyone tries to make a break for it?"

The chief sighed and lowered his cup. "Unfortunately, they are, or at least a few of them are. But I'd rather have them out there than in here working everyone into a tizzy."

"I think the daily dose of murder is what's working everyone into a tizzy. The Guard—not so much. Not as long as they keep their needles to themselves." Seph popped a piece of something unidentifiable into her mouth and stewed while she chewed. "So we still can't leave?"

"No. Not unless your sister figures out a way to call off the dogs. Even then, we have to consider how we're going to separate the healthy from the soon-to-be dead."

Seph winced. "The illness is not an automatic death sentence. A cure exists, remember? There's just not enough of it to go around."

"Like I said, the dead. No one's gonna waste a limited cure on any of us. Remember what happened last year during Hurricane Katrina? At the Superdome? The kind of people who amass in a shelter are considered expendable. And when it comes right down to it, so are we."

Annie interrupted their morbid conversation with a brief spate of announcements. "A second storm is coming. From the west, this time. Not a hurricane, thank God, but we can expect another round of heavy rain and strong winds. No more going outside until it passes. Expect to be here another week until the blood test results are back." The crowd groaned, and Annie disappeared with Alice on medical rounds.

"Fabulous. Just what we needed—another storm. As if morale could get any lower." Seph squashed an errant raisin into a mushy, brown blob on the table with her thumb. "Do you think this rainwater will be contaminated, too? Maybe that's the real reason the Guard left—to protect their own."

"Remember what I said yesterday about you sounding paranoid?" The chief eyed her pulpy mess. Seph swiped her sticky fingers over her wet water bottle and cleaned her hand and the table with a napkin.

"Seph, I'm no scientist, but Annie said the infection came from off the coast of Africa, where Atlantic hurricanes start. This sounds like a home-grown, run-of-the-mill thunderstorm. The water should be fine. It might even help us by washing away any residual contamination."

Chief Bishop took the final swig from his cup. "But what the hell do I know? I could be talking out my ass. I need more coffee." He pushed his chair back but stopped at the strange sight ahead. Father Barney, face flushed, was rushing their way holding a pair of canary yellow stilettos.

The shoes dangling from Father Barney's hand rocked back and forth like a songbird on a swing.

"This ought to be good," the chief muttered.

"Or very bad." Seph arched her brows. "I've never seen someone waddle with such urgency."

The chaplain paused to catch his breath, and a trickle of sweat ran down his cheek and dripped onto the concrete floor. His huffing and puffing continued as he approached their table.

Chief Bishop nodded at the shoes. "I don't think they'll fit you, padre. Not your size."

The priest thrust the shoes in the chief's face. "I found them under my cot when I got up."

"Sounds like someone's playing with you. Someone who obviously knows about your podiatric proclivities."

Father Barney's eyes widened, and he began to stammer. "Um, I don't think so. I mean, at first, yes, I thought the same thing—someone was taunting me, perhaps. But then I noticed the blood on the heels. See?"

The chaplain pointed a pudgy finger at the two red streaks staining the heel of each shoe. "I've searched the whole shelter except for the rear, of course, where we're not allowed to go, and I can't find Angel anywhere. I'm worried something may have happened to her."

Chief Bishop reached into his back pocket and pulled out a pair of latex gloves. Father Barney handed him the shoes. Seph peered over the chief's shoulder while he rotated the stilettos for a full inspection. Each heel had two meandering lines of dried blood, while the toes and soles were clean.

"Pull a baggie out of my belt, will ya? Second pouch on the right."

Seph unfolded the evidence bag and offered it to the chief, who dropped the shoes inside and zipped it shut.

"What do you make of this, Doc?" the chief asked.

"Are you quizzing me?"

"You betcha."

"Well, I'd say Father Barney's concerns are justified. Something bad has happened to our angelic prostitute."

"You don't say?" The chief dangled the bulging bag in front of her face. "Can you be a tad more specific?"

Seph batted the bag away. "If it's so obvious, why'd you ask? I don't like being grilled."

"At least I'm grilling nicely. I could've said, 'No shit, Sherlock.'"

"Please." Father Barney raised both hands. "Please." His distress wiped the glare from Seph's face.

The chief noticed as well, and he switched from teasing to professional. "Tell me about the blood on her shoes. Or rather, what does the blood tell *you*?"

"Angel saw something about to happen and turned to run. The back of her shoes got splashed when she tried to get away."

"Wrong. Think about the ways blood can splatter or flow. If you ignore the unlikely possibility of someone purposely painting the blood on her heels, there's only one way the blood could've formed this pattern on this location of her shoes. She was killed via a through-and-through abdominal penetration which cut a major artery, probably her aorta. The blood flowed out her back and ran toward her feet. The stream split into two where her heels contacted the floor, causing the separate lines of blood you see here."

Chief Bishop held the plastic bag up to the light and pointed to the crimson streaks with his pen. "Angel's lying dead somewhere. We just need to find her. Someone wants us to, or else he wouldn't have left you the shoes, Father."

"Lord have mercy." Father Barney lowered his head to his hands and moaned. "Heavenly Father, haven't we been tested enough?"

The chief punted that ball straight to Seph. "It's a good thing we have such a solid counselor on staff, isn't it, Father?" He patted her on the upper back and grinned. Seph shot daggers but remained silent.

"I'll brief my officers and organize the search teams. Father, you didn't happen to come across Angel's boyfriend while you were heading our way, did you?"

The priest removed his head from his hands. "No. As a matter of fact, I did not."

"Didn't think so. Guess we'll be searching for both of them. Doc, I'll rely on you to bring Annie up to speed."

"Thanks."

"You're welcome. You might also want to pay a visit to Thad. He and Angel got pretty chummy after Delmas's death." The chief strode off, radio in hand.

Father Barney appeared puzzled. "The chief thinks Angel's boyfriend killed her?"

Seph shrugged. "The boyfriend would be the most obvious person of interest. But with everything that's happening around here, the murderer could be anyone. No motive required. Just the disease."

"I suppose." The chaplain pondered her sobering words. "She was such a nice woman. I can't imagine anyone . . ."

Seph interrupted. "*Selma* was a nice woman. Angel turned tricks and stole from the elderly for a living."

Father Barney's color rose, and he straightened to his full five feet five inches. "Unlike you, Dr. Smith, Angel had no education, no home, no family who gave a shit whether she lived or died. She did what she did to survive. When a stray dog digs through a garbage can for scraps, do you blame the dog? How about the owner of the can, who had so much food to waste he threw it away without a backward glance, ignoring the poor, hungry creature outside?"

The priest's eyes flashed with an emotion Seph had not previously seen him display. "You may have given up on God, Dr. Smith, but don't give up on humanity. You'll require a whole new career if you do." He waddled away in a huff.

First came the shock of being reamed out and sworn at by a priest. Then, the guilt set in. Father Barney was right. The transformative power of her experience in the dark and oppressive shelter had drained Seph's sympathy and toughened her soul. She was changing, but the people here still needed her support. She had a job to do, and, for now, her job description included compassion. She could evaluate her relationships with God and society in the brighter light of another day.

The hangar's roof shrieked a warning. Storm number two had started. The shelter populous responded with a moment of silence followed by a surge of nervous babble. *Get to work.* Seph's brain convinced her feet to embark on a search for Annie.

She found Alice first, alone at the nurses' station. "You finished rounds rather quickly, didn't you, Alice?"

"Dr. Parrish isn't feeling well, so we hurried things along a bit."

"Still has her migraine?"

"Yes." Alice, ever discreet, added no details.

"What I have to tell her isn't going to help, I'm afraid. Chief thinks Angel's been murdered. Where can I find Annie?"

"She said she'd be in the control room if anyone needed her. I was hoping no one would."

"I know, Alice. I hate to bother her, but I also know how upset she'd be if we didn't notify her of this latest . . .event. She likes to be kept in the loop."

"True." Alice gave a slight smile and resumed her charting.

The control room's overhead lights were switched off, but despite the darkness, Annie's presence was obvious. Her red shirt reflected the flashing lights of the electronic arrays, making it appear to pulse an urgent, rhythmic warning like the strobe atop an ambulance. She sat at the folding table with her back to the glass door, staring at the blank wall ahead. Her upper body jerked when Seph knocked before entering, but she didn't turn around.

"Annie, I'm sorry to interrupt, but we have a situation." Seph kept her voice low and soft. She'd learned from Grace's debilitating migraine attacks to tread carefully.

"What kind of situation?"

"Father Barney found Angel's yellow shoes under his cot. They have blood on them."

"*The Case of the Missing Shoes.* Sounds like a Nancy Drew story."

"Except in this case, it's more like *The Case of the Missing Feet.* We can't find Angel or her boyfriend, and the chief believes she's been murdered. He's organizing a search party."

"Okay."

"Okay?" Seph aimed a dubious look at the back of Annie's head.

"Yes. Okay. The chief can handle it. Keep me posted."

"Okay. I mean, will do." Seph reopened the door as quietly

as possible and was sidling over the threshold when Annie, still facing the rear wall, stopped her.

"I need you to do something for me."

"Sure. What is it?"

Annie's phone jangled on her hip, and they both jumped. She glanced at the screen, and her eyes widened in surprise. It rang again.

"Later." Annie waved Seph out the door. "Hello, this is Dr. Parrish."

Seph closed the door behind her. She longed to know who was on the other end of that call, but Annie was not in the mood to share. She lingered, watching Annie's figure through the dark glass, but her boss turned her back and kept her voice low. Defeated, Seph decided to move on. She still had to interview Thad.

Thad's cot wasn't far from the nurses' station given his high-risk conditions. His hip fracture predisposed him to developing blood clots, and between his underlying deformities and the ulcer on his rear end, Alice and her nurses had their hands full. Their frequent administrations of morphine kept him docile, and his steady stream of visitors kept him occupied. The corrupted analogue of a man had wasted no time in establishing a network of "friends" after Delmas's death.

Seph loitered nearby while Thad and one of his shady, new associates completed a transaction. The young man placed a knit cap on Thad's head and traded him a lidded Styrofoam cup for an opened pack of Marlboros. A hoodie, cinched at the neck, obscured the man's face, but as he stood to leave, Seph caught a glimpse.

"Hey! Hey, wait!" She lurched toward him, and their eyes met.

Hoodie man bolted, pushing people aside to jostle his way through the central dining area. He disappeared into the crowd. Seph waved a desperate hand at the police officer guarding the front door. Their chase was brief and futile. Hoodie man was gone, intermingled with the mass of humanity in the non-medical half of the shelter.

"What happened? Are you okay?" The police officer reached her side. He had one hand on his radio and the other on his weapon.

"The man in the hoodie was Angel's boyfriend. I'm certain of it." Seph hunched over, gasping for breath after the short, but intense pursuit. "He and Thad were bartering until he saw me and took off running. Where's Chief Bishop?"

"Searching the back."

"Brief him. He'll want to know what I saw. I'm going back to talk to Thad. The chief can find me there if he needs me to fill in the details. Tell him I'm convinced Thad knows something about Angel's disappearance."

"Roger that." The officer raised the radio to his lips.

Seph made a pit stop at the nurses' station.

"Alice, have you noticed anything weird going on with Thad and his visitors?"

"You'll need to define weird for me, Dr. Smith."

Seph chuckled. Alice, cracking jokes. Lew was right—they'd fallen down a rabbit hole after all.

"Thad's last visitor—the guy in the hoodie—was Angel's boyfriend. Angel is, as I'm sure you've heard by now, missing."

"Except for her shoes."

Seph smiled. "Yes, except for her shoes. I saw him and Thad conducting some sort of bedside transaction a few minutes ago."

"Interesting. We had to switch to intravenous instead of oral morphine for that very reason. Thad would pretend to swallow the pills only to spit them out when he thought we weren't looking. He'd sell half on the black market. One for him, one for them. I'm surprised he hasn't concocted a way to suck it out of the IV line. The boy is clever."

"I can think of some better words. 'Sneaky' and 'manipulative' come to mind."

They stared at Thad, who, in turn, fixated on his Styrofoam cup.

"Anything else different, Alice? Any idea what might be in the cup?"

Alice frowned. "Thad's been acting somewhat confused lately. Normally, I'd attribute it to the morphine, but day shift reported his usage plummeted from a peak of every-two-hour dosing earlier this afternoon. He hasn't asked me for a hit since I came on duty. Not sure why he would bother buying or trading for pain meds when we are giving him one for free, but if I had to guess, the cup contains Thad's preferred narcotic. Addicts prefer to pick their own poisons. Shall I alert Dr. Parrish and the police?"

"The police are already aware. I expect Chief Bishop to arrive shortly. Let me chat with Thad first—see if I can outmaneuver him. I've been known to walk on the sneaky side if the situation demands it. Especially nowadays."

"Has Chief Bishop corrupted you?"

"I prefer the term 'converted.' Let's just say he's trained me well. Trial by fire, if you will."

Alice assumed her most solemn demeanor. "Of course, Dr. Smith." She sat back, clasped her hands together in her lap, and prepared to watch the show.

Seph approached Thad's cot and lowered herself into a chair, which groaned an announcement. Thad's eyes were closed, but his right hand jiggled his precious cup, agitating its contents until they sloshed against the inner rim of the lid. A noxious, astringent odor irritated Seph's nose and eyes. She examined the bedside table, covered in an assortment of bandages, alcohol swabs, and IV supplies, for the source of the smell, dabbing at her dripping nose. Alice must have recently cleaned Thad's wound.

"Thad."

"Dr. Smith."

"I saw you talking to Angel's boyfriend."

"So?"

"Angel's missing."

"You don't say?"

"Listen, smart-ass . . ."

Thad's eyes flew open, and Seph rose from her chair in shock. Instead of his usual sardonic expression, Thad appeared feverish—dangerously off-kilter. A blood-red halo surrounded his massively dilated pupils, and he struggled to focus on her face. Seph had seen this expression before in both Lew and Carol after the infection had assumed total control of their minds.

"Alice, I need you!"

The nurse jumped from her seat and scrambled to gather her equipment.

"What's in the cup, Thad?" Seph leaned forward and attempted to ease the cup from Thad's grip.

He yanked it away, releasing another toxic plume of fumes. "I'm having a party. Would you like some tea?" Thad giggled.

"Thad, listen to me. You're sick, and soon you might not be able to talk anymore. Concentrate. Tell me what happened to

Angel. Do you understand what I'm saying?" Out of the corner of her eye, Seph saw Alice hustling her way with another nurse in tow.

"One, two, steal her shoes."

"What?"

"Three, four, mop the gore."

"Thad, I'm not following you." Seph pressed one hand over her nose and the other on her midsection in an attempt to quell the quivering mass of fear expanding in her gut.

"Five, six, take some pix." Thad reached under his pillow and produced his phone, which he handed to Seph. She stared at it as if it might bite her. She wouldn't, couldn't push the buttons until the police arrived.

"Seven, eight, it's too late." Thad cupped his gnarled hand over Seph's and gently squeezed. The phone clicked to life. Angel appeared on its screen, lying in a pool of blood with her yellow shoes pointed toward the sky.

Alice arrived in time to witness Angel's picture before the screen flickered off again. She turned to the nurse behind her. "Go get the police. And Dr. Parrish."

"Nine, ten, evil men." Thad lifted his head from his pillow. "Remember, Dr. Smith—good people die first."

He raised his cup in a mock toast and winked. "You'll live forever." He popped the lid and downed the contents in one gulp.

"Oh, my God!" Alice and Seph stumbled backwards at the onslaught of acrid fumes. Seph fought to focus through the haze of her burning eyes. An orange foam bubbled from Thad's mouth, and she heard snap after snap as his brittle bones broke into pieces. Thad was seizing.

"Get out of the way!"

Seph, now blind to everything except the claustrophobic grey film encasing her, recognized Annie's brusque voice. Strong arms wrenched her from Thad's side and onto the floor. Choking and limp, she offered no resistance as her blurry grey world faded to black.

Seph gasped and struggled to sit upright in her cot, tearing off an oxygen mask in the process. Her flailing triggered a coughing fit, and she was horrified to see ugly blotches of bright, red blood on her palms where she'd covered her mouth.

"The chlorine gas damaged your lungs, but you'll recover." Annie's voice—calm, detached—floated in the grey haze. She forced a tissue into Seph's hands.

Seph wiped her palms and mouth. She blinked, and her vision cleared enough for her to discern the figure sitting by her side. "Alice?" She croaked out the nurse's name. "What about Alice?"

"Alice is fine. Her exposure was briefer and from a greater distance than yours. She returned to duty an hour ago. Insisted on finishing her shift. You know Alice."

I've known Alice for all of six days, Seph wanted to say. Instead, she nodded. "And Thad?"

"Thad drank a cocktail of bleach and orange juice, which is quite effective at killing everything from anthrax spores to your average human being."

"Why? Why would he do something like that?"

"He was infected, I assume, and out of his mind. Otherwise, he had at least a half a dozen other easily attainable and less grotesque ways he could've gone about it. Morphine overdose, to name a blissful and obvious option." She paused, and her flat voice wavered. "He suffered terribly. There was little we could do. It's a horrible, painful way to die."

They sat listening to the whistle of the oxygen tank and Seph's intermittent wheezing. Eventually, Annie reached over and turned the flow of oxygen off. "You don't need this anymore." She pointed to Seph's right. "You have an inhaler sitting next to you. Albuterol. It'll help your breathing. Use it every four hours as needed. Doctor's orders."

Seph nodded and retrieved the inhaler for closer inspection. The weight of it in her hand triggered a flood of disturbing memories: Angel's picture on Thad's phone, his insane mockery of a nursery rhyme, his admission of guilt. "What happened to Thad's phone? I had it in my hand. He killed Angel, you know. I don't know how, but he did. He had a picture of her on his phone."

"Alice told us. The chief has the phone. The police found Angel in the back stuffed in one of the packing crates. She was stabbed through the gut, as the chief surmised."

"Does he know who committed the actual act? Because Thad obviously wasn't physically capable of carrying out a murder by himself."

"No. Shane wants to speak to you about that. I'm supposed to notify him when you're ready and able to talk."

"Shane?"

"Chief Bishop. Tall guy. Young. Smart-alecky. Big biceps. You've met him once or twice."

Seph blushed. "I think I need more oxygen." She shook her head, trying to clear the fog.

Annie didn't laugh at Seph's gaffe. In fact, she didn't respond at all. She sat there, unmoving and unreadable, even to someone as sensitive as Seph. When the silence became uncomfortable, Seph kicked the blanket off her toes and swung her legs over the edge of the cot.

"You know, I'm feeling much better now. I think I'll go find him myself." She leaned forward and braced her arms to get up.

"Sit."

Annie arrested Seph's ascent with a palm flat to the chest. Dumbfounded, Seph curled her fingers around the cot's metal frame and did as she was told. "Do you remember what I said to you earlier today in the control room?"

"You wanted me to do something for you." Seph inched her way closer to edge of the cot, ready to spring and run if needed. Annie was creeping her out.

Annie dropped her hand, leaving a sweaty imprint on Seph's shirt. "Correct. I need you to kill me."

Seph blinked, waiting for her brain to reboot so she could access her training. She forced her fingers to ease their death grip on the cot and smoothed the astonishment from her face.

"Explain yourself, please." The "please" was a stilted afterthought, choked out in an attempt to sound professional instead of horrified.

"I'm infected, or, at least, I believe I am."

"Because you have a migraine."

"Because I'm losing my fucking grip. On myself, on this shelter, and maybe even on reality." Annie pounded her thigh with one fist. "And I will not, *will not* kill anyone on my way out, nor do I want to drink a goddamned bleach cocktail. You asked the chief to kill you if you got infected. He told me so. I'm asking you to extend me the same favor."

"Annie, assuming I had the means to honor your request . . ."

"I can get you the means."

". . . I took a vow, much like you did. The golden rule of health care: First, do no harm."

"My head hurts so bad, Seph. So bad. You have no idea." Annie covered her face and rocked forward, lowering her head to her lap.

"Why ask me? Why not ask Alice?"

"Alice believes in God and consequences."

"And I don't?"

Annie raised her head and blasted Seph with an icy glare. "No. Not anymore, or so I'm told. Alice stinks of virtue. You just stink."

"Not a nice thing to say. Downright rude, as a matter of fact."

"This is not a nice conversation. Look at me. I'm rotting from the inside out—physically, mentally. But you? You're rotting morally. You're the perfect person to ask. You reek of hypocrisy. A psychologist who no longer gives a shit about her fellow man. A counselor who loves the sinner more than the saint. You're an embryonic sin, and you know it. If you don't, you're lying to yourself."

They eyed each other like combatants in a cage, ready to exchange blows.

Seph shook her head. "This conversation is over. My advice: Arrange coverage with Dr. Dodgson. Go ask Alice for some morphine. Sleep it off. Things will appear different once your headache breaks. We'll talk again tomorrow once you feel better."

"Thank you, Dr. Smith, for your words of wisdom. True clinical pearls." Annie's face twisted into a sarcastic grin. Seph motioned to get up, and this time, Annie let her go.

Seph bolted from her bed in a blind search for the chief. When she paused to look back, Annie remained in the exact same position, staring at the empty cot.

Seph exhaled and debated her next move. The chief was awaiting her report on Thad, and he would certainly want to know about Annie's morbid request. But maybe she should talk to Alice first. Unlike Seph, Alice had forged a strong professional rapport with Annie. Perhaps the steadfast nurse could persuade Annie into accepting a night off.

While Seph waffled, Chief Bishop, surrounded by a gaggle of other officers, rounded the corner.

"Doc, nice to see you upright and breathing. How ya feeling?" He motioned for the officers to leave, and they scattered to assume their positions around the shelter.

"Physically? Better. Mentally? Totally freaked out."

"I know. Drinking bleach? I've seen Drano before, but bleach is a new one, even for me."

"Not about Thad. About Annie. She asked me to kill her."

The chief blinked in surprise. "Holy fuckamoli. How . . . unexpected."

"Tell me about it. She thinks she's infected. Sound familiar?"

"Everyone's caught a bad case of paranoia." He grinned. "I'm *dying* to know your response."

"So not funny."

The chief kept right on grinning.

"No, all right? I told her no. As if there were any doubt. But the point is, she may take matters into her own hands. If we were home, she'd be involuntarily admitted to the psych ward and placed on suicide watch. I think we should have someone lay eyes on her every so often, like we did for Joaquin."

"She's not going to appreciate that kind of attention. Joaquin didn't like it either, and he wasn't even the boss."

"Do you have a better suggestion?"

"No." He stroked his chin. "I guess we'll have to be real subtle-like. Good thing it's my middle name. Remember?"

Seph rolled her eyes. "Let's hope we have a better outcome than with Joaquin."

The memory of Joaquin's disemboweled body drove the smile from Chief Bishop's face. "We need to discuss Thad. I got Alice's report, but it's obviously secondhand. You feel up to telling me your side of the story?" He waved her toward their usual spot in the dining area.

"Yes."

"Good. Let me get a cup of coffee, and I'll be right back. You want anything?"

"A bottle of water would be nice."

"Roger that." He strode off, leaving Seph to reflect on the evening's events.

She rested her hands on the table and intertwined her fingers, watching the flickers of light from the countless rows of cots in the non-medical section of the shelter. It was late, and the overhead lights had long been extinguished. The evacuees were supposed to be asleep, but even after a week in the shelter, many had not yet adapted to sleeping in such a tumultuous environment.

These insomniacs held their flashlights like sabers, slicing them through the darkness at the slightest noise. The murders hadn't helped. How many were they up to now? Seph had lost count. She closed her eyes and attempted a mental tally, clenching her fingers tighter and tighter with the resurrection of each bloody memory.

"Dr. Smith?"

Seph's hands and eyes flew open at the sound of Father Barney's voice, and the surprise triggered another coughing fit.

"Are you okay?" The priest patted her on the back, and she shrugged him off.

"I'm fine, thank you."

"You look tense." The priest unfolded the chair next to hers.

Seph frowned. "I am tense. It's been an eventful night, to say the least."

They flinched as the sheet metal ceiling shuddered and screamed with a gust of wind. Distant thunder rumbled a warning. Storm number two had arrived.

"I heard. Another one." Father Barney blessed himself before continuing. "The chief sent me. He wants you to meet him in the back of the shelter. The police found Angel's boyfriend, and Chief Bishop would like the two of you to interrogate him together."

"The chief was just here a minute ago." Seph stretched her neck, searching for his uniform in the kitchen area.

"I know. One of his officers waylaid him at the coffee pot. He told me you were waiting for him, and he didn't want you sitting here forever. He asked me to give you this." He placed a bottle of water in front of her.

"You're sure he said to head to the rear of the shelter? You know we're not allowed back there."

The chaplain nodded with such vigor, the crucifix threatened to bounce off his neck. "I'm positive. I suspect they wanted someplace where they wouldn't disturb those who are sleeping. I can accompany you if you're uncomfortable going alone." Father Barnabas leaned forward, his countenance too eager, his tone too sincere.

Seph stared at the priest. Her muscles quivered, overcome by a sudden and inexplicable urge to run. She pushed both palms against the table and stood. "That won't be necessary. Thank you, anyway."

The chaplain's face fell. "As you wish."

Seph marched stiff-legged toward the back of the shelter, aware of Father Barney's eyes following her every step. She rounded the first rolling barrier and paused to listen. Her ears perked up at the sound of the chief's distinctive New York accent accompanied by the low rumble of two other unfamiliar voices. A dim light flickered from near the utility closet where Joaquin had cowered during his hypoglycemic attack.

Seph approached as if she were trespassing, until the smell of rotting flesh stopped her in her tracks. She must be close to the morgue. She covered her nose and gagged.

"Chief? Are you there?"

The voices ceased. Steps hurried in her direction. Chief Bishop burst out of the darkness and into the beam of her flashlight.

"Seph, what the hell are you doing here?"

She stood dumfounded, and the chief's anger softened at her expression. "Look, I'm sorry I left you sitting, but you know no one is allowed in the back alone. I asked Father Barney . . ."

"Father Barney told me you wanted me here. Is that true?"

"No, it is *not* true." Chief Bishop frowned. "He was supposed to tell you I had something come up, and I'd catch you later. We found Angel's boyfriend, and I wanted to interrogate him myself, before day shift took over. Given the late hour, I didn't have much time."

"Why would he lie? He was adamant I was to join you in the rear of the shelter. Said you wanted my help interviewing Angel's boyfriend."

"And you believed him? I am more than capable of grilling a prisoner myself without a psychologist attached to my hip."

Seph's cheeks burned, and she was grateful for the veil of darkness which hid her crimson face. "I know you don't *need* me, but I thought maybe it was more of the mentoring thing—you know, you and your pathetic attempts to convert me into a criminal psychologist. And besides, I may have renounced my religion, but I still don't expect a priest to lie."

She was interrupted by a retching sound from behind.

"What was that?" Seph peered over his shoulder and into the darkness.

"You don't want to know."

She searched his impassive face, made even more enigmatic by the shifting shadows.

"What are you doing back here, Chief?"

A moan wafted through the humid air.

"Desperate times, Doc."

In a burst of bravado, Seph brushed past the chief, zigging and zagging to avoid his grasp. She sprinted toward the circle of dim light, where Angel's boyfriend sat tied to a chair. He hunched over and retched again, adding to the pool of blood and vomit on the floor. He spat a tooth, which skittered across the concrete and landed at Seph's feet. A police sergeant, fists clenched and ready to fly, loomed over him.

Seph's intrusion prompted the officer to take a step back. His eyes darted to the chief, who raised a steadying hand.

"This is what Father Barney wanted me to see." Her quiet words disappeared into the darkness. The silence stretched while Seph waited for a wave of revulsion to lap at her soul. It did not. She remained as dispassionate as a judge.

"What did you find out?" she asked.

She may as well have dropped a bomb. Chief Bishop, expecting an outpouring of vitriol, fumbled to recover.

"Thad awoke from his morphine-induced haze to discover Angel pilfering through his belongings. He wanted to set an example, so he made Angel's boyfriend an offer he couldn't refuse—not if he wanted to keep all four limbs, anyway. Seems Thad has developed a robust network of thugs in the non-medical half of the shelter."

"Not surprising." Seph nodded at the man strapped to the chair. "If he was so forthcoming, why the heavy hands?"

"He could've come to us for help first instead of slicing up his girlfriend."

"Sure. Because everyone here is in his right mind and behaving normally. Isn't that right, Officer?" Seph aimed a derisive smile at the sergeant, who dropped his eyes.

"Clean him up, and let him go," the chief said to his sergeant. "We have what we came for."

He pointed at Seph. "You and I need to talk." Chief Bishop escorted Seph back to the dining room area, where they both took a seat.

"What—no coffee?" Seph assumed a prim and proper pose in her chair.

"Knock it off, Doc."

"Should we ask Father Barney to join us? I can get my brass knuckles."

"Let's talk about that first. Besides for his little white lie, did he say anything else unusual?"

Seph recalled the strange reaction she'd had when the priest offered to accompany her to the rear of the shelter. "He wanted to come with me. For my safety, he claimed. I declined."

"Of course you did. Because that would've been practical."

Seph scowled. "*Because* he made me feel uncomfortable. He was kind of . . .I don't know, creepy about it."

"Well, that explains it, then."

"Do tell."

"You're the psychologist, but the way I see it: Father Barney had a foot fetish and a crush on Angel. Listening to the boyfriend talk about her murder, how he removed her shoes etcetera—it's a vicarious thing, right?"

"Could be. Or he might have been trying to kick-start my conscience and help Angel's boyfriend in the process. He obviously suspected you'd be using caveman methods of interrogation. Then again, maybe he was trying to lure me into the back to kill me."

"You didn't expect him to lie, but now you're accusing him of premeditation? Murder is a few notches above lying in my book. Don't you think you're being a little, um, skittish?"

"Perhaps. Just throwin' it out there." Seph's shoulders slumped as her energy level ebbed. The overhead lights brightened, and a crowd began to gather for sign-outs. "Guess we don't need to discuss my final conversation with Thad anymore. Case solved. I'm going to bed."

"Aren't you going to wait for Annie's end-of-shift, rah-rah speech?"

"I'll pass. Besides, I doubt she'll be giving one."

Chapter Twelve

The Seventh Night

Seph did not sleep. She fussed and fidgeted until she finally gave up and resigned herself to listening to the antics of an active shelter. *Ring around the rosie* . . . While day shift played archaic games with the children, Seph hid from her dreams and nightmares alike.

She was the first night shifter to breakfast. No line for the coffee pot. Bonus. Seph rarely drank caffeine in any form, but today she'd grant herself an exception and make the chief proud.

Seph poured herself a tall one before cruising in slo-mo to the nearest table. She took a swig and shuddered. Lousy, for sure, but she wasn't drinking it for the taste. She forced herself to take another gulp. Today's coffee was for medicinal purposes only. The jolt of caffeine should help clear the cobwebs from her addled mind.

She slouched over her cup and waited for the caffeine to kick in. Alice approached.

"May I join you?"

"'Course," Seph mumbled. She waved haphazardly at nearby chairs.

"Bad night?" Alice settled into her seat and placed a paper napkin on her lap.

"You could say that."

"Do you think you're still suffering ill effects from the bleach exposure?" Alice knitted her brow and counted Seph's respiratory rate from across the table.

"No, nothing like that." Seph hastened to reassure her. "I couldn't fall sleep. I tried my face mask, ear plugs—every trick in the book—and I was still up the whole damned night—day—you know what I mean."

"Overstimulation. A common problem." Alice buttered her toast and balanced the edge of her knife on her paper plate. "Normally, I'd advise you to lay off the caffeine, but in your situation, it may be helpful."

"How so?"

"Caffeine dilates the bronchial tubes and helps with wheezing. It should eliminate any lingering effects from the bleach."

"Nice to know I chose the right day to indulge. Although this is not much of an indulgence." Seph grimaced with each sip. "Honestly, it tastes like jet fuel."

She sighed and watched the trickle of night shifters reporting for duty. "Did Dr. Parrish say anything important last night at sign-out? I went straight to bed. Not that it helped."

"She didn't speak. I talked her into taking more headache medication before bed, so hopefully she'll feel better this morning."

"Let's hope so." Seph picked at her food, pushing it around the plate in concentric circles, and debated whether she should tell Alice about Annie's suicidal plea.

Chief Bishop arrived, postponing her decision. Judging by the spring in his step, he'd fared far better than she in the sleep department. Seph glared at him over the rim of her cup.

"Top o' the morning to ya, ladies." He eyed Seph's coffee but wisely refrained from commenting. "Today's our one-week anniversary."

"I'm not sure it's an event worth celebrating," Alice said.

"No, probably not. But it means we're one week closer to going home. We have to be, right?" By now, the dining area teemed with employees changing shifts. The chief perused the crowd. "Anyone seen Annie?"

"No." Alice plucked the napkin off her lap and crumpled it into a tight wad. "But I see Dr. Dodgson." She pointed to the day shift team leader as she stood to gather her tray. "I'll see if he knows where she is. If not, I'll find her. After all, I can't do rounds by myself, and the patients need their evening medications." She gracefully excused herself.

Dr. Dodgson positioned himself in Annie's usual spot and addressed the crowd. After dispensing an update and a handful of bland compliments on their hard work and dedication, he scurried away. The crowd dispersed as the day shifters retired to their beds.

Across the room, Seph watched as Dr. Dodgson and Alice engaged in a brief conversation, which ended with the two of them jogging toward Annie's cot.

"Not good," Chief Bishop said.

"Nope. Alice doesn't jog." A sudden rush of jitteriness coursed through her veins as the caffeine hit her system. *Finally*. "Did you question Father Barney about last night?"

"No. It's on my 'to-do' list. I think the whole Angel-murder thing is settled. We've got her boyfriend confined and under one-on-one observation until we can haul his ass to jail. I threatened to handcuff him to Father Barney if he misbehaves, so I think he'll be a good boy." He chuckled. "It's business as usual until we see if your sister comes through for us. Have you heard anything?"

"No." Seph frowned at the bottom of her empty cup. "How would I? My phone doesn't work, remember?"

"Didn't stop you before."

Seph snorted with exasperation. "Let it rest, will ya? The only phone call of which I am aware is the one Annie got yesterday."

"About what?"

"I don't know. I was summarily dismissed from her glass castle before I heard anything valuable."

"Was this before or after she asked you to kill her?"

"Before. Why? Do you think they're related?"

"Might be." The chief shrugged. "Or not. It's hard to tell. The only one who knows for certain is Annie, and she appears to be AWOL. Why don't you attach yourself to Alice and see what you can uncover while I chat with our fibbing friar? Let me know if I have to organize another search party. I'm hoping Annie just curled up somewhere due to her headache. If you find her, ask her about the phone call."

"I doubt she'll want to talk with me. Our last conversation was a doozy. As a matter of fact, she called me stinky."

Chief Bishop threw his head back and roared with laughter. An indignant Seph pursed her lips. "It was quite insulting, actually."

"No doubt." The chief wiped an imaginary tear from the corner of his eye. "Funny as hell, though. Do the best you can with her, okay? I know she's a tough nut to crack. If you can't get the information we need, I'll pump her after I'm done with Father Barney." He nodded at her empty cup. "How about a refill?"

"No. I think I've had enough for today. Now, if it were tequila . . ."

Chief Bishop laughed. "You're hardening up, Doc. I'm telling ya, there's a career in criminal psychology waiting for you on the other side."

"I'm beginning to believe you're right."

Seph started her search at Annie's cot, which was empty. Next she headed to the nurses' station, where Alice sat documenting her patient encounters.

"How's Dr. Parrish doing?" Seph asked. "She must be better—the two of you finished rounds pretty darned fast."

"I rounded with Dr. Dodgson. He was motivated by his fatigue." Alice frowned as she attempted to decipher his handwritten orders.

"Oh. I gather she's not doing well, then?"

"I'm not sure," Alice replied. "When we found her, she was sitting on the edge of her cot, staring at her phone. Dr. Dodgson asked her how she was feeling, and she told him her headache was gone."

Alice's frown deepened, and she put down her pen. "Said she felt fine. She didn't *look* fine, Dr. Smith. Not fine at all."

"If everything was hunky-dory, why didn't she do her own patient rounds?"

"Precisely. Supposedly, she got an important message from Central Office and has a pile of administrative work to do. Asked Dr. Dodgson to do rounds for her. She's been holed up in the control room ever since."

Alice pointed over her shoulder at the glass-enclosed telecom office where Annie sat facing a computer screen. She tapped feverishly at the keyboard; the printer next to her responded by spewing out papers. Every few moments, she paused to retrieve the documents, collating them on the clipboard by her side.

"What's going on, Dr. Smith?"

"I have no idea, Alice. But I'm going to try to find out."

✚

Seph strode to the front of the shelter and was met outside the control room door by a dawdling Henry. He shrugged at her inquisitive look.

"She threw me out. Said she had some 'highly sensitive' work to do. Not that I mind. I'm sick of staring at the same four walls, even if they are made out of glass."

"I bet. Why don't you go get a snack or something, Henry? I want to chat with Dr. Parrish."

"Excellent!" The young man beamed at being released from his tether. "Be careful she doesn't bite your head off. She's moody like that." He loped away.

"I hadn't noticed," Seph muttered under her breath. She squared her shoulders, rapped on the glass, and barged in.

"Annie, I . . ."

"Go away."

"Um, no. Not without some answers."

Annie spun away from the keyboard, and Seph gasped at her ghastly appearance. Sallow and drawn, she was a shadow of her former haughty self. Annie noticed Seph's reaction and seemed to deflate. Her shoulders sagged, and she fixated on an invisible spot on the floor.

"Forget about what I said last night, okay? I wasn't thinking straight. The headache had me half crazy, you know? How would you know? You don't suffer from migraines."

Annie swiveled back to the computer, and Seph seized the opportunity to peek over her shoulder at the clipboard. The papers appeared to be lists, labeled at the top with a number and along the side with names.

Annie continued mumbling. "Trust me. If you did, you'd understand where I was coming from, why I asked what I did." She rested her fingers on the keyboard. "I have a lot of work to do. I've gotten some guidance, you might say, with regards to the demobilization of the shelter. Turns out those blood tests didn't take a week after all. They lied. Imagine that. I need to make arrangements."

"You have the results?"

"They have them."

"Who's 'they'? Annie, I must know. Am I infected? Are you?" Seph sidled around the table toward Annie and the clipboards.

"I don't know." Annie stood to cut her off at the pass.

"You're lying. I can feel it." Seph contemplated taking the papers by force. Instead, she tried another tactic. "Is this what yesterday's phone call was about?"

"Yes."

"Is Dr. Dodgson aware?" If Annie wouldn't talk, perhaps he would.

"No. I outrank him, seniority-wise. I alone am responsible for everybody in this shelter, living or dead." Annie shuffled forward. "I need you to leave."

She put her hand on Seph's right shoulder. The gesture was gentle, apologetic, and totally unlike Annie. "You were right, you know."

"About what?"

"About everything. Now go on." Annie nudged Seph toward the door before repositioning herself in front of her keyboard. A bewildered Seph paused at the threshold to stare at Annie's back.

"Seph?"

"Yes?"

"Take care of the shelter for me."

Seph stood outside the control room and gaped into space, completely flummoxed by Annie's behavior. Her eyes vaguely registered Chief Bishop and Henry loitering in the distance. Lost in her turbulent thoughts, she missed their approach and jerked when the chief waved a hand in front of her face.

"Wakey, wakey, eggs and bakey." He grabbed her by the elbow and led her away from the glass enclosure. "Stay here, Henry, in case Dr. Parrish needs your assistance." A disappointed Henry resumed his dawdling.

Once they were out of earshot, the chief dropped his hand from Seph's elbow. "Do you want to go first, or should I?"

"You go first. I'm still processing." Seph shook her head, trying to jostle her thoughts into some semblance of order. "I might need another hit of caffeine."

The chief grinned. "The upshot is Father Barney denied everything. Said you must've misunderstood him." He laughed at Seph's incredulous expression. "He's not a good liar, Doc. Scratch that—he's a *terrible* liar. You two should play poker together someday. Would be a hoot to watch. Anyway, don't worry. I'm on your side. Now, what've you got for me?"

"Perverted little bastard!" Seph fumed.

A clap of thunder boomed overhead. "Careful, Doc. You're talking about a man of the cloth." Chief Bishop gazed toward the heavens.

"I don't care who I'm talking about!" Seph paced a tight line. "You wait until I see his hairy ass again . . ."

The chief winced. "Now *there's* an image I'd like to forget." He leaned forward to whisper in her ear. "How do you know it's hairy?"

Seph uttered a series of expletives which would've made Lew proud and her mother blush.

"Feel better? Good. Now back to Annie . . ."

"I do not feel better! You're going to let him get away with it?"

"Seph, what can I do? He didn't break any laws, and it's his word against yours. The man is disturbed. Probably fried his brain with all the drugs. Did he tell you his life story?"

"Of course he did."

"God may have saved Father Barney's soul, but He didn't do a thing for his grey matter. Let it be. We have more important things to worry about, like how we're busting out of this joint. What did you learn from Annie?"

Seph fluttered her hands. "Our talk raised more questions than answers. She implied she has the results of the blood tests. Said she'd been contacted about plans for closing the shelter. She printed out lists of names. Each list had roughly forty names per page, but they didn't seem to be organized into any particular pattern. I didn't get a good look, though. She hid them from me.

"One minute, she was Ms. CIA; the next, she was Mother Teresa. It was a bizarre conversation. I don't know what to make of it, unless she truly is infected and has lost her mind, like the others. She sounded suicidal, just like before. I'm telling you, we should put her on one-to-one observation."

The chief stroked a pretend beard. "Hmm. Curiouser and curiouser. That's the million-dollar question, then, isn't it? Is Annie sane and plotting our escape, or has she gone bonkers and become a threat to us all? The key is: She *may* know who's infected. I, as the person in charge of the security of this shelter, have the right to know who's on the list. I realize quarantine's a dirty word, but putting the potential psychopaths in one contained area would concentrate my resources."

"I get the distinct impression she doesn't want to share."

"Then Dr. Dodgson, myself, and you, as our star psychologist, will deem her incompetent to make decisions. We can remove her from her position if she's too ill to continue. And the only way we're going to know is to see if her name is on that almighty list."

Rule #4: Never antagonize the one in charge of your way out.

"This doesn't sound like a good idea," Seph said.

"I'm all ears."

"You still have *your* phone. Why don't you use it?"

Before Chief Bishop could answer, the shelter foretold their fortune with a deep, ominous growl. The hangar shook, and, as they raised their eyes to the sky, the roof fell on their heads.

Strips of jagged sheet metal sliced through anything in their path before caroming off the concrete floor. Their reverberations mingled with the terrified screams of those caught in the crossfire of the collapsing shards. When the onslaught abated, the only noise which remained was the sound of thunder and the pounding rain.

Seph extracted her legs from under the chief's and gingerly rose to her feet. He groaned and rolled onto his back.

"Are you hurt?" Seph, shaken, but unharmed, offered him a hand. He waved it off and pushed himself to his knees.

"No. I'll survive, anyway." He winced as he dabbed at an oozing abrasion on his cheek. "You?"

Seph tried but could not respond. Wide-eyed, she absorbed the catastrophic scene around her. The shock stole her voice.

Rain poured through a gaping six-foot hole above the employee rest area. Four cots had been decimated by the debris. Two of the occupants had escaped unscathed, thanks to a combination of quick reflexes and poor sleep habits. The other two were not so lucky.

Dr. Dodgson, eye mask in place and plugs planted firmly in his ears, remained in his cot, but his head was no longer attached to his neck. The young nurse to his right had awakened in time to see her death coming. Her eyes, frozen wide with horror, gaped at the three-foot chunk of metal protruding from her chest.

The remainder of the day shift stood, stunned and silent, at the edge of the tangled mass of cots and metal roofing. A stoic few went straight to work, moving cots and personal belongings away from the flow of water and blood. Chief Bishop sprang into action, organizing the recovery.

"Alice, triage any injuries. Where the hell is Annie?"

"I'm right behind you."

The chief spun around to see Annie dispassionately viewing the carnage. He pointed at her decapitated colleague.

"Dr. Dodgson is dead."

"I can see that."

"Is that all you have to say? You're their leader." He swept his arm toward the bedraggled employees, some of whom clung to each other, weeping. "You need to *lead,* goddammit. You remember leading? It's what you used to do, back in the day."

Annie ignored his sarcasm. She stepped onto a pile of rubble and projected her voice over the roar of the wind and the rain.

"Compress the dining area. Move half the cots there and the other half into the medical ward. It'll be tight, but it'll work until morning." She turned to Chief Bishop. "Have your men move the bodies to the morgue."

The chief wasn't satisfied. "The hurricane may have loosened whole sections of the sheet metal roofing. It could've been hanging by a thread this entire time. Then storm number two came along and blew down the house of cards. The military decommissioned this base, if you recall. Now we know why. We could have similar weak spots in a multitude of areas, just waiting for the next gust of wind."

"We might." Annie twirled a strand of short, dark hair as her eyes, bright, but unfocused, wandered the shelter. "But it's not enough."

"Not enough for what?"

"Enough to order an evacuation."

"What?" Chief Bishop shook his head in disbelief. "Who said anything about an evacuation?"

Annie turned to stumble her way back to the control room. The chief yelled after her. "Where the hell do you think we're gonna go—Paris?" The glass door slammed shut.

"Jesus," he said.

"I told you." Seph had watched the interchange carefully, observing Annie's every twitch. "Initially, I thought her symptoms were headache-related, but now I know otherwise. Either she's truly sick, or she's got herself completely convinced and is manifesting psycogenic symptoms. Either way, she has more than a migraine. Grace never acted like this with hers."

"Annie should know. First of all, she's a physician, and secondly, she has the list of test results. But she wasn't exposed to the contaminated water."

"Not that we're aware. Maybe she's a closet smoker. Or she might be suffering from something else entirely, like the brain aneurysm she used to obsess over. The list of differential diagnoses is broad. Either way, Annie's savvy enough to realize what's happening. She's fighting it. I think she's trying to help us, to do her job, but her mind is slipping away."

"Great. And now we've got no Dr. Dodgson and a wounded shelter." The chief stared at the yawning hole in the ceiling. "We do have another medical doctor on day shift. We could ask him if he's willing to function as team leaders. Remember the old guy we shared the bus with? What was his name?"

"He didn't deign to introduce himself." Seph sniffed. "I'd rather have you in charge."

The chief chuckled. "Thanks—I think."

A sergeant approached. "Dr. Smith, we could use your help in the medical ward. We've got a bunch of patients freaking out. I think this incident triggered their PTSD, or something."

Or something. Seph and the chief exchanged worried looks.

"I'm sure that's all it is," Seph replied sans conviction. "Sergeant, try to locate Father Barney. Ask him to make rounds on the other side of the shelter. I'll work on settling the folks over here."

"Yes, ma'am." The sergeant departed in search of the chaplain.

Chief Bishop sighed as he watched the chaos swirl around him. The hole in the roof created a vacuum, with each gust of wind outside triggering a maelstrom of loose papers and fluttering debris inside.

"I suspect it'll be near dawn by the time we get this mess cleaned up and the new sleeping arrangements organized. I'll come find you later. We'll nail down our final plan then." He glanced at his watch. "Day shift won't be able to work on patching the roof until after the sun rises."

The pouring rain had slowed to a trickle. A drop of water landed on the chief's forehead and slalomed down the bridge of his nose. He dashed it away with the back of his hand. "Let's hope this baby stays together until then."

Seph arrived in the medical ward as Alice was finishing her last triage. A jumbled mound of dirty gauze, bottles of peroxide and alcohol, and surgical scissors blanketed the nurses' station.

"What's the toll, Alice?" Seph asked, marveling at the experienced nurse's quick hands and calm demeanor.

Alice taped a bandage onto her patient's forearm and sent him on his way. "The physical toll isn't bad, minus Dr. Dodgson and Nora." Her voice trembled. "I talked to her a few times during change of shift. Gave her some advice. She was fresh out of nursing school. She came for the experience."

Alice bent over the table to hide her face. "Besides them, we had only a few minor lacerations here, a contusion there. A miracle, considering what might have been." She gathered the disposable equipment and tossed it, along with the bloody gauze, in a red biohazard bag.

"The emotional toll is much worse. I'm glad you're here." She stripped off her gloves and added them to the garbage. "I have a list of patients for you to see."

"I wish I believed in miracles, Alice. I'm afraid I'm not much of a counselor anymore."

"Nonsense. Of course you are." Alice startled her by grasping Seph's hands in her own. "You don't have to believe in miracles to be a good counselor. They need to talk, Seph. Someone to listen. That's all."

She dropped Seph's hands and reached into the pocket of her scrubs, producing a slip of paper. "Now get to it, Dr. Smith."

The list, written in Alice's elegant, cursive script, was a long one. Seph did her part, roaming from one patient to the next to sit and soothe, hold hands, and wipe tears. Faking but not feeling. Aiding despite apathy.

By the time she reached the final name on Alice's list, Seph was depleted. Last night's insomnia had ground her emotions to a dull nub, and she longed for morning so she could retire to her cot—wherever it might be.

Chief Bishop found her in the cramped dining area, slumped over a black cup of coffee. "Wow! You've gone hard core, Doc. Drinkin' before bed, even."

"The pharmaceutical companies need to develop a sustained-release form of caffeine. Surely the world would pay for such a wondrous thing?" Seph struggled to sip from her cup without raising from her slouched position. "Everything under control?" she mumbled.

"More or less. It's six a.m. We have an hour 'til change of shift. I swung by the control room, but Annie's not there. Did you happen to see her during your rounds?"

"No. Did you check her cot?"

"I would, if I knew where it went." The chief grimaced at the jumble of cots crammed into any available space. An arm's reach from their table, a day shifter tossed in his bed.

Seph's nose twitched. "Do you smell something?"

"Bad coffee and body odor. Thanks for pointing it out."

"Wait for the next breeze." Seph stared at her napkin until it fluttered on the table. "Now!"

The chief raised his chin and sniffed. "I do smell something. It smells like . . ."

"A gas station!" Seph jumped out of her seat, sending it skittering into the cot behind her. "Tell me we don't have gas cans in the shelter."

"Sure we do. How else do you think we run the portable generators? They don't run on hopes and dreams, you know."

"We store it here, in the shelter, among all these people?"

"We have to. We can't be running outside during the middle of a hurricane to get gas. It's standard operating procedure."

The wind howled its disapproval, and the odor intensified.

"We need to find the source. Now!" Seph, sniffing like a bloodhound, spun around in circles, trying to pinpoint the origin.

Chief Bishop radioed his officers and activated the search teams. "The hole in the ceiling has the air currents spinning every which way. It's hard to tell for sure, but if I had to guess, I'd say the smell's coming from the back."

"From whence all good things emanate." *Drama plus caffeine equals anxiety.* The fumes didn't help. Seph's chest tightened, and she curled her hand around the inhaler in her pocket.

The chief shrugged. "Yeah, whatever that means. At least it'll cover the stench from the morgue."

"Thank you, Pollyanna."

Intent on reaching the rear of the shelter, Seph and Chief Bishop navigated the tangle of cots together. Alice stopped them at the DMZ. The petite nurse plowed through the rolling barriers, stumbling in her haste to reach them before they disappeared into the dark void.

"Chief! Dr. Smith! Someone's stolen our oxygen. We had three full tanks when I came on shift. I inventoried them myself. One of our asthmatics started wheezing, so I went to get him some oxygen, and it's gone."

Chief Bishop dismissed her with a wave of his handheld radio. "One crisis at a time, Alice. I'm guessing a piece of the collapsed roof punctured a gas can. We could have a major fuel leak somewhere. Let me find it first; then I'll hunt for your oxygen."

"Wait." Seph grabbed the chief's arm. Alice caught a whiff of the noxious air, and she and Seph gaped at each other in horror. Gasoline plus oxygen. All they needed was a match.

It's not enough. Seph heard Annie's disembodied voice from when she'd gazed at the hole in the roof. Seph echoed her words.

"We need to evacuate the shelter."

Chapter Thirteen

The Eighth Day

"Alice, gather all the nurses, day and night shift's, and mobilize the patients as best you can. Wheelchairs, walkers—carry them out in their cots, if necessary."

"Right away, Dr. Smith."

"Wait a minute." The chief pried Seph's fingers from his bicep. "Who's in charge here? I love ya, Doc, but it's not you. It's Annie. At least for the time being."

Alice glanced sidelong at Seph and darted away.

"Where the hell does she think she's going?"

"To carry out her orders. Alice knows I'm right, Chief. Annie planned this."

"Why? Give me one logical reason."

"Who knows why? Maybe because she's sick. Or batshit crazy. Or pissed off. Possibly all the above. I don't know why. We'll figure it out later. It doesn't matter right now. What matters is she plans to blow this place to high heaven, and we need to get these people out of here. You wanna be in charge? Fine. Run with it. But evacuate first, debate later. You can blame me afterwards if I'm wrong."

"Don't worry. I will." Chief Bishop prowled the edge of the DMZ. "Where do you think we're gonna go, Seph? We have no place to put the staff, much less hundreds of evacuees. It's dark, and it's raining. These people will get soaked, not to mention totally freaked out, if we leave them outside for long."

"So they get wet. They won't melt, but they might burn." Seph's glare met the chief's scowl. She blurted out a flash of inspiration. "We'll use base housing. Remember? We drove by it on the bus ride here. We'll have to break into each unit, I'm sure, but it's an option."

The availability of safe shelter seemed to sway the chief's opinion, and he softened his stance. "They probably don't have power . . ."

"We have the portable generators."

". . . But we have the generators." Chief Bishop conceded. "I'll get on the horn and make an announcement. We'll rendezvous at the farthest edge of the parking lot, in case this thing does blow. Let's keep this as calm and organized as possible."

"You go. I'll meet you there. First, I want to find Annie."

Seph watched as Chief Bishop wrenched open the electrical panel by the hangar door and flipped several switches. The hangar was bathed in light as, row by row, the fluorescent tubes flickered to life. The evacuees sat upright in their cots, and a buzz of anxiety went through the shelter as they checked their watches. For seven days and seven nights, the lights had come on at exactly seven a.m. Something was up. The employees knew it, too, and they filtered into the dining area for instructions.

The chief gesticulated like a football coach, drawing circles and X's on his clipboard and separating the staff into smaller subgroups. When the team huddle broke, he put the bullhorn to his lips.

"Attention, attention. We have a gas leak in the rear of the building. You are in no immediate danger, but we need to evacuate the shelter. Take your valuables and nothing more.

Line up in rows. Please allow families with small children at the front of each line. A through H here . . ."

Despite the chief's even voice and cool composure, the shelter erupted as panicked evacuees grabbed what little they had and charged toward the hangar door. While the police dispersed into crowd control formation, Seph, emboldened by the light, crossed the DMZ and pushed deeper into the shelter. Maybe she still had time to stop this.

She passed the container where she'd retrieved Joaquin's insulin pump and skirted the blood stain where she'd found him and Lew. She paused when she reached the closet where Joaquin had sat paralyzed with fear. The next room had a sheet of plastic taped over the door, sealing it shut. The morgue. Seph pinched her nose. The chief was wrong. The gas fumes *weren't* strong enough to mask the smell of rotting flesh. A gust of air stirred the odors, and Seph gagged. The combination of the two was worse yet.

With the bright lights shining overhead, the vast space appeared far less sinister than it had on her previous incursions, but this didn't lessen Seph's apprehension. She crept past the morgue and around the corner into an area she'd not previously explored. No man's land. Sitting in the center was Annie.

She didn't acknowledge Seph's arrival. Her head flopped on her neck, and her phone lay dormant in her lap. She was surrounded by empty wooden crates and a mishmash of blankets, papers, and other flammable debris. Kindling. A green oxygen tank sat to her left.

Seph stepped forward, and her shoe squished on the wet floor. She crouched to dab at the liquid with her finger. Gasoline. She squinted across the room at the glistening concrete and traced a pattern of concentric circles, which ended at

Annie's chair. Seph opted not to approach. If this was a bluff, it was an elaborate one.

"Annie, it's Seph. Look at me."

"I figured you'd come."

"You've accomplished your goal. The shelter is evacuating."

"I know. I can hear it."

"You can stand down now. No need to blow us to bits."

"You can leave. Your legs aren't broken."

"Neither are yours. Why are you doing this?"

"Your sister called." Annie raised the phone from her lap and fiddled with random buttons. "She sounds like a nice person. Good at her job, too, with all the right contacts. She got everything arranged in no time. All I had to do was provide the reason. A reason why we can't stay. As if a brain-eating parasite wasn't reason enough."

"Grace told you to destroy the shelter?" Seph's mind reeled with confusion. Her sister would never suggest something like that. Would she?

"Of course not. She told me to figure it out. We have to be outside by seven a.m. today. They're taking the crazy ones, the infected, away by bus. Make sure you take my lists with you. Follow them to a T. I left them on the table in the control room so you could grab them on your way out." Annie glanced at her phone. "Looks like we're right on time."

She tossed the phone through the air to Seph, who managed to catch it without slipping into a puddle of gasoline. Annie reached to her left and cranked the valve on the oxygen tank, turning it as far open as it would go. A loud hiss filled the air.

"Annie, hold on a minute. Let's talk this out. I'm sure we have other options here."

"I'm not getting on that bus, Seph." Annie pulled a pack of Virginia Slims and a book of matches out of her shirt pocket. She raised a cigarette to her lips.

Seph froze as a million scenarios raced through her brain. She might be able to make it to Annie in time . . .

"Seph?" Annie ripped a match out of the book.

"What?"

"Run."

Seph made it as far as the dining area before it all went to hell. The blast blew her off her feet and underneath a nearby table, which was itself perched precariously upon two topsy-turvy plastic chairs. The makeshift shield protected her from the flying debris, and as soon as the toxic rain ceased, Seph was on her feet. She scrambled for the exit, breaking stride long enough to root for Annie's precious papers amid the glassy ruins of the control room.

Fortunately, Chief Bishop had the foresight to open the hangar's main door. The entrance, wide enough to admit a cargo plane, prevented a stampede. It also created a glorious backdraft; as Seph raced to break free of the shelter, flames followed behind, whooshing out of the cavernous gate like a fiery hand reaching to drag her back to the belly of the beast.

Blinded by smoke and fear, Seph ran as far and as fast as her legs would take her until someone called her name. The ringing in her ears muddled the distant sound, and, confused, she slowed her sprint to a jog before lurching to a stop as her adrenaline tank ran dry. She lifted her face to the weeping sky and felt the rain drizzle over her flushed cheeks. The water dripped onto Annie's papers, which Seph clutched to her chest. Gasping for breath and alone in the darkness, Seph waited for the world to converge into view.

She occupied the farthest edge of a lengthy runway leading to the hangar. The parking lot, their rendezvous point, was the other direction. A horde of people stood, transfixed like moths between two flames, illuminated by the blazing shelter on one side and a long row of bobbing lights on the other. The misty rain blurred Seph's vision, and she blinked. The orbs of light focused into pairs of headlights. A fleet of buses idled, lined up and ready to go.

Seph pulled Annie's list away from her chest and strained to read the heading at the top of the page: "Bus 1A." A drop of water landed on the first name, smearing the red ink into an angry streak. Seph thrust the papers under her shirt to protect them. She wheezed her way into motion and jogged toward the crowd. The sun pierced the horizon, and she shaded her eyes from the glare. Dawn had finally arrived.

"Seph!" Chief Bishop's tense figure jumped out of the crowd as soon as she approached. "Jesus! I was yelling at you the whole way. Haven't you ever heard of 'Stop, Drop, and Roll'?"

"I wasn't on fire, was I?" Seph rasped out the words, punctuating them with a harsh cough.

"You sure as hell looked like it, the way your heels were smokin'. And I mean that *literally,* not figuratively." He eyed the cuts on her face and hands. "Are you okay?"

"I think so." She whipped the papers out from under her shirt. "These are Annie's lists. She said it's critically important everyone gets on the proper bus. Has anyone boarded yet?"

"No. We've been trying to settle the crowd and count heads first. Make sure we didn't leave anyone behind." He paused. "You talked to her, then? Before . . ."

"Yes." They stared into the flames, which had burst through the collapsed roof to lap at the polychrome sky.

"She didn't follow you out, did she?"

"No." Seph refused to make eye contact. "Subtract one from the head count."

The chief nodded and cleared his throat. "I'm told these buses are under the command of TDEM, the Texas Division of Emergency Management. TDEM falls under the direct jurisdiction of the governor of Texas, who gives them a lot of operating authority—more so than any emergency management system in any other state. TDEM was established way back when Texas was its own country."

"My sister arranged this."

"I'd assumed as much."

"Grace gave Annie the results of the blood tests, and Annie divided the buses into the healthy versus the not. The lists are a who's who. The infected, whether they be staff or evacuees, go off to quarantine if they're lucky, or research labs if they're not. The healthy go . . . where?"

"Good question." The chief's mouth was set in a grim line. "I guess anywhere is better than here. We don't have much choice at this point. The building's gone. Our supplies are gone. Morale is broken. We're at TDEM's mercy. Let's hope your sister's contacts believe in good old-fashioned Southern hospitality."

The door to the first bus opened and disgorged a burly man with an even burlier accent. "We need to start boarding, y'all. We're behind schedule. You done countin' yet?"

"I didn't know we had a schedule," Chief Bishop replied. He snatched the papers from Seph's hands and thrust them into the man's huge paws. "This is what you were asking for. You read the names."

The man subjected Seph to a cursory inspection before giving the chief his full attention. "New York, right? Guess that explains some things, don't it?" He shuffled the lists. The first two were written in red ink. The others were in black.

"I'll take it from here." He winked at the chief. "Nice accent. Ma'am." He nodded at Seph and loped back to the bus.

The chief gritted his teeth. "So much for Southern hospitality."

Seph grimaced. "At least he was polite."

"His name is 'Bubba,' for the record."

"You're kidding, right?"

"Decide for yourself."

The Texan pounded on the door to bus 1A. It opened, and eight heavily armed men wearing star-shaped badges disembarked.

"Are those Texas Rangers?" Seph whispered.

"I have no idea." The chief stepped forward and turned to address the crowd. "We're going to begin the boarding process. Each of you is assigned to a specific bus . . ."

The Texan put a bullhorn to his lips and spoke over the chief. "Listen up! When your name is called, get on the bus." He read the first name on the list.

Chief Bishop balled his hands into fists and returned to stand at Seph's side. The rain had stopped with the sunrise. By the light of dawn, they watched the parade of bedraggled souls rushing to climb, no questions asked, into the first bus. Seph recognized some; other she did not. Their faces shone with a mix of relief and anticipation, and it made her weep. She swiped her palms over her wet cheeks and turned away.

"I know." Chief Bishop rested a warm hand on her shoulder. "I can't shake the feeling they're being carted away to the gas chamber."

Seph stifled a sob. Isn't this what they'd wanted? "They trusted us to do the right thing. Look at them. They still trust us. And we've betrayed them." Before the chief could respond, a scuffle erupted in front of the buses.

Bus 1A was filled to capacity. The last two people to enter were armed Rangers. The folding doors closed behind them with a soft whoosh followed by a clank, as if it'd been barred from the inside.

Bus 1B was almost full. Bubba bellowed the final three names in one, long breath. A man approached, dragging his wife by one arm. Her other arm held their baby. Behind them, two scrawny teenagers clung to each other with the desperation of youth. The boy's face was a sullen mask, but the quivering chains on his leather jacket gave him away. The girl glanced over her shoulder and tightened her grip on his waist.

A middle-aged woman, hair piled higher than meringue, thrust herself in front of the teens, blocking their path. "That's my granddaughter. I demand to go with them."

The man piped in. "Same here. I'm not leaving without my wife and son. Why would you split us up?"

Bubba was unmoved. "Get on the damned bus. You have assigned seats."

"What difference does it make what bus we're on?" The man released a string of expletives in Spanish.

"Please!" The woman interrupted his tirade to plead her case. "My granddaughter's pregnant . . ." Her voice trailed to a halt when Bubba smirked in response.

"You asshole." She grabbed her granddaughter by the hand and yanked her away from her boyfriend. "C'mon. We're boarding." They made a run for the bus.

The Texan barely seemed to twitch, but the tip of the Taser hit its mark with deadly accuracy, and both women fell, rigid and foaming at the mouth, to the ground. The crowd of evacuees uttered a collective gasp.

"Oh my God, oh my God, oh my God." The girl's boyfriend surrendered his tough guy pretense with a whimper. He fell to his knees by her side, his hands roaming the air around her body, but too afraid to touch her.

The man cowered, as stunned as if he himself had been tasered. His wife, tears streaming down her cheeks, stroked his forearm. They turned their faces toward the crowd, searching for someone, anyone to speak on their behalf.

Seph fought the urge to hide behind Chief Bishop's broad back. *They know.* Her conscience screamed from within.

Ultimately, it was Father Barney who stepped forward to fill the moral void. He lowered his head and his voice to quickly confer with the couple, grasping their hands in his as he spoke. Then, he walked over to where Bubba lounged against the front bumper of the bus. Another brief conversation ensued. Bubba shuffled through the papers; the chaplain waved his crucifix. Finally, Father Barney returned to the couple and nodded.

The man wiped his eyes and kissed his son on the forehead. He pushed his wife closer to Father Barney, who wrapped one arm around the sobbing woman's shoulders and gave her a protective squeeze. The man touched his wife's chin and whispered something in Spanish. "You will be safer on the next bus," he said aloud and in English, glancing at the chaplain. He clenched his teeth and strode through the open doors, pausing only to spit on the ground at Bubba's feet.

Bubba made a subtle motion, and a pair of Rangers hoisted the paralyzed but conscious teenage girl off the ground and onto the bus. Her glassy eyes briefly touched on Seph, who screwed hers shut in a childish act of denial. Bubba tapped the girl's boyfriend on the shoulder, and he bolted onto the bus as if the devil were nipping at his heels. The door closed behind him. Another clank. Both buses revved their engines and chugged out of the lot, away from the remains of the burning shelter.

A moan drifted through the silence. The girl's grandmother had regained muscle control. Alice slipped out of the crowd to crouch beside her. Father Barney, his arm still around the woman's shoulders, guided her in Seph's direction. "Matilde's boarding with me now. I promised her husband I'd see to it she and little Tito are taken care of."

Seph stroked the baby's chubby cheek. He cooed in response, oblivious to the tragedy unfolding around him. "I'm so sorry." She attempted to console the distraught woman, but Father Barney shook his head and gently interceded.

"Tillie doesn't speak any English." He murmured a few quiet words in Spanish, and Tillie lowered her eyes to the ground and rubbed her cheek against her son's.

The chaplain cleared his throat. "I snatched a sizable peek at those lists while the Texan . . ."

"Bubba." Chief Bishop interjected with a grim smile. "We're calling him 'Bubba.'"

". . . While Bubba was searching for my name. The two of you are on the final bus. I'm on the second-to-last. Tillie and Tito were supposed to be on the third, but Bubba agreed to shuffle a few names."

Chief Bishop cocked his head in Bubba's direction. "How'd you manage to convince him to play nice? He doesn't seem to be the negotiating type." The chief glared at the Texan, who had already begun boarding bus number three.

"No. No, he does not." Father Barney dropped his arm from Tillie's shoulders in order to finger the crucifix around his neck. "He refused at first, until I threatened to curse his soul. Told him he'd burn in hell for all eternity."

"And he bought it?" Seph raised her eyebrows. "You can't be serious."

Father Barney gave a nonchalant flick of his wrist. "I guessed he was Baptist, and I guessed right. They usually respond well to the fire-and-brimstone stuff. Besides, I got the impression the first two buses are the critical ones. Did you notice how they were boarded by a mix of evacuees and staff? The next few pages listed only evacuees, and the last two consisted of nothing but employee names. At this point, I don't think it matters who gets on when. Bubba's just holding on to the charade."

In support of Father Barney's theory, they watched as Bubba split the pile of lists in two. He handed half to one of the Rangers, who began calling names for bus number four.

"Two buses of infected people." Seph counted rows of seats through the tinted windows. "That means we're talking about what? Eighty people?"

"More or less." The chaplain sighed. "Mercy."

"I don't think they'll be getting any, Father." Chief Bishop monitored the lines forming behind each bus, but there were no further disruptions. One by one, eight hundred people squeezed onto twenty buses. By the time they'd reached the final two, the sun shone high in the sky, and the shelter was nothing but a pile of twisted metal and smoldering ash.

Bubba called Tillie's name, followed by Father Barney's. "Everyone else will ride the last bus with me."

Figures. Seph cringed as she pictured herself trying to make small talk with Bubba. Chief Bishop noticed her reaction and scowled.

"Yeah, me, too. We may have to sit on the roof." He put a hand on the small of her back. "C'mon, Doc. Let's get outta here." They joined the stragglers filtering toward the bus.

Father Barney walked Tillie to the door, but to Seph's surprise, he didn't board. Instead, he returned to stand by her side. He reached into his pocket and pulled out her necklace.

Seph gasped. The last time she'd seen it, the necklace was lying on the concrete floor, twisted between Carol's dead fingers.

He displayed it in front of her, letting it dangle off his palm. The yellow gold sparkled in the afternoon sun. The cross had been cleaned and polished, all traces of blood scoured from between the links of its dainty chain.

"Take it, Dr. Smith. You may decide you miss it once you return home."

Seph hesitated, then raised a tentative hand to caress the familiar object. Out of the corner of her eye, she saw Bubba sauntering their way. Father Barney had arrested the boarding process in order to save her soul.

Her stomach twisted into knots, and she dropped her arm. "No. Give it to Tillie. Better yet, give it to little Tito. Tell him it's from his papa."

Father Barney frowned and closed his fist around the necklace. "Your faith, Persephone—it will come back to you someday, someday when you least expect it. When you need it the most."

Seph pressed her lips into a tight, thin line. "Bullshit." She pushed past the priest and boarded the last bus out of Hell.

Chapter Fourteen

Seph and Grace clasped hands and stared grimly into the cold drizzle of a grey Sunday morning. Behind them, a portly woman with a too-bright umbrella leaned forward to whisper in Seph's ear. "April showers, love."

Seph did not turn around. The priest droned onward, intent on reciting the complete Mass for the Repose of the Soul of the Departed despite the thick fog lapping at his ankles. He finished with a hymn. "Amazing Grace." Seph felt her sister cringe. By the time they'd returned to their car, Seph and Grace's black suits were as soggy as their spirits.

The drive home was short.

"I hate that song," Grace said.

"I know." Seph kept her eyes on the slick road ahead.

"Why'd you let him use it, then?"

"I didn't know he was going to. You made the arrangements."

Grace began to sob.

Dammit! Seph tightened her grip on the wheel. Their mother's death—slow and unmercifully painful—had been a bitter blow on top of Grace's rape and military separation. Her sister's emotional stability was precarious at best, and she refused to consider treatment.

"Not much longer," Seph murmured. "The day will soon be over."

Grace sniffled. "Then what?"

Seph avoided her sister's question by clicking on the radio and cranking the volume to max. Elvis's smooth voice filled the vehicle. "Amazing grace. How sweet the sound . . ."

✚

They managed to sit through the entire wake, enduring hugs, pats, and condolences uttered in both English and Italian. Uncle Chick hovered in the background, deflecting as many questions as he could. When the crowd finally cleared, Seph and Grace sat, emotionally exhausted and silent, in their mother's tiny living room.

"We have enough leftovers to last a lifetime," Seph said, sipping the residual sweet drops from a spent bottle of anisette. Meat and cheese platters blanketed the dining room. Dozens of cookies intermingled with empty cups on the coffee table.

"It'll take us all night to pack everything up." Her tone was matter-of-fact. She was too tired to be anything else.

Grace nodded and twisted a partially shredded tissue in her lap. She fixed her gaze on a bowl of meatballs. "Seph, I'm leaving. I found a job in Maine."

"What?" Seph dropped a stack of napkins. She and Grace had been too busy caring for their mother to discuss the future. Seph assumed, after six brutal months, they would take some time to recover.

"I can't stay here. My military career is over, and without mom, this house is nothing but a box full of memories. I have a friend in the Coast Guard. She says one of the private lumber companies is looking for a logistics person to manage their fleet. Says it's right up my alley. I can stay with her until I get settled. I'll sign my part of the house over to you. You can do whatever you want with it."

Seph swallowed the lump rising in her throat. The idea of Grace relocating didn't bother her. The military had kept her sister roaming the globe ever since she finished the Academy. However, if Grace moved on with her life, then Seph would need to make some hard decisions as well. Grace was forcing her hand.

Her sister stared at her with expectant eyes. Seph searched for a response, blurting out the first thing that came to mind. "We'll sell the house. Split the proceeds. That'll allow you to get your own place in Maine—an apartment, at least."

Grace wasn't satisfied. "What about you, Seph?"

"I'm formulating a plan as we speak." Seph smiled, hoping to inject some levity into the heavy room. In truth, an idea had been festering in Seph's mind since her return from Texas. She'd tried to return to work, but after a month of awkward counseling sessions, she'd taken a leave of absence. Used her mother's relapse as an excuse. Never planned to go back. Dr. Persephone Smith, counselor extraordinaire, had been lost to the storm.

Grace always knew what her sister was thinking. "You're good at what you do, Seph. Don't throw it away."

"I was once, before I disengaged. I like that word. Sounds better than saying I had a meltdown." A rain cloud passed by the window, darkening Seph's face. "But I think I found something which suits me better. The new me, that is."

Grace studied her sister's rigid posture before settling on the crevice of her neck, where her cross used to lay. "I don't think I like the new you."

Seph snorted. "You'll get used to her." She squeezed her sister's hand. "C'mon. Let's get this mess cleaned up." She hoisted a tray of amaretti into the air and headed to the kitchen.

Later, when order was restored, Seph muttered an excuse and hopped the city bus to her own apartment. She'd slept at her mother's for months now, but tonight she needed her own room, her own bed . . .and the bin.

She hurried to her bedroom and opened the closet door. She paused, eyeing the bin warily as if it were a cobra, coiled and waiting to strike from beneath the piles of shoes and clothing. She hadn't bothered to unpack upon her return. Her duffle had burned with the shelter, so she'd come home from Texas with only a secondhand purse and some clothes from Goodwill. She'd tossed the whole lot into the bin and shoved it into the farthest corner. Out of sight, out of mind.

She removed the purse and dumped its contents onto the floor, splaying the items out with her hand. A half-empty bottle of hand sanitizer, a gum wrapper, a few coins . . .and a crumpled business card. She picked it out of the jumble with two fingers and held it up to the light. *Dr. Whitmer Burton, forensic psychologist, NYPD.* Chief Bishop's handwriting triggered a flood of unpleasant memories, and her stomach twisted.

"Whitty's always looking for talented interns. I could put in a good word for you." The chief's voice echoed in her skull. "Besides, he owes me one."

Seph glanced at the clock. It was late, but he'd still be up. The chief probably wasn't sleeping any better than she these days. Seph pounded his number into her phone before she could change her mind. She didn't wait for him to say "hello."

"Chief. It's Seph. I'm in."

About the Author

Dr. Jennifer Delozier submitted her first story, handwritten in pencil on lined school paper, to Isaac Asimov's magazine

while still in junior high school. Several years later, she took a creative writing elective at Penn State University and was hooked. She received her BS and MD degrees in six years, which was followed by the blur of internship, residency and the launch of her medical career. But she never forgot her first love.

From the deductive reasoning of Sir Arthur Conan Doyle to the cutting-edge science of Michael Crichton, she remains inspired by facts that lie on the edge of reality: bizarre medical anomalies, new genetic discoveries and anything that seems too weird to be true!

Dr. Delozier spent the early part of her career as a rural family doctor and then later as a government physician, caring for America's veterans. She continues to practice medicine and lives in Pennsylvania with her husband and four rescue cats.

Acknowledgements

To my readers: The best compliment a writer can receive is a 5-star review. I hope you enjoyed the ride!